EMERGENCE

C. MICHELLE JEFFERIES

WALNUT SPRINGS PRESS

To Noble—the heart of the story, and my dearest friend

ACKNOWLEDGEMENTS

I am deeply grateful for everyone I have associated with on the journey to making *Emergence* a real book. To those who read it and gave suggestions, you're awesome. To my Tooele and Castle Dale writing groups, I couldn't have done it without you. Thanks to my critique groups over the years, for hours of reading and critiquing. To those I've not named but who have left a huge dent in my heart, I thank you, too.

Thank you to Karen Hoover and Weston Elliot, for being there. To Jodi Meadows, who turned this book in the right direction. To Tristi Pinkston, AKA Darth Editus, my friend and teacher: the force is with you in all ways. Special thanks to Paulette Inman, for everything, especially the *what if*s and the long on-the-phone plotting sessions.

To Linda Prince and Amy Orton at Walnut Springs, thanks for bringing the story to life, and for your excellent effort and time spent.

To my husband, my children, and my family, who have been there every step of the way. Thank you. You guys are my everything.

1

Antony Danic let the slide of his Glock .357 slam home. The sound echoed against the sterile surfaces of the industrial kitchen where he waited. Rows of stainless-steel appliances and stark white counters filled the room that was half the size of his whole apartment. *Elite would love this kitchen.* A machine-like calm settled over his body as his thoughts turned from his wife to the hit.

"HQ, this is Viper," he said as he double-checked the blade strapped to his calf and adjusted his blue-lensed Lanzen sunglasses.

"Viper acknowledged," a female Corporate operator said over his silver and red earpiece.

"Viper in recon position."

"Roger that, Viper. Radio silence commenced."

The earpiece went silent. There would be no more contact until he initiated it.

Mr. Bennett held to a strict schedule when he was in town. He would arrive at exactly eleven to do a final walk-through of his restaurant before locking up for the night. Somehow, after chasing the man for three weeks, through the United States and the Middle East, Antony was now less than twenty minutes from home.

"Thank you," a voice echoed through the kitchen, coming from the direction of the dining room. "I'll talk to you later."

A phone snapped shut and Antony heard heels clicking on the tile floor. He slid his finger from the side of his Glock to the trigger well. A wide man entered the kitchen, checking the small refrigerator by the door and wiping his finger on the counter.

Meticulous and well-fed, Antony thought as he stepped from the shadows, training his pistol on the man. *Pretty oblivious, too.* They now stood a mere ten feet from each other.

Antony cleared his throat—he refused to shoot a man in the back—and pulled the trigger. He grimaced at the splatter of blood on his pant leg and made a mental note to stand farther back next time. *I should know better—the larger targets always bleed more.* Especially that third signature shot to the femoral artery. At least it wasn't obvious on his black cargo pants, although Antony could feel the blood growing cold and sticky on his skin. The door of the restaurant hissed closed behind him, and the smells and sounds of the city drew his attention from his last hour of work. He stood on the corner of Bonython and Gale for a moment, then headed for the nearest train station.

A siren echoed and a lone car rolled past him, the tires crunching on the blacktop. There were still a few of them around. Older cars were a luxury, too expensive for the common man, or a major expense for the "old-timers" who didn't like or trust newer technology.

"Time," he said into his earpiece.

"It is 11:56 PM, April 26, 2087," answered a woman from headquarters.

"When does the next train leave the Phillip Avenue Station?"

"At 12:06, sir."

Phillip Avenue was still a city block away. Ahead of Antony, a community shuttle hovered at the curb of a stone apartment building. A young woman stumbled down the steps toward the shuttle. Behind her, a man followed.

"Inform Catelyn that the package is delivered and Viper is going home," Antony said. Then he ran, his titanium sniper-rifle case bouncing against his back in a calming cadence. Above him, a few shuttles flew along the appointed routes. The city was unusually quiet tonight.

"Yes, sir," said the voice in his ear.

"Viper out." He nudged the earpiece with his shoulder. The station was just ahead of him.

He swiped his access card at the turnstile and rushed up the stairs. He reached the platform just as a large shuttle rose in the distance. *Trans-World Flight,* he thought, *a cruise ship in orbit.* He intended to take Elite on one someday.

"Welcome to Canberra ACT, the national capital of Australia," the automated voice said.

Antony turned the corner and walked into the station. A maze of tracks crossed through the large room, and metal stairs and ramps led to each of the bays. Bright florescent lights bleached the color from everything in the station. The digital sign projected on the wall indicated that Antony's train would stop at a bay to his left in 3.32 minutes.

"God loves those that come to him and confess their sins," a man said. He stood next to the access card dispenser, with a metal can on the ground at his feet. He held a book in his hand, and his frayed clothes reminded Antony of the homeless he'd seen around the city. "What about you, young man—have you given him your sins?" he asked, grabbing at the sleeve of Antony's jacket.

Antony felt strong fingers pinching at his muscles. Sighing, he closed his eyes for a prolonged second; all he wanted to do was get home to his wife and bed. He pulled his arm up, the fabric sliding out of the preacher's grip, and sneered at the him. "Hardly," Antony said, then continued to the left.

"The path you choose leads to darkness—your heart yearns to be free from sin." The man maneuvered himself in front of Antony.

Antony stopped to avoid running into the man. "Religion is placation for the weak-minded," he growled. "It's slavery in itself."

The man met Antony's gaze, and he noticed that in spite of the man's speed and strength, he was older. The lines around his dark, almond-shaped eyes were evident at this distance. When the man reached for his arm again, Antony grasped the front of his coat.

"Get your hands off me, old man." Antony pushed the preacher away from him. The man stumbled back a few feet before he stopped his own fall. "There is no God. It's all in your head."

Antony stepped back as the train pulled into the station. *If there was a God, my mother would still be alive.* Clenching his teeth, he shoved the thought into the back of his head where it belonged.

"Everything all right here?" asked a police officer dressed in traditional khakis. He stepped between the two men and reached out his hands, placing one on Antony's chest and one on the preacher's.

"Tell that freak to leave me alone." Antony pushed the officer's hand away and stormed past him to the open train doors.

"Simply a difference of opinion," he heard the preacher say from behind him.

Two people stepped off the train before Antony got on. He found a place to sit against the wall in the rear of the train car.

He leaned back in his seat, the bloody fabric on his leg feeling coarse against his skin.

An old woman turned on her bench to stare at him with watery eyes. He groaned and looked back at her, raising his eyebrows.

"What?" he snapped. She turned away and looked down. He punched the volume up on his earpiece. "Music," he said, and closed his eyes.

2

Antony watched the station disappear out the train window, the lights fading behind him, the stars appearing as the train picked up speed. Above him, the track stretched ahead until it vanished in the distance.

His foot bounced as adrenalin rushed through his veins. With his assignment finished, he'd be getting a large bonus. There was no such thing as a promotion with his job. As far as he knew, he was the only company soldier in the corporation. His reality revolved around his handler, Catelyn, who gave him his assignments. He reported either to her or headquarters, and the monthly paychecks and bonuses were electronically deposited in his account from some foreign bank. Years ago, the in-house accountant had the devil of a time deciding what accounts payable his salary went under. Antony laughed long and hard when his first check listed him as an employee of human resources.

He did his job, and he did it well. This hit was done just in time for his vacation. He couldn't wait to take Elite to Tahiti. When they came home, she would draw a thick black line through the words "Stand on the beach of Riangora," written on the textured watercolor paper tacked to the corkboard in their walk-in closet. Every time she crossed an adventure off the list, she added a new one.

He imagined her face as he gave her the tickets. Her excitement wouldn't be containable. Visiting the beaches of Tahiti was one of the first on her list of things to do. The islands, closed to tourists starting with the island Riangora in early 2000, only allowed a few people a year to visit now, the ecology too fragile to return to the days of constant tourism. Antony had placed his and Elite's names on the waiting list over five years ago, and they'd notified him in January of the visitor passes.

His smile widened as he thought of his wife standing in the surf. She would thrill at the feeling of sugar-white sand between her toes and would want to go skinny-dipping at midnight just because. No doubt she would drag him, swim trunks still on, into the water.

The train entered the station just before reaching Antony's building. He stood and moved to the back door. A quick trip up the stairs, into the building, up the lift, and he would be in her arms.

It was dark when he entered the apartment. *Elite must be asleep for once,* he thought. Never in his life had he met someone with so much energy. It was her love of life that had attracted him to her in the first place. They had met when they were volunteer coaches for the Special Olympics. Antony had started years before when his best friend, Gage, invited him to help. Gage's younger sister was born with a birth defect, and his family volunteered regularly. When Antony overheard Elite say she spent the weekend skydiving, he knew he had to introduce himself. He learned she was an adventure/adrenaline junkie like him, and it gave them something to talk about, and do, as they became friends and fell in love.

Antony unlocked the door to his office and pulled the large corkboard out from the wall. After punching in the code, he opened the metal door located in the wall, then placed both his pistol and his rifle in the gun safe and locked it. He pushed the corkboard back into position, then locked the office and quietly entered the master suite.

He dropped his shirt and pants in the metal basket in the closet, then stepped into the shower and let the water rinse the dirt of the last few days from his skin. He hated the filth of his work—not the blood, but the vile lives of some of the people he met. The blood was just part of his job. What bothered him were the people who thought they could do whatever they wanted without paying for it, like the men who attacked and killed Antony's mother when he was young—too young to do anything to save her. They had never been punished. They deserved to die.

Bright light spilled across the dark wood of the closet and bathroom. Antony could see through the glass of the shower stall that everything was immaculate, as usual. Soon, dressed in flannel pajama pants, he opened the door from the bathroom to their bedroom. It was good to be home.

Tacked to the corkboard in the closet, next to the list, was an application for volcanic geology summer camp. *Typical Elite, finding adventures to occupy her time,* he thought as he imagined her with a rock hammer in hand. His brow furrowed when he saw the camp was actually four weeks long. It would be a good time to immerse himself in a supplemental intensive training regimen to keep in shape. He would spend the day working out, meditating, and training at the dojang where he practiced tang soo do twice a week. His master instructor, Sa Bo Nim Rick, would be happy to see him focus on his training. It would be the perfect time to reset his mind and body.

Elite's head lay on her pillow in the shaft of light from the bathroom. Her dark brown hair had streaks of blue in it today and curled softly around her face. The short style she loved made her look younger than her thirty years. Her tan shoulder peeked from under the blankets. There was an open book on the floor by her side of the bed; she must have fallen asleep while reading. Antony turned off the light, stepping from the rougher rock floor of the bathroom onto the smooth wood floor of their bedroom.

He walked to his side of the bed, touching the knobby wooden post, then pulled the denim comforter down and slipped in next to her. She shifted as he laid his arm across her stomach. He hadn't seen her in over three weeks. Pulling her close, he breathed in the familiar smell of her shampoo and closed his eyes, the exhaustion of a finished assignment making his eyelids heavy. Soon, he felt his body surrender to sleep.

"It's almost time to go. Are you ready?" Elite asked as she came out of the bathroom, fastening a long, dangling earring in her ear. She wore a bright azure sweater that matched the blue in her hair, and a long, dark gray suede skirt. The richly embroidered hem of the skirt covered the tops of her black leather boots. Antony had spent the last hour watching her get ready through half-closed eyes.

"Antony?" she said. He stretched his arms over his head, yawning. He had forgotten how comfortable his own bed felt.

"What?"

"You're not even out of bed, and the ceremony starts in just over an hour. It takes forty minutes to get there by train."

"Ceremony?"

"Yes." She walked back into the closet and grabbed a shawl from a hook. They sometimes laughed at how his almost all brown, black, and blue clothing contrasted with her multi-colored wardrobe. "Sara and Michael's bonding is this afternoon."

"Ugh, Elite, that's church stuff."

She stopped at the doorway of the closet and blinked, her lip quivering.

He cursed inwardly. He didn't like that face.

"You promised." Her voice was small and timid.

Antony groaned and rolled over. He wondered sometimes at the hardened soldier he was that became mush the instant his wife started blinking, trying not to cry. Her power over him was confusing, as if she had woven herself around his black heart and infused his lack of love with her abundance of it.

She left the room, and he heard her searching for the keys. She never put them in the same place, no matter what he told her.

He had gone to church with her before, but he hated the way being there made him feel, as if he were being burned alive right there on the bench for his lifestyle and occupation. He didn't believe in a higher being, but after an hour of Elite's church, he was apt to believe there was a hell and he was going there.

"Fine," Antony said loudly and sat up. *I want her to be happy, even if it's not where I want to be.*

"What?" She entered the room, her bag over her shoulder.

"Fine, I promised you and Michael. I'll go. Just give me a minute."

She smiled and reached for his black suit, still draped in the dry cleaner's plastic.

"Not that," he said. "I'll wear my khakis and a button-down shirt. I'm not going more dressed up than you are." He saw her hang up his suit and pull out a pair of pants, a shirt, and sweater as he turned on the shower. Great, he would be hot and stuffy *and* feel like he was burning from the inside out all at the same time.

This is going to be a pain in the . . . But it was the least he could do in their current circumstances. In fact, the first item on Elite's list was to be bound in her religion. Just being married wasn't enough. Her religion believed they could not only marry flesh to flesh, but soul could be bound to soul.

"We're going to be late," she said as he rinsed off.

"We'll take a taxi."

"It's almost noon."

"But it's Saturday. We'll be fine." He stepped out and grabbed the thick Egyptian-cotton towel hanging on a hook by the shower. His feet felt cool on the rock floor as he gave himself a rigorous once-over.

"Did you get them a gift?" he called out.

"I ordered it weeks ago. It should have been delivered on Thursday," Elite said from the kitchen, her mouth full of something.

Antony pulled the sweater on and filled his pocket with his wallet, knife, and keys. Then he checked his pistol. It was loaded. He grabbed his phone in case things got boring.

"Let's go." He found his shoes in the basket by the door and dropped them on the floor to slip them on.

Elite came out of the kitchen, several crackers in her hand. "I called the taxi. It should be here by now," she said.

He looked at the crackers and smiled.

"What?" she asked. "I was hungry."

He shook his head, opened the door, and escorted her out by the elbow.

Antony didn't pay attention to the address she gave the driver as they stepped into the taxi, but he soon realized they were in the opposite part of town from her church.

"I thought this was a bonding," he said as he turned his gaze toward Elite. She sat with a book in her lap, silently reading.

"It is."

"Then why are we going this direction?" he asked.

She looked up at him. "They're having the bonding at her parents' house."

"But I thought bondings were performed at the church."

"It's not *where* they're performed, but by whom," she said and shut her book. "Sara got someone high up to do it, but I think she's being a little vain. Her own father is an elder, and he could have bonded them with permission."

"Elder?"

"Elders run the local churches. There are people higher in the chain of command who oversee the elders." She grimaced, suddenly looking pale.

"Honey, are you okay?" Antony asked.

She shook her head. "I'll be fine, just a little car sick. You know how I get." He nodded. They usually took the train because it was easier on her stomach. Planes and trains were okay, but cars were a completely different story, which was why he hesitated to buy a car or a shuttle. Why own either if Elite couldn't ride in them?

"I'm sorry, I forgot I told you I'd go," he said. "It's my fault we were too late to take the train. We'll take one on the way home, okay?"

She nodded. She was extremely claustrophobic when she was sick like this. Antony longed to calm her, but she wouldn't let him near.

He opened his window a little and watched as she sat back and closed her eyes. How he wished for a little boy or girl with chocolate eyes just like hers. He frowned. He hadn't thought about a baby for a long time. He and Elite were going to be surrounded by members of her congregation, and he knew many of them would ask when he and Elite planned to have children. She would be in a bad mood after the celebration because it wasn't them being bonded, or having a baby.

She had mentioned adoption again just before his assignment to Pakistan. The fight had been mean, she'd gone to bed silent, and he'd left early the next morning. Was it so wrong to want a child of his blood? They could take home a baby anytime from the orphanage Elite owned, but it wasn't the same.

Abandoned as an infant on the steps of a church in Dunedin, New Zealand, Antony wanted a child of his own, a blood relative in a world where he had none. Yet, he wanted more than anything in the world to erase the sorrow in Elite's eyes.

He vividly remembered the day she was diagnosed with infertility. She locked herself in their bedroom and wept for hours, insisting she had ruined his chances to be a father. To get to her, he had to unhinge the door and climb over the dresser she had somehow moved to bar the way. He made it across the floor, which was cluttered with anything she could throw, and held her in his arms, promising her it didn't matter, that he still loved her, that she was the most important thing in the world to him.

The sound of the taxi's air jets on gravel drew him out of his thoughts. They were pulling up to a grand house set on top of a small incline. He stepped out and paid the driver two international credit notes before Elite could open her bag. Then Antony walked around to her door, opened it, and held out his hand.

"Allow me," he whispered. She reached out a thin hand and he pulled her up. The book had disappeared into the bag, no longer needed—if she concentrated on something else besides riding passenger, she didn't get as sick. "I love you, Elite Danic."

She blushed. "I love you too," she said as the taxi flew off.

Antony stopped her as she took a step forward. "Elite," he said. She paused and looked into his eyes. "Let's turn in the papers and take a baby home. I hate seeing you alone. I want you to be happy. It doesn't matter to me anymore whether our child is of our blood or adopted." He hoped she couldn't see through his façade. His chest hurt at the thought of lying to her. It was the reason he had confessed to her what he was even before he proposed.

"I'm an assassin," he remembered saying.

"You kill people?" she asked, backing away from him. Her eyes were wide, the skin around her mouth tight. Antony regretted the decision to be honest as soon as he saw her face. "Do you just go up and shoot anyone you feel like killing?"

"No," he hurried to explain. "Only those who pose a threat to our country and the citizens' safety."

"So you're in the military?"

"Actually, I'm retired. I work for a military contractor as a corporate soldier."

She paused, her arms folded across her stomach, her lower lip between her teeth. "It's like that National Security thing. You go after terrorists," she said after several seconds.

"Yes. If they pose a threat to the people I work for, they send me to take care of it."

"Is that all you do?" she asked.

"I'm also a courier. I transport documents or objects too valuable to ship through normal channels. I act as a bodyguard if needed, too."

Elite was quiet a moment longer. "You protect the innocent like I do," she said at length. "I work at the orphanage my mom owns. Some of the children who live there have been removed from abusive parents. We go to court all the time, and sadly, sometimes the parents lie and they get their kids back in spite of the evidence against them."

"Sometimes, even with the most terrible evidence or solid eyewitness, the accused still gets off," Antony said. "The justice system is an imperfect machine with human people running it and working for it. When that happens in my realm, I'm called to take care of it."

He looked at Elite, trying to read her face. It was obvious she was thinking about it. As her eyebrows lowered and her face relaxed into something calm compared to the alarmed look when he first told her, she reached out for his hand.

"I think I prefer the word 'soldier' instead of 'assassin,'" she said.

He refused to live a lie with her. No one else mattered.

"You're ready to apply for adoption?" she asked now. Her eyes searched his face, intensely flitting from feature to feature. He still felt wrong about it, but secretly hoped the idea would grow on him.

"I think so. I want to see you sitting in the nursery, rocking a baby to sleep in the antique chair I bought," he said. That part wasn't a lie. Her eyes reflected less sorrow and more joy, and he smiled.

"It's time, isn't it?" she asked.

He pulled her close to him. "It's time someone called us Mom and Dad."

3

Antony took Elite's arm as he stepped to the door. He turned to see a pleasant smile on her face. She was happy, and that's what he wanted. It was better for both of them that he not be so selfish. *Who am I to deny her what she really wants?*

The large oak double doors were propped open, welcoming guests to the bonding. A garland of ivy and ribbon framed the entryway, and candles and white fabric decorated the grand room. Roses and many other flowers Antony couldn't identify covered nearly every open surface, and the air was heady with the fragrance. White chairs were set in rows in the living room. Tables nestled here and there against the walls held pictures of the bride and groom.

Elite led Antony to two empty seats near the back. Soon, the crowd grew silent as an Asian man stepped forward, his dark navy robes flowing around his aging body. Long black hair hung down his back, and a gold earring with a single black bead adorned his left ear.

"Family and friends, welcome to the bonding of Sara and Michael. I'm Sori Katsu, and I'll be performing the ceremony."

Antony sat perfectly still as he saw heads bow and tissues raised to some of the women's faces. Elite sniffed and blinked. He suppressed a groan.

"Would the couple come forward?" Katsu said. He stood behind a pedestal that held a fabric-covered book. Just in front of him, on the first chairs across the aisle from each other, sat the groom in a tuxedo and the bride in a white wedding dress.

The groom was an old friend of Antony and Elite's, the bride a young woman from Melbourne. They met her at the fall feast last year when the couple had announced their engagement. She seemed nice enough, though a little young for Michael, in Antony's opinion.

The groom stood and took the bride by the hand. He kissed her cheek before he led her forward, and they knelt on cushions in front of the pedestal.

Katsu touched his forehead and the people in the audience touched theirs. Elite had explained years ago that it was an acknowledgement of a higher being, and a reminder to pray. She began her prayers the same way and often made the motion when her thoughts turned to thankfulness or she was in need of help.

"Michael and Sara, marriage is a gift from our God, an institution of joy and prosperity."

Antony looked at his hands, a thought tickling his brain. Although it wouldn't be completely honest, what if he and Elite were bonded like this in their own home—no guests, just an elder? Antony could get through the requirements, couldn't he? Then Elite would be able to cross it off her list. Even if he didn't believe in it, couldn't he do it for her? If he was making her happy, just like the adoption, was it lying to her?

Elite sniffed again and Antony turned his attention back to the couple. Katsu took the bride's hand and placed it on the fabric.

"Sara, will you accept Michael as your life and soul mate, and honor him forever?" Katsu asked.

"Yes," she said.

The elder took the groom's hand and placed it on top of Sara's. "Michael, will you accept Sara as your life and soul mate, and honor her forever?"

"Yes," he said.

"Then I bind you together, for all time."

Katsu laid his hands on top of theirs. Michael leaned over and kissed Sara, and someone whistled. Elite laughed lightly and clapped her hands, making her bracelets tinkle. Antony reached over and took her in his arms. She sighed, laying her head on his chest. He knew exactly what was going through her mind.

"Do you regret marrying me?" he asked, and instantly wished he had kept his mouth shut. "I mean, if you had married someone from your church, you would be bound to him by now." He felt her stiffen under his arm, and she didn't answer for a moment.

"Regret marrying you? No. Wish you were a member? Yes. Sometimes. Antony, I knew who I married. I knew I fell in love with an atheist. It was my choice. My parents didn't have a problem with you, and I don't either." She brushed at the wrinkles in her skirt. "This is Michael and Sara's big day. Let's not ruin it with a fight." Elite's eyes, the color of melted chocolate, looked deeply into Antony's.

"Sure, El, no fight."

She brightened and grasped his arm. "Let's go congratulate them."

Antony stood, and she pulled him into the aisle. Elite leaned to see around the man in front of her and dashed into the gap, stopping when they entered a small clearing in the crowd. The photographer guided the bride and groom to the dining area, and the crowd stood watching as the couple posed by the mountainous cake. Elite moved to the right, Antony in tow.

"Elite!" a woman said as they passed her.

"Donna, how are you?" She released Antony's hand to give the woman a hug. He stepped just a few feet from Elite in case she wanted to introduce him. He studied the painting hung on the wall, a floral done in thick strokes. Blues and greens mixed and melted with lilac and pink.

"It's a Matisse original."

Antony turned to see Sori Katsu standing next to him. Antony looked back at the painting, searching for some obscure signature.

"I've always loved this piece," the elder said. "It calms the mind."

Finally, Antony found the scrawl in the corner. "I like the colors." He wondered how much an original like this cost; it had been a while since he'd added to his investments.

"Walk with me," Katsu said.

"Why?" Antony glanced at Elite, hoping she wanted him.

"I'm sure she will be fine for a moment. Please, amuse an old man."

Antony followed out of curiosity. They walked into an adjoining room filled with musical instruments and desks.

"You've got quite the woman there," the elder said.

Antony stood opposite him, resting a hand on the smooth black lacquer of a grand piano. "I do." He folded his arms and faced Katsu.

"She has good taste in men," the elder said, a smile bending one corner of his mouth. When Antony didn't respond, he asked, "Do you know who I am?"

"You're an elder in my wife's church—she told me that much. Look, what's this about?"

"It feels like I've known you for a long time now," Katsu said.

Antony scoffed. "What can you possibly know? We've never met."

"I know you're an atheist. And that your day job is less than desirable."

"What?" Antony's hand clenched at his side. *Impossible. Viper is invisible.* "How do you know that?"

"And I know you would do almost anything for your wife."

Antony stole a quick look at Elite through the doorway. The wedding guests had gone silent, frozen like statues. A man stood, a wide grin on his face. The woman at his side leaned toward him, her hand to her mouth as if she was whispering in his ear. A woman sat, her mouth open, a glass tipped sideways in her hand. Liquid hung in a waterfall above her lap. The house was quiet, as if the world was on mute. Antony could hear the old man's slow breaths and his own quick ones.

"Do anything for her, that is, except give her a child not of your blood."

"That's none of your business," Antony snapped as he looked through the doorway again. The scene was eerily the same. Katsu moved closer, forcing Antony to step back.

"How are you doing that? Why?" Antony gestured toward the dining room.

"I'm just giving us a little privacy so we can talk," Katsu said. Then he whispered in Antony's ear, "Why are you so opposed to the adoption? Don't you care about her feelings?"

"You think you're cool with your fancy parlor tricks," Antony said angrily. "But you aren't fooling me—you must have talked with my wife's friends."

Antony placed his hands on the elder's chest and pushed. Katsu stepped back, raising his hands to shoulder level.

"What do you think you're accomplishing with your stupid assumptions?" Antony asked.

"Nothing, my dear boy. I'm not trying to intimidate you in the least."

"Good, 'cause you're irritating me instead."

"So how was your trip to Pakistan?"

Antony raised an eyebrow. "Pakistan?"

"I don't like the Middle East—too hot." Katsu gave him a knowing smile.

"Who do you think you are?" Antony's left hand touched the grip of his pistol in the waistband holster at the small of his back, a subtle move he had perfected over the years.

No, I can't . . . he's just trying to mess with my brain. Antony forced his hand to release the weapon, thinking instead of the blade at his side.

"The question is," Katsu said, moving forward and pinning Antony against the wall, "who do *you* think you are?"

"I asked first," Antony growled, pulling out his knife. He stepped sideways, out from Katsu's grasp, and shifted his feet, turning to face him. In a second, he had Katsu pinned against the wall, his blade arching toward his throat. Katsu brought his own arm up. He held a Sai, the hilt in his palm and the three blades parallel to his arm. Antony's blade clanged loudly against it.

"Patience, boy. My time is not yet."

"Who are you? Why are you bothering me?" Antony asked, his voice raised to a shout. He could feel the anger boiling inside him. His head fought his instincts as to whether the elder was a real threat.

"I knew you the moment I saw you walk into the home. Your Kai energy is very high."

"That's all in your head," Antony retorted. The scene was strangely similar to the one last night at the train station.

"God wouldn't lie to me. I've been waiting for you," Katsu said.

"I don't care what you think."

"What I think doesn't matter. It's what he thinks."

"You're delusional."

"He has plans for you. Big plans." Katsu pushed at Antony's arms, staring at him. "Antony Danic, I extend to you the position of Speaker and High Elder in training."

Antony loosened his grip on Katsu's throat. His arms were going numb, probably from holding them at an odd angle. "Yeah, right. In your dreams."

"Exactly." Katsu smiled.

"Whatever." Antony put his dagger in its sheath. "Crazy old man." He walked away.

"You will come to me when you're ready," Katsu's voice called over the distance.

Antony waved his hands over his head as he stormed out of the room. The guests began to move again. Antony found Elite in an adjoining room. She held a plate of food and a cup.

"Antony?" She set her dishes on a table covered with mounds of food. "You look horrible."

He needed to touch her, the center of his universe. She reached for his face. He grabbed her hands and held them, kissing her fingertips.

"Antony, you're hurting me," she whispered.

He released her hands. She looked worried.

"I need a drink," he said.

"I have one right there."

"No, I need something stronger." His heart slammed against his ribs. He sucked in again, but it didn't reach his lungs. He turned. He needed fresh air. It was too hot in the house, and there were too many people. He hated crowds. He looked at one wall. There were doors leading into the rest of the house, and more people. The front door was too far away. He looked the other way. There was a side door much closer. He gasped again.

"Antony?" He could hear the panic in Elite's voice. She held his arm as he made his way to the exit. "Somebody help us!" she said loudly.

He shook his head. Everyone in the room stopped talking. Antony pulled at the air—it felt warm and humid. A man approached as Antony and Elite stepped toward the door. A few feet and he would be able to breathe.

"Are you okay?" the man asked, reaching out.

"Don't touch me!" Antony barked and took another step as he hit the man's hand away.

"Is he choking?" someone asked.

"He's having a heart attack," said another voice.

"He looks so young."

Antony was almost to the door

"Antony!" Elite cried as he pushed a woman to the side and careened down the stairs. He stood on the grass and bent over, placing his hands on his knees, gasping for air. He sank to the ground as Elite knelt by him, her hand on his shoulder, rubbing in small circles. His stomach clenched and he retched onto the ground, his fists pulling up grass by the roots.

"Let me through." A soft-voiced man broke through the crowds. "I'm a healer." Antony felt warm hands on his back.

"Please, I . . . I can't lose him," Elite sobbed.

"Just relax," the voice said. "Breathe deep calm in, fear and confusion out."

Antony turned his head. His breath caught as he spied the elder's blue robes. He pushed himself up, lurching backwards.

His anger at himself rose—the situation should not have thrown him. *When exactly did I begin to lose control? Come on, Viper, get it together.*

He coughed and pushed himself back farther, knocking the elder's hand off his back. "Leave me alone. Don't touch me!"

"Antony, what's wrong?" Elite wrapped him in her arms. His chest flared in pain with the effort to breathe, and he could taste bile in his mouth. Everyone was looking at him.

"Home. I want to go home." He looked at her, his hands shaking. *I'm so pathetic,* he thought.

"Somebody call a cab, please," she said.

Someone pulled out a phone and Antony heard it dial. He watched as Sori Katsu walked away, his robes swirling around his ankles with the cool breeze. He stopped and looked back at Antony.

You will come to me when you're ready. The voice echoed in Antony's head. He couldn't tell if it was memory, or if the elder could actually speak into his mind.

Get out of my head, you freak! Antony screamed silently, just in case it was the latter. Katsu smiled, turned, and disappeared into the crowd of people.

4

"I appreciate you coming to our home, David," Elite said as she held open the door.

Antony watched from the couch as a heavy man, not much taller than Elite, stepped in. His gray hair curled just past his ears, and his brown eyes were faded with age. The man looked familiar, but Antony couldn't place him. Antony's thumb reflexively hit the remote button again, and the scene changed from a cooking show to a line of old cars racing around a track.

"No worries," the man said as Elite took his jacket. "I promised your parents I'd look after you when they died." He pulled a pair of glasses out of his pocket and set them on the end of his nose. "Now, where's the patient?"

"In here." She led him from the entryway into the living room.

Patient? He means me, Antony thought as he threw the remote aside and stood. "Elite, can I talk to you?"

"Antony, this is Dr. David Spalding. I asked him to take a look at you after what happened this afternoon."

A memory of puking on the grass flashed through Antony's mind. "I told you, I'm fine. There's nothing wrong with me."

Are you sure? asked a voice in the back of his head.

"There may be nothing wrong now, Antony, but there was something *really* wrong earlier," Elite said. "What if it's serious and you just ignore it?"

"What exactly happened?" David asked as he opened his old leather bag. The seams were cracked and it looked faded beyond normal wear.

"Nothing," Antony said.

The doctor pulled a stethoscope out of his bag.

Nothing? the voice asked.

Shut up! Antony told it.

"We were at the bonding. He came up to me and he was shaking," Elite explained. She pulled her arms tight against her chest, and Antony could hear her voice tremble. "He was gasping for air, and I could see his veins bulging. He asked for a drink, but then he headed for the nearest door. Once he got outside, he collapsed and threw up."

"This guy was playing tricks with my head," Antony said. "It kind of freaked me out. I've been away for a few weeks. It's probably a bad case of jet lag." *Great, Antony—he's going to think you're crazy.*

"It was Sori Katsu," Elite said.

"You met the High Elder? Did he say or do something to make you react like Elite described?" David asked.

"I don't want to talk about it." Antony folded his arms.

The doctor held out his stethoscope, and Antony fixed him with a hard stare. "Would you please pull up your shirt?" the doctor asked.

Antony didn't move.

"Antony, please," Elite said.

"I said I'm just fine. This is stupid." He still wondered at the fact that Elite would call a doctor at all. *She must think something's really wrong with me.*

"Do it for me?"

He saw the glint of tears in her eyes. He knew she'd been scared by what happened—she had babied him the rest of the afternoon. She even got someone to take her job at church tomorrow so she could stay home with him. He wasn't going to complain about that—he hadn't spent time with her in almost a month.

He let out a breath and rolled his eyes. "Fine. For you, I'll let this guy stick that . . ." Elite didn't approve of Antony's swearing, and he had gotten good at long pauses and under-the-breath cursing. ". . . cold thing on my back."

David didn't hesitate. He listened to Antony's heart and felt the glands under his chin as Antony sat on the couch, annoyed that he couldn't see the television screen. *Doctors are so invasive, poking their heads where they have no reason to be.*

David stepped back, returning his instruments to the bag. "I don't hear anything abnormal. His heart is strong, and he's healthy and young. I am going to say it was what we call a panic attack. It's possible that he has a panic disorder and the symptoms will return."

"So it wasn't a heart attack?" Elite asked.

"I'm fine," Antony interrupted.

"I don't believe it was." David wrote something on a pad of paper, tore off the top piece, and handed it to Elite. "This is a prescription for a relaxant. Antony should take one in the morning for a week. Then, if the symptoms arise again, he should take one of these and call me immediately. Call the emergency line if the symptoms don't lessen within fifteen minutes." David tore off another piece of paper and handed it to her.

Antony felt like a little kid. "I'm still here. You don't have to talk like I disappeared."

Elite's gaze flashed to his face and then back to David. "Thank you, doctor." She walked David to the door. Antony shook his head in disbelief.

"One more thing," David said, turning back. "Get some rest. Elite says you have some vacation coming. Take advantage of it. Stress can bring on the symptoms you experienced."

Antony grunted and looked at the television screen, wishing the doctor would just go away so he could get on with his life.

Elite shut the door and returned to the living room. "I'm relieved it wasn't a heart attack," she said, holding the papers in her hand.

"Elite, I told you I was okay. I don't need a doctor telling me I have some stupid disability."

"Panic disorder."

"Whatever. I'm fine, see? He said I'm healthy." Antony stood and stepped toward her, holding his arms wide.

"I was worried." She clutched the papers to her chest, the concern evident in her face.

He breathed out hard. "You worry too much." He plucked the papers from her hands, then leaned over and kissed her on the forehead. "I'm going to bed."

Who opened the blinds? Antony thought as he rolled over. He grabbed another pillow and pulled it over his head.

"Elite," he groaned. A headache was beginning behind his eyes. He could hear her talking in the kitchen. Was she on the phone? He tried to remember if he'd heard it ring.

"No, the doctor said he was healthy. Something set him off. I don't know. He's awake—do you want to talk to him?"

Elite walked into the room and held out the house line headset, then placed a bottle of pills from the pharmacy on the bedside table. Antony frowned. He had crumpled the prescription and referral and thrown them in the garbage. *I should have burned them,* he thought.

"Who is it?" he whispered.

"Just take the phone," she whispered back.

"I don't feel like talking." He pulled the blanket over his shoulder and closed his eyes again.

"You can't hide in the bedroom for the rest of your life."

"That's not what I'm doing."

"Really? How many days have you been in here?"

"One."

"More like a few. It's Wednesday. That's three days."

"Just answer the phone!" they heard from the earpiece.

"Crap. Cate!" He reached for the phone and took it.

"Catelyn!" He looked at Elite and mouthed, "Why didn't you say it was Cate?"

"I told you to answer the phone," she said and walked off.

"It's a good thing you finally decided to pick up," Cate said. "I was about to tell Corporate you disappeared."

"I'm here. You don't have to tell them anything."

"Elite says you're healthy, and a doctor confirmed it. Is it true?"

"I'm just fine."

"Eyewitnesses at the wedding say you freaked out, had a heart attack or something."

"I said I'm just fine." He placed his legs over the edge of the bed but paused as he went to stand. "Wait, are you having me followed?" Silence on the phone. Faces from the bonding flashed through his memory. Did he see anyone there that looked out of place? Why would Catelyn have him followed? He stretched and ran a hand through his matted hair. He was way overdue for a shower.

"Were you still planning on taking three weeks off?" she asked.

"Yes." He walked to the bathroom. "I cleared it with you months ago."

"I expect you to report back to work in seventeen days. I hope your plans don't overlap that at all."

Elite returned to the bedroom, folded towels in her arms. She placed them on the shelf and smoothed them before walking back out.

"Seventeen—"

"You already used four, Mr. Danic, or did you forget that? Have a nice day."

5

Antony sat at the kitchen table, his laptop open in front of him. He closed out of his online bank account. The deposit was there from his last job, and he'd paid the bills for the month.

"I'm going shopping," Elite said as she set a plate on the table. She held her hands out, in one a tiny blue pill, in the other a glass of water.

Antony sighed. She wasn't going to give up on this. "Shopping?" He moved the laptop to the side and pulled the plate toward him.

"Last-minute things for the trip." She gestured with her hands. "Are you going to be okay?"

"Elite, I think I can handle myself for a few hours." He smiled, then took a big bite of scrambled eggs.

"What if something happens and I'm not here?" she asked, offering him the pill again.

He pushed her hand away. "Nothing's going to happen. Your doctor friend said I'm healthy."

"But Antony." She closed her eyes.

"Nothing's happened since Saturday. I'm going to the dojang to practice with Sa Bo Nim for a few hours, and then come home. Nothing will happen." He turned her to the door and gave her a gentle nudge. "Go shopping and forget about Saturday."

"Take the medicine." Elite turned back and handed him the pill and the glass of water. He opened his mouth to protest. One look at her face, though, and he pinched the little pill between his fingers and placed it in his mouth, between his gum and cheek. Then he took a drink of water.

"There," he said. "Now go and have fun."

She smiled and walked to the door. As soon as the door closed behind her, Antony grimaced and gagged, spitting the blue pill into a napkin.

He had dutifully taken the first few, but hated how numb they made him feel. At least the mocking voice in his head had disappeared. He disposed of the rest of the pills in a similar fashion when Elite turned her back. Besides, the doctor declared him healthy. He could explain the events of Saturday morning with a bad case of jet lag. The proof lay in the fact that nothing had happened since the bonding.

He dumped his plate and napkin, with the pill, in the trash and grabbed his tang soo do bag. He already wore his canvas karate pants and a black T-shirt. He listened for the master lock to set and took the lift to the lobby. A fifteen-minute train ride south and he was at his training hall.

"'Bout time you showed up. I was beginning to think you were dead under all that human resources paperwork," Rick said as Antony dropped his bag on the edge of the mat.

"You know my schedule. I'm out of town a lot." Antony slipped his shoes off and bowed, then stepped onto the blue-padded floor.

"I haven't seen you for two months. You're probably as rusty as a shipwreck." Rick stood with his arms folded, a scowl on his face.

"Not a chance—I practice all the time. Besides, I pay you whether I'm here or not."

"That's not what I meant, Antony. Sure, I teach karate for a living, but my intention, especially with my serious students, is to keep you in the best shape possible and your skills current. I'm concerned about you as a person and a black belt." Antony looked down at the floor. "I have a responsibility as your instructor," Rick went on. "Besides, I want to think we're friends."

"We are. I was gone out of town for three weeks, and two weeks before that, and so on and so on," Antony said.

"Well, then, I want two hundred of all your warm-ups. Then we'll work on your forms for your test." Rick walked to the other side of the mat as Antony began with jumping jacks.

Antony had been home a couple hours when the doorbell rang. Laying down the digital reader that held the latest book he'd downloaded, he stood from the couch where he'd been icing his ankle. After landing wrong from a spinning 360-degree back kick, he had to admit to his master instructor that he was a bit rusty. He looked at the door scanner screen to find a blond, gold-eyed surfer dude wearing loose khaki shorts and a bright Hawaiian shirt. He had expected Elite, with too many packages to grip the doorknob or find her keys.

He opened the door. "Gage," he said, not hiding his surprise.

"Nice jammies, brother," Gage said.

Antony opened the door wider as his best friend from his teenage years walked in and set his pack on the floor. "I'm on vacation," Antony said, looking down at his pajama pants.

"What are you doing here?" He pulled his friend into an embrace.

"I was in the area. I thought I'd stop by and see how you're doing."

"Liar. You never come to Canberra."

Gage shrugged and picked up his pack. "When I've got business to conduct, I do."

"Business?" Antony asked.

They had shared a dorm room while training at the Royal Military Academy in Duntroon. Gage had dropped out after his required service contract, while Antony went on to become an intelligence officer and then retired to join the world of Corporate. An inventor at heart, Gage always had his hands in some sort of business venture.

Gage set his bag on the kitchen table and pulled out his laptop, a model that made Antony's look like a toy. "Have a seat," Gage drawled in his Aussie accent. "I want to show you something."

He opened the computer and pushed the ON button. Antony limped over to the couch and grabbed his ice pack. He sat at the table and elevated his foot on another chair, then placed the pack under his ankle.

Gage looked down as he aligned the computer with the wireless electricity transmitter. "What'd ya do?"

"My foot? I landed wrong today at practice."

"Only insane people practice karate. I prefer cricket." Gage started typing. "You still have that strange thing on your ankle."

A dark brown ring, almost black, wrapped around Antony's leg just above the ankle. It looked like a rough drawing of a snake biting its own tail.

"It's a birthmark. They don't go away," Antony said. "What'd you want to show me?"

Music started, and he and Gage watched the screen, which showed a close-up of a metal hinge with a bolt in it. "Welcome to Helping Hands," a voice said. "My name is Mat, and I'll be your guide today." The picture panned back to reveal mechanical hands pulling plates out of a sink full of soapy water and loading them into a dishwasher. "With this remarkable program, you will never fall behind on housework again." This time the screen showed the hands loading clothes into a washing machine. "No time to cook dinner? Company coming over unannounced? No worries, mate—we've got you covered," the voice said as several pictures of hands doing housework dotted the screen. When the screen went dark again, Gage sat back and looked at Antony.

"This is the program you made for your mother?" Antony asked.

Gage nodded. "The very one. I reprogrammed it and worked out the kinks. I installed it at my house, which is where we shot the footage. It works perfectly—the arms are flawless. I call her Mat." He tapped the mouse pad, and a hologram appeared on the keyboard.

"Good morning, Gage. How may I help you?" the tiny figure asked. She wore loose pants and an attractive blouse, and her pale blond hair was pulled up in a messy bun.

"No worries, doll," he said, "I was just showing you off."

"Yes, of course," she said before disappearing.

"Mat, as in Mathilde? Your dead girlfriend?"

"Fiancée. Yeah, that's the one," Gage said. "Look, Antony, I've come here for a very specific reason. I need an investor, someone who knows this idea isn't just a figment of my imagination. I need enough money to mass produce an initial stock and market it."

"So you're asking me?" Antony leaned back, two chair legs on the ground as he regarded Gage with raised eyebrows.

"I've been turned down by every major bank in Sydney. They think my idea isn't marketable, but I swear I have ten of my mother's friends just waiting for this thing to go public so they can get one. Plus, they'll tell their friends and they'll tell theirs. I can't lose."

"These are the metal arms, like you showed me a few years ago?" Antony asked.

"Yeah. I've added more joints to make them even more flexible. The fingers are coated with a non-skid finish. No dropping Grandma's antique china." Gage paused to look at Antony while working with his laptop. "I found you only need one pair in a laundry room, but three or four in a kitchen, depending on how big the room is."

"Three to four pairs? Where are they stored? Elite would have a fit if there were all these metal arms hanging around."

"So would every other woman on earth. No, the arms are installed in boxes set into the wall, covered with doors designed to the customer's liking. I have options such as ceramic or tin tiles, wood, and some that look as if the wall is still intact. I usually install the arms in between the cupboards and the counters, although they also work in the space above the cupboards, too. So, what do you think?"

"I know your inventions are good—I've used them myself. What are the terms?"

"I need this much." Gage slid a paper across the table. "In return, I'll pay you thirty percent of every program I sell until I pay you off."

Antony looked at the paper, calculating in his head. "At this rate, you'd pay me back in about twenty years."

"I know this sounds like a bad investment, but when the business picks up, I'll pay you more."

"No."

"No? Antony, what?" Gage looked crestfallen. He pulled the paper toward him, but Antony placed his fingers on it and stopped him.

"I'll give you the money, but instead of you paying me back, I'll buy a percent of your company and sit on it as a silent partner. You will be the decision-maker, but I'd like my investment to do something. Perhaps I'll use my assets sometime. I think you've got something here, and I'd like to be part of that wild ride."

"Sure," Gage said, his voice cracking. "So . . . you invest the money for the program and marketing, and in exchange, I'll sell you eighty percent of the business until I can buy twenty percent back."

"I'll buy forty percent," Antony countered. "Still your company, and your ideas."

"Seventy-five."

"Fifty."

"Sixty. No less. Your money—you own the majority percent, even if I'm the decision-maker," Gage said.

Antony paused. "Okay, sixty percent."

"Deal." Gage pulled his computer toward him. "We'll work out a contract we can both live with, and I'll bring a witness here to notarize it."

"Elite can witness it. She's a notary." Antony stood. He winced as he placed weight on his foot. Gage nodded as he began to type. "So speaking of beautiful girls," Antony said, "when are you going to ask someone on a date?" He retrieved a bowl of fruit from the fridge.

"Never," Gage answered.

Antony placed the bowl and a loaf of bread on the table. "Never? Gage, it's been years since Mathilde died. I know you loved her, but isn't it time you moved on?"

"We were going to get married. It's not so easy to just pick up your life and move past it. Your father never remarried after Emilie was murdered."

"My father died in a plane crash after the murder."

"Years after. Did he ever date before he died?"

"Well, no," Antony said. "But—"

"How are the plans for the orphanage fund-raiser going? I got the invitation last week. The idea of a luau in the middle of winter is smashing."

"It's going well. Elite found another donor. He said he would double all donations up to ten thousand dollars. And you're changing the subject."

Gage popped a chunk of bread in his mouth. "It's a subject I'd rather not discuss right now. I hope you understand," he said after he finished chewing. "So, this new corporation in which you're the silent partner—what should we name it?"

"How should I know? You're the businessman," Antony said, then dished up two smaller bowls of fruit.

"Something Technologies. I see this being bigger than just the housekeeping program. I have plans, huge money-making plans."

"Therefore the reason I've invested in your ideas. Make me rich, Gage."

"Pshaw, you're already rich."

"Yeah, but I want to fulfill every darn thing on Elite's list, and I need money to do it. I'm sending her to volcanic geology field camp this summer, and she just added visiting the pyramids of Giza."

"See why I don't get hitched? Women are too expensive."

"What about Gage and Antony Technologies?" Mat's voice offered. "We could call it GA Technologies, or GA Tech, for short."

"Perfect," Gage said. "Mat, you're a genius."

"I know. The contract is ready. Should I print it?"

Gage looked at Antony. He nodded.

"Sure, doll," Gage said. There was a whirring noise and two papers shot out from the bottom of the computer. Antony raised an eyebrow. "Mat made it for me," Gage explained. "Computer and printer in one. You want one?"

"Heck yeah," Antony said.

"I'll have it shipped to you next week. Consider it a welcome to my family corporation."

"What color, Antony?" Mat asked.

"Color? I don't care—I just want a computer like that."

"I'll make it green, your favorite," she said.

Antony laughed. "Sure, Mat, whatever you want."

It was late afternoon when Elite came in, her hands full of bags. "There, we're ready to go to Tahiti," she exclaimed as she shut the door to their penthouse apartment. "Oh! Hello, Gage. It's been a while." She set the bags down. "What's the occasion?"

Antony gave his best friend an "I told you" look. Even Elite noticed how rare Gage's visits had become.

"Good afternoon, Elite," Gage said. "Nice to see you."

She walked into the kitchen and kissed Antony on the cheek, then turned to Gage and gathered him into a hug. "You look good," she said.

"So do you, doll." He brushed at her hair. "I like the blue."

"It matches his eyes." She nodded toward Antony and turned to the fridge. "So, what brings you by?"

"I'm investing in his new company, and we need a witness so we can sign the contracts," Antony said. "Will you do the honors?"

Elite took a water bottle out of the fridge, sat next to Gage, and pulled one of the contracts toward her. She scanned it and then looked at Antony. He could see she was testing his resolve on the decision. He retuned her stare for a moment. She sat back, her blue-streaked hair disheveled from the wind outside, and placed the bottle on the table. The condensation ran down the sides to pool on the glass-top table.

"Go ahead, Antony. It's your money. Besides, everything Gage touches seems to turn to gold." She watched as they signed, and then she added her name in the witness spot. "Well, here's to your success," she said, raising her water bottle to take a drink.

Antony nodded, and Gage smiled as he filed the contract in his bag. The other copy he pushed over to Antony, who stood and placed it on the counter next to his laptop.

"Anyone for Chinese? We should celebrate," Antony said. He touched his phone screen. If he had one weakness, it was Chinese food.

Elite smiled and began to clear the table. After placing the order, Antony put his laptop away and helped her set the table with chopsticks and three square plates as black as obsidian. He opened the fridge and reached for the champagne he had stored in the back, but hesitated. He remembered how happy Elite had been when he didn't drink one night a few weeks ago. He grabbed a carafé of apple juice instead and set it on the table.

The things I do for love, he teased himself. The buzz drinking gave him helped him relax from the stress of his life and occupation. Stalking his hit, scoping the area, and getting to know his victim took him away from home for one to three weeks at a time. He would come home for a week and then he was at it again. If Elite hadn't been diagnosed with infertility, he would blame his work schedule for their lack of children. For tonight, for her, he would forgo the alcohol and make her happy.

The knock from the delivery guy startled Antony out of his thoughts. He limped to the door to pay for the food before Elite or Gage could. This was his celebration. Investing in Gage's company felt right and solid, a move so contrasting to Antony's day job, something he and Elite could fall back on if his employer ever became unhappy with him or decided to remove him from his position—if he lived through that kind of Corporate decision.

This was not a job you just quit. Years ago, when he asked Catelyn what had happened to his predecessor, she said he had retired with a bullet to the head. Whether true or not, Antony knew her words were a warning to him, her calm voice and emotionless face a tactic in subtlety. At any rate, if something happened to him, Elite could rely on his percentage of GA Technologies.

He placed the white paper boxes on the table and opened a few of them. The aroma of garlic and onion filled the kitchen. Elite touched her forehead and clasped her hands, her hair falling into her face as she offered a silent prayer. Gage lowered his head as he crossed himself.

Antony bit his bottom lip. When had Gage gone back to the religion of his childhood? Antony would have to have a talk with the boy.

"I love the salt and pepper chicken from this place. Too bad they don't have a location in Sydney," Gage said as he loaded up.

Elite took a small amount of everything, and Antony scooped chicken, sweet and sour pork, and pot stickers onto his plate. He had missed Gage—they'd been friends since they were seventeen. They were troublemakers when they were together, too adventurous to stay out of trouble, although Gage had changed since Mathilde died from meningitis three years ago. She caught it as she cared for her parents, who worked as doctors on the northern island of New Zealand, Antony's home country. Gage was more cautious, less adventuresome, and definitely not as happy since Mathilde died. Antony had strongly suggested he start dating again, but it seemed Gage's heart would be forever linked to a hologram and program that shared her name and memory.

Darkness covered the Australian landscape when Gage climbed into his Land Cruiser and drove home. Antony sat back in the leather couch in the living room. He was now the majority principal of a corporation. It felt comforting— something solid and permanent.

Elite finished packing her bags and left them at the door. The taxi was scheduled to arrive at six in the morning to take her and Antony to the airport. He watched her walk across the wood floor and onto the soft brown rug, her hips swaying in the tie-dyed skirt she had made as a teenager. She sat down next to him and pulled a real paper book off the table behind the couch. He laid an arm over her shoulder, and she snuggled into his chest and opened the book. This was the life he desired—peaceful and perfect, his occupation a small black spot on an otherwise clean white sheet.

He grabbed at the book in her hands. She resisted, but laughed as he finally managed to remove it. Leaning over, he kissed her on the lips.

"I can't wait to have you alone for a week," he whispered in her ear.

6

"Come on—the water's great." Elite ran ahead of him, splashing into the bright blue expanse. He watched her over the edge of his sunglasses as she laughed, spinning, her hands making waves on the surface. "Antony!" she called.

"I'm fine right here, El. Go on." He held his towel and his paper book under his arm. A warm breeze carried the heady scent of tropical flowers and a touch of salt. The white expanse of sand stretched as far as he could see. Palm trees of every size dotted the beach.

With the one o'clock tour of Huahine canceled, they had the afternoon free until dinner. Tomorrow they would visit Bora Bora, then fly home the next day, and this amazing trip would be over.

I wish I'd scheduled the fourteen-day trip instead of the ten, Antony mused. The first day consisted of scuba diving at Riangora, a hike into the forests of Tahiti itself the next. He and Elite had gone deep-sea fishing and tried their hand at surfing, too. Yesterday was a catamaran trip around the island of Moorea. Breakfast on the balcony of their hotel room and snorkeling preceded this afternoon's chance to be lazy. He decided he was actually enjoying the trip as much as Elite was. It was hard to watch her be so happy and not get caught up in it.

Antony spread his towel on the sand. He dropped his shoes, sat down, and set the book at his side. His intention was to relax in this place of no distractions. If he decided to read, he would. If not, that was okay too. The islands were such a direct contrast to the modern world, and he enjoyed the lack of technology. It had been amazingly easy to lock his phone and earpiece in his gun safe and leave the world of corporate soldier at home.

I could get used to this, he thought. He stared out at the ocean. It felt good to be still.

Suddenly, Elite looked startled, and then her face broke into a wide smile. "Look, Antony! It's a huge ray!" she shouted.

Even from a distance, Antony could see several of the giant creatures scatter as she yelled. As one swam near Elite again, she leaned over and brushed her hand across its back. Antony could almost feel her excitement as he watched her.

Soon, he felt his eyelids grow heavy and he lay back, listening to the sound of the breeze in the palms and the occasional tropical bird, and drifted into a memory.

"Elite, what in the— What are you doing?" Antony asked as he walked into the room. The floor was draped in sheets, and all the furniture had been moved to the center.

"Painting." She wiped a stray piece of hair out of her face, smearing paint on her cheek.

"Bright red?" Two walls were covered in the new color.

"It's the guest room, honey. You don't have to sleep in here. Besides, I had this awesome idea."

"I don't think anyone will be able to sleep in here again." He watched her pick up the roller and attack the wall with energy he only wished he had.

"Dinner's in the oven. Go ahead and serve yourself." She paused. "Isn't that your phone?" she asked. Sure enough,

he heard the theme music to The Pink Panther *coming from behind him.*

"Hello?"

Antony opened his eyes. A man sat near him in the shade of the same palm tree, talking on his phone. It must have the same ring as Antony's. "Of course. Goodbye," the man said, then pushed a button and put the phone in the pocket of his swimsuit.

Antony sat up and looked toward the ocean. Elite stood in the water, still playing with the rays.

"Beautiful day, isn't it?" the man asked.

"It is." Antony stretched his arms over his head. He hadn't slept that long, had he? Without his earpiece, he had lost all sense of time. That wasn't necessarily a bad thing, he reminded himself.

"Are you enjoying your vacation?" The man dug his toes in the sand; white grains spilled to the sides of his feet. "It's much warmer here than in Canberra."

Antony said nothing. *Who is this guy?*

"Speechless, eh? They told me you were a hard case to crack." The man's voice sounded gravelly, like that of a smoker. Antony could see the outline of a body holster—a pistol was strapped on the man's hip. The swimsuit wasn't baggy enough to hide that.

"Who are you?" Antony wished he had his Glock right now, but it was locked in the inside compartment of his bag, in his hotel room. A handful of scenarios of how he could kill this man and get rid of the body paraded through his head.

"You don't need to concern yourself with who I am. You should be more worried about why I'm here."

"Which is?" Antony watched Elite through his dark lenses, his body suddenly hyperaware. The man was about six feet tall, a muscled two hundred pounds. Dark hair and eyes, medium skin, no facial hair. A scar marred his right cheek near his mouth, and another snaked into his hairline at the temple. His hands were scarred, indicating either a life of hard work or street fighting. Antony bet it was the latter, but he was pretty sure he could take him.

"The corporation sent me to deliver a message," the man said.

Antony's body stiffened, ready for fight or flight, the muscles on his arms tightening against his will. Elite was about one hundred yards away. The nearest building was about five hundred yards from where he sat, through the trees.

"They're not happy with you, Danic, despite your handler's reassurances. This vacation and your recent bumbling are out of character for an employee of the corporation. Your last assignment took way too long, causing you to miss a window of opportunity for another job." The man turned his head from Antony to stare at Elite, who walked toward them from the ocean.

Antony moved his hand, pointing his fingers down and splayed wide, a signal not to approach him at this time. They'd worked that out a long time ago. She stopped and examined the water at her feet.

"If you continue to frustrate them, I can't guarantee that you, or anyone around you, will be . . . safe." The man stood, still looking at Elite. "I hope you understand. I'm just the messenger." He stood and walked away.

Antony folded his hand into a fist, the signal that it was okay to approach now.

"Who was that?" Elite asked as she sat down next to him.

"Some guy. He wanted directions to the hotel." Antony breathed in deeply. He hated lying to her, but this was their vacation—they were going to have fun.

"Why did you stop me then?" she asked as she brushed the fine sand from her legs.

"He was checking you out and I didn't want him to get a closer look," Antony said. Her cheeks turned pink and he laughed. "What do you say to watching the fire dancers again tonight after dinner?" He wanted to be in public, someplace with a lot of witnesses. Elite's safety was his priority right now.

"I'd love that." She lay back in the sand, putting her sunglasses on.

I'd do anything in my power to keep you safe, he thought.

7

The gray building took up a large piece of the land inside the fence, although there was enough room for basketball hoops and a decent expanse of green grass. Diagonally from the hoops, an old jungle gym stood in the midst of wood chips. They needed a new one, but Elite wouldn't let Antony buy it. "Let someone else help for a change," she said. "If we fix everything, the public isn't going to want to help or think we need it." He had entertained the thought of donating something anonymously, but he knew she'd figure it out. The old one was okay for now, he consoled himself.

Antony paused and looked at the fence. It was ten feet tall, and he knew adding razor wire at the top would make it more secure. He wondered if that would pass zoning in a residential area, or if he should just install an iron fence with pointed tips at the top.

He closed his eyes against the memory of the man on the beach at Huahine. Had he also been at the bonding ceremony? Antony didn't remember his face. Was the corporation really watching Antony's every move? If they were so disturbed by his work lately, why were they even making an effort to tolerate him? Why didn't this man just do Antony's job? The simplest reason was that Antony was better than him. The guy was just the corporation's insurance policy. Either way, Antony needed to make sure Elite was as safe at work as she was at home. This was the real reason he was here at the orphanage today.

Three boys dribbled balls on one of the courts. Antony nodded as two of the boys raised their hands in greeting. The other kid just stared. He must be new; Antony didn't recognize him. *Motion detector floodlights along the fence would be nice too—maybe security cameras.* Antony jotted that down in his small notebook and placed it back in his pocket.

"That's Antony," he heard one of the boys say. "He's married to Miss Elite. He's really cool."

"Miss Elite's married?" the new boy said.

Antony laughed to himself. *Who wouldn't have a crush on her?* He made his way to the back entrance. He punched in the code and the metal gate opened. Gage had designed the system and installed it years ago, right after Elite took control of the orphanage and added the Sanctuary. The Sanctuary was a women's shelter, a respite care center for foster parents, and a safe house for children removed from their parents. They'd had security issues in the past, trying to keep women and children safe from their abusers. The shelter still stayed on top of security, but now Elite was in danger, and that was Antony's priority.

He shut the gate and walked across the blacktop to the back doors adjacent to the kitchen. *A better camera over the back door,* he noted. The kitchen entrance was dark and secluded.

"Good afternoon, Antony," a middle-aged woman said. She stood on the top of the stairs, pouring a pan of grease into the dumpster.

"Good afternoon, Mrs. Moore."

"Are you eating with us tonight? I made your favorite—barbequed chicken."

"For your barbequed chicken, I'd climb Everest," he said. "Have you seen Elite?"

"Mrs. Danic was in the library last time I saw her."

"Thank you. I can't wait for dinner."

"If you're late, the boys will eat your serving." She laughed.

"I won't be late." He headed for the offices. Another thought—*have Gage run more extensive background checks on all the employees at the orphanage.*

"Uncle Dan, Uncle Dan!" he heard and turned around. A young girl with a walker headed down the hall toward him. The younger children found it too hard to pronounce "Antony," so they tried Uncle Danic, and after a while it was shortened to Uncle Dan.

"Hello, Miss Lisa. How are you today?" Antony knelt to see her face to face. Her hip had been broken when she was an infant—her parents threw her down a flight of stairs—and she never healed correctly. She was removed from her home as a toddler and had been a resident of the orphanage since. She wore braces to minimize the turn of her legs so she could walk. Antony and Elite had spent hours at the hospital with her through her many surgeries.

It angered him to know what the little girl had suffered at the hands of those who were supposed to love her most. Lisa was special to him—she was just tiny when she first came to the orphanage. Elite had brought her home and cared for her all day and night for months until she was well enough to leave with the overnight staff. In spite of Antony and Elite's requests to the courts, Lisa had never become eligible for adoption.

"I'm doing really well in my classes," Lisa said. "I just got an A on my English test."

"An A? That's wonderful." Antony pulled out his wallet and gave her a dollar. He did that for all the kids, encouraging them to try hard in school. She smiled and placed the money in the bag on the front of her walker. He stood and looked down the hall. "I need to talk to Miss Elite. I'll see you around, okay?"

"Bye," Lisa said.

Antony's heart broke to look at her and know her disability was caused by abuse. Her parents were never convicted for their crimes against her, but when she was three years old, they were arrested in a drug bust and sent to jail. Lisa then became a ward of the state. Children removed from their homes who weren't reunited with their parents were declared ineligible for adoption and for the foster system, and were raised here in the orphanage. Elite's goal was to have it be as much like home as possible. She took no income from the orphanage, thinking it was better to use the money on things for the kids.

These were Elite's children, in a way. When her mother managed the orphanage, Elite would come home from school and do her homework in the library with her friends. When her parents died, it was natural for Elite to take over. The day after the funeral, she sat at her mother's desk and immediately went to work. With her brilliant ideas and fundraising abilities, she had started the Sanctuary in the unused wing of the building.

Her mother had maintained the orphanage well and always kept the foundation in the black, but Elite's fresh blood and vivacious personality started a larger influx of money, more than the orphanage had ever seen before. *Elite's good at everything she puts her mind to,* Antony thought, then wondered if he should put cameras in all the rooms, or just the hallways and Elite's office.

"Hey, Dan, come see," a voice called as Antony passed the teen recreation room.

He stopped and saw Chris, one of the newer permanent residents, facing the TV with a game controller in his hand. The teen sat on a donated couch with threadbare cushions. They could probably reupholster it instead of getting a new one, Antony decided. The more money they saved on maintenance and furnishings, the more children they could house. The teen room had a large-screen TV on one end with the couch and beanbags. At the other end of the room, numerous tables and shelves lined the walls, full of games, books, and art supplies. The kids' room was similar, but the TV was locked in a cabinet. Elite insisted the children read books before watching movies.

"What did you do to earn your enable card?" Antony asked as Chris pressed the buttons with his thumbs, holding his tongue between his teeth.

"Huh? Oh, I got a white card for behavior last week." White signified good behavior—black was bad.

"Good. Does this mean you're going to take school and the rules here seriously?"

"Uh, yeah. One week in detention was enough for me. She had me hauled off in a cop car."

"But those are the rules, Chris, and you were made aware of them when you came here."

"Yeah, I know," the teen grumbled as he pressed the buttons harder. "I made it to the fourth level."

"I see," Antony said. "That's good. Did you find the secret points on level three?"

"You mean the chest in the old hotel? Yeah, I got them."

"Good," Antony said as he sat next to Chris. He picked at the loose threads on the cushion, then forced himself to stop, knowing Elite would note his behavior and say something about his being nervous. He wasn't nervous.

"Hey, Dan," another teen said as he came in, a laptop under his arm.

"Hey, Dallin, how's the story going?" Antony asked.

"Good. I fixed the plot after I showed it to my English teacher. It's sounding a lot better." Dallin opened his computer. Elite had talked a manufacturer into donating laptops for all the older students.

"I want to read it when you get it done, remember?"

"Sure, when it's done." Dallin looked down.

From the brief excerpts the boy had let him read, Antony thought he was a good writer. Antony enjoyed the story; he felt himself drawn into Dallin's imaginary world. Books were Antony's way of escaping the real world. When he read, his mother's memory lived warm and sweet.

He found himself pulling at the threads again and decided to move before he unraveled the whole couch. "I still need to talk with Miss Elite. I'll see you guys later," he said as he walked to the door of the teen room. Both of them muttered some sort of goodbye, and Antony turned left toward the library and Elite's office.

Suddenly, he stopped walking and took his notepad out again. *Bars on all the windows, not just the Sanctuary,* he wrote. When he got home, he'd talk to Gage and see if he'd contract the work that needed to be done. Gage would understand why Antony felt shaken by the threat at Huahine. They had served in combat together. Despite the fatigue of battle, they'd talked long into the night that first evening as the fighting faded with the sun.

Standing at the door to the library, Antony could see that the few couches and rows of books were undisturbed. He thought it strange—as a teen, he would have loved to have access to this many books. His mother used to read him volumes of fantasy and science fiction as he fell asleep. Her favorite had always been a story about a planet covered in desert sand.

He kept walking down the hall and ended at the door to Elite's office. He pulled out his keys, and as he touched the doorknob, it swung open. *How do I convince her to lock her door?* he asked himself. She needed to be accessible to the staff and residents, but someone could just walk in, and she would be caught unprotected. This room was empty, too. *Where is she?* Turning, he scanned the room, looking for the best place to install one or two lenses. *So much for having any privacy,* he thought.

"Aw, El, I'm sorry to do this to you," he said as he noted a corner where her desk would be visible.

"Sorry for what?" her voice came from in front of him.

"Nothing!" He jumped, hiding the notebook in his hand and pulling his arms back. Elite stood up from the floor, holding a bunch of pens in her hand.

"I was opening the package and they exploded all over," she said, her cheeks coloring slightly. "What's that?" She leaned to the side, attempting to see behind him.

"Nothing." Antony put the notepad in his pocket as she dropped the pens in her drawer and came around the desk to stand by him.

"What are you doing here? I thought you were working on those things Catelyn sent you while we were gone." As much as he hated lying, he couldn't tell her the truth. She would call him "paranoid" and think he was being ridiculous. The corporation was beginning to make him nervous. The new security here needed to be installed, yesterday.

"You're not busy, are you?" he asked.

"I always have time for you."

"Good. I was at home, and I realized we forgot something."

"Oh?" Her brows furrowed.

"Yes." He leaned in close. "You forgot to give me a kiss goodbye this morning," he whispered. He took her face in his hands, and his lips met hers.

The bright green and blue GA Technologies logo streamed across the side of the high-gloss box on the kitchen table. It must have arrived after Antony left for the gym, but before Elite left for work. He hadn't been involved in the design process at all, but he was impressed with the professional image presented by the packaging alone. He could imagine giddy homemakers' reaction to getting their shipments of software and the mechanical arms that came before Gage's installers arrived to finish the job. Antony slid the dagger out of his calf sheath, opened the box, and removed the paper.

A slick, second black box opened to reveal a heavy-duty laptop case. He pulled it out, letting the other boxes and material drop to the floor. Within seconds, he had the metallic green laptop out and plugged in.

"Good morning, Antony. I was wondering when you'd open me. So, do you like?" Antony grinned as a hologram of Mathilde appeared on the mouse pad. "I'm programmed to recognize your voice."

"I like it," he said. "So, I'm connected to you. Cool."

"Of course. What would be the point of having just another regular laptop?"

"Now, if I had you in miniature . . ." Antony said.

"I'm working on that. Are you going to try me out?"

"Okay, what's the foot pound per second of a .308 bullet at four hundred feet?"

"What shape and how many grains?" Mat asked.

"One hundred eighty grains, pointed, not round."

"Altitude?"

"Ten thousand feet."

"Temperature, barometric pressure, and relative humidity?"

"Twenty-nine degrees, twenty-one inches, and seventy-eight percent."

"At 400 feet, the foot pound per second would be 2,124." Antony put down the calculator as Mat gave her answer. "That was easy," she said. "Ask me something more difficult."

He stood and pulled out a drawer in his filing cabinet, then opened a small box and removed two small tubes of glass with red liquid inside. He laid the first one on the optical sensor.

"Who is this?" he asked.

After a few seconds, Mathilde replied, "Antony Danic, age thirty-two, born in Dunedin, New Zealand. Six foot two, one hundred eighty-seven pounds, blood type A negative. Department of human relations for a local corporation. Married to Elite Danic. Retired lieutenant of the Australian Defense Force. Scout sniper and munitions expert."

"How do you know all that?" he asked. "I'm supposed to be invisible."

Mathilde paused. "I scanned you when I was at your house last time. According to the world database, your blood sample doesn't match with any person on the planet."

"That's not funny," Antony said as he walked into the kitchen to grab a drink. He didn't like the thought of being in some database where he could be found.

Mat laughed. "Yes, it is."

Antony's black hair slapped against the back of his neck as he ran. It still smelled of chlorine—he never showered between running, biking, and swimming. He had only paused a moment as he pulled on his pants and shoes, then took off from the Olympic-sized community pool into the cool air. Before his laps at the pool, he had ridden his bike for ten miles. He would run ten miles, then return home to shower and dress.

Gage had agreed to contract the work for the orphanage and sent some of his men for the assessment. They would be back to install the new equipment next week. It hadn't been hard to convince Elite that a wrought-iron fence would look much better in the residential area than the chain link.

Meanwhile, Antony had an assignment—the message on his phone told him to meet his handler at eleven this morning. He looked at his watch. He had an hour until he was supposed to be in downtown Canberra. *Not enough time,* he told himself. He would retrieve his bike from the pool area later. Passing the two-thirds mark, he poured on the energy and sprinted to the doors of his apartment building. He would be late if he didn't hurry, and Catelyn hated it when he was late. She was normally a congenial person, but she got grumpy when he made her wait.

He touched the UP button, then paced in front of the elevator to cool his muscles.

"Good morning, Mr. Danic," an elderly woman said as he passed her.

"Mrs. Vant. I'm sorry, I didn't see you." He stopped at her side, leaning over and placing his hands on his knees, breathing hard.

"Out getting your exercise, I see," she said.

"A man's gotta stay in shape for the girls."

She smiled and patted his bare shoulder. "I don't see why a corporate type such as you needs to almost kill himself running, though."

"Kill myself?" Antony laughed. "I was in the military before I retired and decided to become a desk jockey. I guess I like to stay in the best shape I can."

"Well, we ladies aren't complaining when you don't wear a shirt, my boy," she said and stepped into the lift.

Antony smiled and followed her. He stretched, bringing one knee to his chest, and then the other.

"You've been in town for a while. I bet that sweet wife of yours has enjoyed the time."

"Yes," he said. "Elite and I went to Tahiti for ten days. It was nice."

"It must be easy for the two for you to pack up and just go, with not having kids," Mrs. Vant added as he stretched his back.

Antony stopped and breathed deeply as the emotional pain gripped his heart. "Not as easy as you think," he said, forcing himself to sound neutral. Mrs. Vant wasn't trying to hurt him, he reminded himself. She was just an elderly woman who had made it her job to mother them. Besides, she was on the building's community board, so it wouldn't be good to anger her. "With my job and Elite's charity work, it took almost a year to get the time off to go," he said as the woman raised her eyebrow at him. "I'll probably be out of town again by tomorrow. Such is the life of an executive."

Mrs. Vant grimaced, then looked at the lift's display as she gathered her bags. "Well, I'll see you when you get home."

Antony mentally hit his forehead. He had offended her. "When I return from my trip, we'll have you and your husband over for dinner again. You know Elite and I had a lot of fun the last time."

The elderly woman's face brightened at the invitation, and she smiled as the doors started to shut.

Antony leaned his head against the metal of the door and groaned. She didn't understand—no one who had children would. Silently, he walked to his apartment and opened the door. Elite was making breakfast, but he walked past her into the bedroom.

"Antony?" she asked as he slammed the door.

He stripped and stepped into the shower, letting the water drum some of the tension from his muscles.

"Antony, what's wrong?" Elite called.

He ignored her, knowing if he opened up right now, it would all come flooding out and there would be no immediate end to his frustration. He had no time to deal with this now.

He jumped as the water turned cold. "Elite!" he yelled.

She stood outside the shower, her hand on the faucet knob at the sink. The hot water streamed out like a flood. Her other hand was folded across her chest in defiance. "What's wrong?" she asked again.

He stood in the cold water, rinsing the soap out of his eyes and hair. "I think I alienated Mrs. Vant."

"What? She's on the board. What if she doesn't approve our lease renewal?"

"I know. I didn't mean to . . ."

"What happened?"

"I saw her in the lift on the way home," Antony said. "She made a comment about us not having kids. I tried to be nice—I forced myself to be nice—but I think she saw through it. I told her we would have her and her husband over for dinner again. I think she liked the idea."

Elite frowned. "Catelyn called and asked if you were home."

"What did you tell her?"

"That you were out running."

"And?" he asked.

"She wanted to move the appointment up. She said something about errands she had to run."

"Move the appointment up?" he said. He turned the water off and lunged out of the shower as Elite turned the hot water off. "Crap! If Catelyn calls again, tell her I'm on my way. And tell Mrs. Vant I'll be home in a few weeks. I have another assignment." He couldn't call Catelyn directly—her number came up as private on his phone and he had to go through headquarters to contact her. There was no time. Besides, she would be grumpy no matter if he told her he was going to be late, or just showed up late.

"Sure," Elite said, frowning.

He paused. "What is it?" He ran his hand through her hair.

"The fund-raiser is Friday. I was hoping you'd be here this year—some people think my husband is imaginary."

"But I have to go when the corporation says go."

"I know, but I hoped."

"You'll do just fine. You always do. The orphanage has been making a profit since you took over."

"I wanted you here."

She turned away and he followed her out of the bathroom, his shirt flapping behind him. He took her by the shoulders and turned her around. "Sorry—I don't have a choice."

She held her lips tight against the words she obviously wanted to say, and he rushed to button his shirt and slip on his shoes before he ran out the door.

Antony's phone bounced against his chest as he ran up the stairs to the station. The westbound train was just arriving as he stepped onto the crowded platform. Above him, the north-south lines were just as busy. He pulled the phone out of his chest pocket and placed it in his pants pocket with his keys and his knife. His hand hit crumpled paper—he pulled it out and smiled. It was a receipt from a little trinket store on Riangora in Tahiti.

He remembered the pareao he had given Elite. She'd really wanted it—he knew from the way she kept coming back to it repeatedly at the little roadside shop. After sending her off to buy some fruit, he purchased the pareao. He gave it to her that night in their hotel room, and her squeal of delight was enough thanks for him. She immediately wrapped it around her waist, tying it on her hip.

The trip to Tahiti had been pure bliss, though definitely not long enough. One day on each island didn't give them enough time to really relax—it was more of a rush-around-and-enjoy-the-sights trip. Next vacation, he would plan a stay in one hotel in one place and sleep in, with a spend-the-day-at-the-beach itinerary. Even with the rushing around, the islands had been beautiful and the culture purely enjoyable. It frustrated him, how with all their moving from island to island, the man from Corporate still found them. *How did he get a visitor's pass so easily? It took me years,* Antony thought.

His mind went back to Elite. He hated to leave her when they were arguing, but he'd had no choice. Catelyn ruled his life. His contract with the corporation was in effect until he died or they released him. He hoped he never got on their bad side and experienced what they meant by "releasing" him. After the strange conversation with the man on the beach, the threat was much more a reality than it was years ago when Antony signed the contract.

In a few blocks, he got off the train, walked a block north, and turned east. He stood on the corner and looked around. Catelyn was nowhere to be seen.

Dang it! She knows it takes me an hour and a half to go through my whole course. Across the street stood a busy convenience store, and the other corner held an empty lot, with no sign of any recent traffic. A greenhouse occupied the third. Antony slammed his hands in his pockets and stood there fuming. He grabbed his phone and dialed Elite's speed number. He got her voice-mail greeting. *Stupid caller ID,* he thought. She wouldn't answer her phone after this morning.

"El, this is Antony. Look, I'm sorry," he said as he turned away from the traffic so he could leave a clear message. "Has Cate called? I'm at the meeting spot and there's no one here." He looked up and stopped. On the corner where he stood was an old cathedral, the gray stone reaching toward the sky. "Never mind. I'm sorry. I'll talk to you when I get home."

He shut his phone and ascended the steps toward the large oak doors. He walked into the church and looked around. A woman sat on a pew near the front, her head down in the silence of the chapel. He sat behind her to the right.

"You're late," she said.

"And you've got one heck of a sense of humor, dragging me in here when you know I'm an atheist."

"I thought it was funny." She sat back and Antony leaned forward, as she had been doing. A manila envelope dropped to the floor and she pushed it under the bench with her feet.

"Boss said this one's important—no mess ups, no misses."

"Catelyn, I haven't missed in almost ten years. You know me."

"I repeat your instructions, that's all. And I'm docking your pay one hour for making me wait."

"What?" Antony gasped and looked from the floor to his handler.

She chuckled. "Have a nice day, Mr. Danic."

She stood and walked past him, her perfect red lips smiling. Her long brown hair was pulled back in a tight bun, so formal compared to Elite's casual grace. He watched Catelyn's slim figure leave the church. He leaned over and picked up the envelope, then stuffed it under his shirt. In his haste to get here, he had forgotten his pack.

Antony sat for many long minutes in the pew, looking at the religious icons of this particular faith. He didn't feel like he was burning to ash in this building. He wondered if it was just his guilt or the fact that he was usually sitting by Elite when he felt that way.

When he knew his handler was long gone, he stood and walked toward the doors. There was a single candle lit in the bank of candles against the wall.

He wondered at people's faith. *Does lighting a candle send a message to their God any easier than touching your forehead and asking for Providence? What makes these people, in a world so degenerate, believe there's something up there that cares? If it cared, wouldn't it do something about this trash heap called earth? If God existed, wouldn't people like me be struck by lightning? My life is proof there is no supreme being. Religion is for those who need a crutch to get through their life.*

Antony left the church and stopped on the steps. It was raining. He cursed under his breath and ran for the train station. The cold rain soaked his shirt, and his feet grew wet in his sockless shoes. He was cold by the time he made it to the station. He hated being late, he hated forgetting things. He was a soldier—he shouldn't forget anything, ever. He would be punished for this if he were still in the Australian Defense Force.

He had quickly grown weary of the military. The rigidness and lack of freedom had worn at him, and when it was time to retire, he did it willingly. He needed to be free. He needed to be his own person, rule his own life, make his own decisions. Sure, a little structure was nice, but to be told when to wake up, brush your teeth, eat this, march this long, do this and that—it was too much, and his free spirit rebelled. He was thankful for the training and experience, though. It had made him who he was now.

No looking back. It was a promise he had made himself a long time ago. *Do not examine the person you're killing longer than you need to. Once the case is closed, file it neatly in the back of your mind and never open the file again. Never bring it up with either your employer or spouse unless it's absolutely necessary. Do not give details of a hit to anyone—it could be their life if you do. As an assassin, you're expendable, but they are not. She's not. Elite is your priority, period.*

His train arrived two minutes late—the rain always did that. His shirt clung to him, dripping on the carpet as he opened the door to the apartment.

"Antony?" Elite said from the kitchen. "You're soaking wet."

"I'll be done in a minute," he said as he passed her and headed straight for his office. He locked the door behind him. This was the only time he shut Elite out of his life—when he had an assignment from Catelyn. He pulled his shirt off and threw it to the floor. Water from his hair dripped onto his shoulders and ran down his back. Elite would have a fit. He smiled as he pictured her hands on her hips as she went to clean his office. He considered it payback for the cold shower he had taken that morning. Sitting at his desk, he opened the envelope. The damp papers slid out onto his desk and he tossed the envelope to the floor next to his shirt.

The hit was a man named Kyo Yuji, an Asian man, seemingly innocent in appearance. Some of Antony's hits looked very criminal in nature. He was never given a reason for a hit. Not only was it unnecessary, it was hazardous for him. He killed on command, and if he ever knew the reason why, it would make it harder to go through with it. Plus, it wasn't his business. He slid the papers into his drawer, picked up his soggy shirt, and headed to the bathroom for the second time.

Soon, he was dressed, with his shoulder-length hair pulled back. He stepped behind Elite as she stood at the kitchen sink. He reached his hands around her and took the plate from her. He wrestled the towel from her hand, and she fought him for a second.

"Look, hon. I'm sorry." He kissed her neck. "I didn't mean to upset you."

"I know. I shouldn't be," she said as she turned and reached her arms around his neck. "I knew full well who I married. I know you're at the beck and call of your employer. I was just . . . hopeful that you'd be here this year."

"I might be. I still have some research to do."

"I won't hold my breath," she said, then smiled. "You know, we should put blue streaks in your hair, too."

"Why? So the unseen, obscure assassin will be more easily identified?" He kissed her forehead.

"No, silly. Because they would match your beautiful eyes."

9

According to Antony's computer, Kyo Yuji was a merchant who lived in Kyoto, Japan. He dealt in traditional and antique artifacts. Besides the store's address, there was no other information online or anywhere else Antony searched, as if outside of Kyo's store, he simply disappeared. He was a model citizen, no tickets or debts that Antony could find. It was easy to find someone who had a criminal record or who used credit to buy things. *This guy? Nothing!* Antony thought as he shut his laptop.

He had planned to wait a few days before leaving so he wouldn't miss Elite's fund-raiser, but now he began to think he needed to leave as soon as possible. Three factors contributed to his decision: the way Catelyn talked about this hit, the complete lack of information—with the exception of a business license with Kyo Yuji's name on it—and Antony's gut feeling. What if it took weeks to find the guy, like Mr. Bennett in Pakistan?

Elite left early, without kissing Antony goodbye. He would pack his bag and leave for the airport in half an hour, knowing she would not be home before he left. He placed a pair of lightweight pants and a shirt in the pack. It was the middle of summer in Japan. His earpiece, his Corporate-issued phone, and several food bars and water pouches joined the sniper rifle and Glock .357. Last, he added his paper-thin woven Kevlar undershirt. It wouldn't stop a bullet at point blank, but it protected him from lesser injuries. Packing light was a necessity—he didn't have time for luggage. When he was on assignment, his pack stayed on his back all the time. It was security for him—easy to move, easy to escape. The extremely light titanium gun cases were also waterproof. Once, on an assignment, he had jumped in a river and floated to another city to get away.

The train rushed through the industrial area and out of the city. Tall steel and glass buildings gave way to rural homes and then greenery as the train raced toward the airport on suspended tracks.

Antony wondered how long it would take Elite to forgive him this time. They had been getting along well lately—until this morning. He didn't know how to explain that this mission was a priority, that Cate had warned him this hit was of the utmost importance. Antony had no idea why, since Kyo was just a merchant. What did the man know, or do, that had ticked off Corporate?

The train stopped and Antony looked up at the sprawling airport buildings. He exited the train and walked through the doors. The Canberra airport was busy. He had to walk sideways to avoid some tourists having their picture taken in front of a brass statue of a wallaby family. Antony stopped and back-stepped to avoid a man in black pants and shirt. Black sunglasses covered his eyes, and his short brown hair was immaculate. The man snarled at the inconvenience of having to move.

"Do you have any luggage?" a voice asked. Antony looked down at the self-motorized platform. "I'm cheap and reliable."

"I don't have any," Antony said, then turned to search the departure boards for his terminal.

"I'm better than the competition," the platform said as it moved forward on a cushion of air.

"Obviously you don't have an optical sensor, or it's broken." He placed a foot on the bed of the machine, preventing it from bumping into his shins. "Look, I have my pack, and that's it." The cart gave what he could only assume was a sigh, programmed to guilt people into using it, and floated off.

Antony hated most modern technology—it was unnatural to see something that wasn't human talking to you. He swiped his Corporate card at the turnstile and passed through. His boarding pass would be ready when he reached the terminal. He loved to travel for the corporation—it was first class all the way, if things went well. If not, it might be a slow barge from Kyoto to Fiji and then a flight in a small plane with a pilot who had a death wish.

A high-pitched wail caught Antony's attention. A young girl stood rigid while the contents of her backpack spilled at her feet. Her blond curls streamed unkempt down her back, and her dress was clean, but thin from wear. The woman traveling with her stopped and turned back at her cry. Antony assumed she was the girl's mother. The woman knelt and dropped the two large duffel bags she carried. The baby who slept on her shoulder squirmed.

"Delia, please. We have to hurry or we'll miss our flight," she said as she rushed to grab the toys. She scanned the crowds as if looking for someone, and Antony could see the whites of her eyes.

"My baby," the girl said, her voice trembling. Her doll and a few small items were still scattered on the floor.

"We'll get you more dolls after we reach our new home." When the woman looked up, her body stiffened and her eyes went wide. She reached down to grab the doll and shove it into the pack. Deep purple bruises marred her arm.

She's running from somebody, Antony thought. His fist clenched on the strap of his pack.

"I'm looking for Lydia Mathis. I know she has a flight with you guys!" A large man stood at the ticket counter, his voice booming over the crowds. It wasn't hard to link the two of them together, judging by her reaction to seeing him.

"I'm sorry, we're not allowed to give personal information about our passengers," the counter attendant said.

"So, she's on your flight."

"That's not what I said, sir."

"She left this at home." The man waved a piece of paper. "I know she had a flight with you today. Look, she's my wife. I need to talk to her."

Antony stepped forward, quickly grabbed the remaining toys, and placed them in the pack.

"There you go." He zipped the girl's pack and settled it on her shoulders.

The mother smiled cautiously. "Thank you," she whispered.

"Eh, no worries. What terminal do you need? I can help."

Her eyes narrowed. "I'll be fine, thank you." She stood and picked up the two overstuffed duffle bags. The baby still lay on the woman's shoulder, asleep. The woman watched the man for several seconds, then hissed to the little girl, "Let's go."

Antony stood and looked back. The man was searching the crowd with his eyes as the clerk did something on the phone. Antony positioned himself between the woman and the guy, hiding her with his bulk.

"Look, I've got nothing to do with him." Antony held her, his hands on her shoulders, so she wouldn't be able to look around him. "You're in trouble, and I can help."

"You can't help me."

"I might be able to ensure you get on that plane," he offered.

"Look, mister, I appreciate it, but I can do this myself."

"Not every man you meet is going to hurt you, ma'am."

She didn't reply, but her eyes told him she didn't believe him.

He moved her away from the lobby. "Just give me the terminal number," he urged. Then he noticed her eyes were tinged with tears. "I'm sorry," he said, backing off. "I didn't mean to scare you. I just wanted to help."

"C2," she said, her voice catching with emotion.

Antony looked up at the departure screens. A flight for Hawaii was leaving from Gate C2 in twenty minutes. The man still stood at the counter, alternately talking with the clerk and looking around for his wife. Antony pulled her to the right—the lifts to the terminals were a few meters from where they stood.

"Let's go this way," he whispered, taking her arm in his. He pulled her to the rows of lift doors and punched the button. He stood against the wall, his body blocking hers from the direction of the ticket counter. As he ushered the little girl into the elevator, Antony could still hear the man arguing with the clerk. Antony held the doors open for the mother and pressed the CLOSE button several times. The doors shut before anyone else could get in the lift car.

"I can get you on the plane and distract him." Antony tried to hide the scowl on his face—he wasn't a monster, yet she still looked terrified. Although, if he'd told her he was an assassin, she would have probably run from him screaming.

The woman simply nodded.

Antony pulled out his wallet. He had withdrawn a large amount of yen, but still had some Aussie dollars. He handed her the wad of cash. "Use this to get far away from him." He held it out to her, but she resisted. "It's not poisoned, and there is no tracker. I'm just a retired soldier, turned corporate courier. Please take it. Let me help your children."

The woman hesitated, then took the money. Antony wondered if the man had harmed the two innocent children in her care. His blood boiled at the thought.

The lift stopped one floor up and Antony looked out the open door before he led the woman out. Time was running short—the flight left in less than ten minutes. Looking back, he caught her gaze.

"Do you trust me?" he asked. When she nodded slightly, he scooped up the girl, took the woman's thin hand in his, and took off toward the terminal. The girl stiffened in his arms, and he wished that for this floundering family of three, things could be different. He stopped at the counter gate and let the girl down. She immediately moved to stand close to her mother.

"Danielle Tourrant," the woman said to the clerk after a moment. Antony knew this wasn't her real name—it took too long for her to remember it.

"I'm sorry, the flight is full," the attendant said. "We loaded on standby, and your seats are gone."

"What?" Danielle looked behind her, and Antony felt her panic. "I need to get on that flight, or I'll miss my connection."

"I'm sorry. We stress the importance of arriving early."

Antony looked at the attendant. "She needs to get on the plane," he said, his face cold and hard. The woman at the desk looked at him and took a step back while smoothing her brunette hair away from her face. "What about first class?" he asked as he reached for his wallet.

"There are a few seats left in first class sir," she said as she looked at her screen from a distance.

Antony pulled out his Corporate charge card. "Fine," he said as he swiped the card in the machine. "Upgrade her connection, and take good care of her." He stared the attendant down. She swallowed hard and typed a few things on her computer, then handed him two ticket stubs.

Antony turned to the woman with the children. "Here," he said, pulling her aside and handing her the ticket stubs. "Have a better life." He turned away.

"Thank you. I don't even know your name."

He turned back. "Perhaps it's better that way."

Another attendant led the woman and her children onto the plane. Antony waited until the door shut and he could hear the engines roar as the plane backed away. Walking through the crowds, he spotted the woman's husband rushing toward the gate. Antony smiled. The plane was on the runway, and the man would not be able to touch her. Antony watched him slam his fist against the counter and pull out his wallet.

No! he thought. *He's going to follow her.* Antony stopped and watched from a distance as the man took his ticket stub and pocketed it, then walked away from the counter. The poor clerk looked frazzled.

The man stopped and looked at his watch. He was a big man, middle class from the looks of his clothes. He walked into the restroom, and Antony followed. There was no one else in the room. The man stood at a long bank of urinals, his head thrown back. Antony stepped next to him and placed the barrel of his pistol in his ribs.

"Let's talk," he growled and jerked his head in the direction of the stalls. The man zipped his pants in haste turned to look at Antony.

"You're the one who helped her get away," he said, but shut his mouth when Antony pushed the pistol harder into his flesh. Antony led him to one of the stalls and pushed open the door.

"Sit," he said, and the man sat on the toilet. A thread of sweat appeared on his balding forehead. Antony's high-tech pistol wouldn't make any more noise than the sound of the hammer hitting the cartridge. "You think it's okay to beat on someone because she's smaller than you?"

"You know nothing of my life, mister. She took my kids. Did she tell you her sob story? She tells everyone. She made it up."

"I suppose the hand-size bruises on her arms were just makeup," Antony answered. "According to you, her fear was manufactured, too."

The man punched Antony in the mouth. He blocked a second hit and placed the gun under the man's chin. Blood tainted Antony's mouth as he wiped his sleeve over his lips. No visible mark. Good.

"You think it's okay to hurt a woman because you're better than her?" Antony moved the barrel of the pistol from chin to temple. "Well, you're not," he whispered, and pulled the trigger.

Click.

The man's body jerked and then slumped against the stall wall.

Antony stepped back and used his knife to lock the door to the stall. He washed his hands and rinsed his mouth out—the water ran pink down the drain. He looked at his watch; he had fifteen minutes until his flight was scheduled to leave. After pulling his shirt down to cover the pistol against his back, he left the restroom and took off running.

He arrived at the gate as the attendant was reaching for the jetway door. He grabbed the door and smiled, then raced past her and onto the plane. He sat back in his seat, his pack in his arms, and closed his eyes.

"Your seat belt, sir," a female voice said. "Are you okay?"

He opened his eyes and focused on a young, blond-haired flight attendant. "I'm fine," he said.

"You're bleeding." She motioned at the corner of her mouth. Antony reached up and touched his. He looked at his fingers—the pads were smeared with crimson.

"I pulled a door open and hit my mouth. Perhaps a napkin and a little ice?"

She nodded and left for the galley.

Antony's mouth hurt and his teeth felt loose in his gums. That man had quite a punch. Antony wondered how long "Danielle" had lived with the monster. She wouldn't have to worry about him anymore. Antony smiled and took the white cloth napkin and the ice pack from the attendant.

"Thank you." He wiped at his mouth, then placed the ice pack in the napkin and held it against his face. He pulled out his phone, put on his headphones, and closed his eyes, letting the sounds of almost one-hundred-year-old Depeche Mode help him relax.

10

The humidity hit Antony as he emerged from the airport in Kyoto. It felt like Sydney, where Gage lived. Antony pulled a folded paper out of his pack, shoved it in his pocket, and zipped the pack shut. He stepped forward, his shoes half on the curb, and raised his hand. A small taxi turned out of the stream of traffic and pulled up next to him. It bounced once as the air cushion adjusted beneath it.

His hotel was only a few blocks from Mr. Yuji's shop. Antony reserved it that way on purpose—it gave him a place to start looking. Leaning forward, he showed the address to the driver. The driver nodded and pulled the shuttle out into the heavy, late afternoon traffic. As the vehicle cleared the airport, it took a tight turn and stopped, floating straight up to the next light, then stopped again, waiting for the hovering light to change. The red bar turned into a green circle, and the shuttle accelerated and eased into a line of shuttles above the road. Antony sat back and watched the buildings slowly pass by. After every building began to look the same, he closed his eyes.

Elite stood in the doorway to his office. Looking tired, she leaned into the doorframe, her light blue shirt marked with tears. His pack lay on his desk, along with new supplies. He put a magazine in the handle of his pistol, pulled back on the slide to chamber a round, and let it close. He placed the gun in the holster and left it on his desk. He looked up at her, but said nothing. Words right now would be heated and damaging. He placed his rifle case in the pack, then added food bars and water pouches. Glancing up, he caught her eye, but she looked down. He frowned, shoving the first-aid kit and a change of clothes in the pack, then zipping it shut.

"Elite." He stepped toward her.

She turned and walked away.

Now Antony sat forward and stared at the glass and metal buildings until his eyes hurt. He hated fighting with Elite. He would give everything up for her—this lifestyle, this job. But to leave meant death; he knew too much, had seen too many things. Until he was disabled—he winced at the thought—or the corporation decided it was time for him to retire, he worked for them. Period.

The taxi turned and the big glass buildings and wide streets turned into the smaller shops and narrow passageways of a small merchant district. Although built in the last few hundred years, it resembled feudal Japan. The point was to allow tourists to experience the quaint side of the country, to take a break from the urban sights of the modern city. Antony had never been here before, but the district was featured prominently on the tourist sites he had browsed before the flight.

The hotel sat on a large piece of land surrounded by gardens. Trails led to shrines, temples, and other sights that reminded Antony of the Sento Imperial Palace Grounds. He used his phone to calculate proper fare and tip, then handed the driver two bills and got out of the taxi. He dodged a young woman rushing toward the city center, a white mask with black stripes embroidered on the back of her jacket.

At the top of the stairs that led to the hotel, he turned around and examined his surroundings. According to his map, Mr. Yuji's shop was two blocks down a side street and to the left. Antony turned back toward the hotel and opened the red doors, then entered the cool of the lobby and made his way to the front desk. He slid the reservation paper across the counter and was greeted by a young woman with jet black hair and pale skin.

"Place your hand here," she instructed him. A blue laser slid down the screen as his handprint was mapped and made into a key. "Thank you," she said in a heavy accent.

Technology was nice, but Antony preferred things simpler and old-fashioned. One of his treasures was a set of metal keys on a large ring. His father found them and gave them to him when Antony was young. They didn't open anything, but they were his. Perhaps that's why his taste in music was so outdated, too. The old-fashioned record player Elite had found for his birthday a few years ago was one of his favorite gifts. They spent long evenings dancing to the records they would play.

At his hotel room, he placed his hand on the key pad and opened the door. The room was hot and muggy, so he quickly found the temperature control. Tapping the button, he watched the numbers go down until the cooler clicked on. The room was typical—a bed, a desk, and an armoire with a TV. A small fridge sat on the floor next to the sink. Antony opened it and felt the cool air hit his face. There was a large assortment of soda and a few foreign beers. He reached in and pushed aside some of the cans on the top shelf. There, in the back, were four bottles of water. He grabbed one, opened it, and drained it in a few gulps.

Time to locate Mr. Yuji's shop. Antony closed his eyes and breathed out, then threw the bottle in the trash bin. It landed with a *swish* in the round container.

"Score," he said to himself. The room would be cool when he got back. Besides, it was dinnertime, and he was craving authentic Japanese food.

Soon, he stepped out of the hotel, letting the red doors shut behind him. The crowds surged and waned. Antony looked up and down the street. Many people wore colorful costumes, and street-side booths sold food and trinkets. It must be a festival of some sort. How annoying—the streets were congested and it would be hard to move freely without being pushed along with the flow of the crowd. His target's schedule might also vary and be harder to predict. Antony hadn't thought to check the computer for information about festivals.

No worries. He maneuvered to walk on the outside of the crowd, hugging the curb. The first part of a hit was to locate the target and verify identification. He stepped into the road and in front of a shuttle. The horn blared and he raised his hand and smiled as he dashed to the corner. Then he started down the street he had looked at earlier. He seemed to be going against the flow of traffic and spent a lot of time dodging people as he made his way. By the time he found the shop, the sky had dimmed and the throngs of people were thinning.

Walking into the store, he glanced around. A young girl dressed in a traditional kimono stood behind the counter. The floor looked like bamboo. To his right was a colorful display of kimonos. Pottery and other trinkets filled one wall. Behind the girl was a large section of jade carvings. There were paper lamps, Buddhas, fans, and parasols.

"Can I help you?" a voice said behind him.

Antony turned. A man in a black suit stood next to him, hands behind his back. Antony leaned away from the smell of cologne and cigarettes.

"I'm fine, really. I was just looking." He walked to the door. The store was unique in this modern world—it was a store he would frequent if he lived close by. He wondered if it would survive when Mr. Yuji was gone.

It shouldn't matter, Antony thought. He looked up just in time to avoid running into Kyo Yuji himself. Antony's target was dressed for the festivities in red and black satin, his long black hair pulled back in a braid. A small, secondary braid was tucked behind his left ear. Antony looked down and moved to the side to get by. Strange—Mr. Yuji looked a lot like Sori Katsu, the old man at the bonding. At any rate, Antony now had a positive identification on his target.

The traditional Japanese had it right, Antony mused a short time later as he sat at a booth in a café. While those who practiced the Shinto religion believed in Kami, or spirits, they also deeply respected their ancestors. He could do that— the ancestors, not the spirit thing. He had loved his adoptive parents; they had taken him in and cared for him as if he was their blood. He'd worshiped his father, the man who taught him everything he knew about martial arts, firearms, and shooting. And Antony had adored his mother, a loving and sweet woman. His only regret about his life with his parents was that he hadn't told them how much he cared before his mother was killed and his father disappeared and was assumed dead.

Antony knew nothing of his biological parents. As an infant, he'd been left on the steps of a church on a cold winter morning in Dunedin, New Zealand. The note claimed that his mother was too young to care for him and asked those in the church to find someone who could. A woman had seen the basket on the steps on her morning walk, snatched it, and ran home like mad. She and her husband paid an official a lot of money to approve the adoption without the state getting involved. It was a fair exchange—Antony's adoptive parents were older and had never been able to have children. They doted on him and loved him unconditionally.

Walking back to the hotel was easier than getting to Mr. Yuji's store had been. It was growing late and the crowds were moving in the same direction as Antony.

When he got to his hotel room, he put his pistol under his pillow, then slid between the cool sheets, closed his eyes, and let fatigue overcome him.

Elite stood in the living room, her flannel pajamas rumpled from sleep. She held a baby in her arms. He cried, and she bounced him softly to quiet him. Antony stood in the doorway of the bedroom, fingers gripping the frame as if he could pull the wood off it himself. A man stood next to Elite and the child, with Antony's own gun pointed at her head. He was a large man and nicely dressed, and Antony swore he had seen him before. Elite's eyes pled with Antony to save her, but he was frozen to the spot. He didn't dare move for fear the man would pull the trigger.

Antony waited for a chance to get to Elite before the man killed her. The man sneered at him, and Antony's eyes widened as he recognized him. It was the man from Huahine—the one who had threatened them. Antony could feel his pulse pounding in his head and hands. He wished the gun in the man's hand was in his—Antony would kill him without a thought. Watching every move the intruder made was his only chance at the moment. A phone rang and as Antony flinched, the man jumped. Elite closed her eyes and Antony heard a gunshot.

Covered with sweat and gasping for air, Antony sat up in bed, his fists grasping the sheets. Where was he? Elite! Reality came slowly as he focused on the banner with the Kanji symbols running down it. He was in Kyoto—he was on a hit. He rested his head in his hands and closed his eyes tight.

Just a dream, he told himself.

It was almost six in the morning before he could breathe normally. He had never dreamed like that or felt so vulnerable. He dressed and made his way to the streets. He took off at a jog toward an area famous for its temples and shrines. He needed to run the nightmare out of his head so he could function—so he could kill his target and get back to Elite.

As he ran, Antony remembered the training his father had begun and that Antony had finished in the military. He suppressed the dream and all the feelings that came with it and pulled the soldier in his brain to the front of his consciousness. He allowed himself to harden, to wish the feelings in his heart away.

He remembered coming home the first time after he had joined the ADF. His parents' home was quiet and empty. After his father's funeral, Antony had ordered the sale of almost everything. He couldn't cry or grieve—he simply couldn't find a way to weep. No effort of his could start the tears falling, and he had walked away from his childhood home numb, unfeeling.

With his room's contents stored in a small unit, he had signed the real estate contract and gone back to Duntroon. It wasn't until he had met Elite and married her that he could finally grieve the loss of his parents. She brought out the human in him, but in this case, he needed to be a soldier, leaving the human locked away.

An hour later, Antony stopped near the green trees of a Shinto shrine, panting and coughing. He felt like gagging, even though his stomach was empty. He collapsed to his knees and gasped, closing his eyes against the sweat that ran down his face to the ground. Every muscle in his legs and chest felt like fire. He hadn't run so hard or so fast in a long time.

I feel so much more in control now. So different from this morning. Nothing would stop him from completing his assignment. The soldier had taken over. He chastised himself for letting thoughts of home break through his walls. He shook his head as he regained his breath.

"When you deny who you really are, it causes pain, yet when you accept your path, joy is felt." A voice invaded his awareness. Antony's eyes snapped open and he looked at a short monk with a wooden rake in his hands. His rough brown robes were wide in weave and dusty. A triangular, woven reed hat shielded his face from the morning sun. The tines on the rake were wooden dowels spaced far apart. The man had been raking the gravel in patterns around larger rocks and trees at the base of the shrine trail.

"What?" Antony said, still winded. "You know nothing about my path."

"I know when someone denies his true course," the monk replied.

"I don't believe as you do." Antony began to walk away.

"Believe what you may, but the path you walk is one of pain," the man said quietly.

Antony picked up his pace and ran toward the shrine. He slowed as he entered a series of orange and black gates placed close together to form a tunnel of sorts. A sign at the entrance identified it as a Torii archway at the Fushimi Inari Shrine. The sunlight flashed between the pillars as he ran. He could see the greenery at the end as he made a slight turn and came face to face with Mr. Yuji again, tripping over him and skidding to a stop on the gravel.

As the man spun and fell to the ground next to him, Antony reached for the pistol at the small of his back, but he paused. To draw any weapon within the shrine grounds was a serious crime in the Shinto faith. Whether he believed or not, his respect of other cultures and religions was a professional courtesy. Yuji didn't look surprised to see him, almost as if he expected him to be there.

"Yujisan! Yujisan!" Antony released his grip on the butt of his pistol as three children surrounded his target. Yuji laughed and started to talk to them in Japanese.

Antony scrambled to a stand and took off toward the end of the archway. He couldn't breathe again. *If I'd killed Yuji at that moment, it would have been witnessed by three young children and shown disrespect to the sanctity of the shrine. Bad timing and poor planning on my part.* He was losing it. How had he lost his concentration so easily?

He couldn't wait to get back to the hotel. He needed silence, and the noises of the city celebrations were pounding in his ears. He walked, ran, and stumbled to the station and boarded the next train heading in the direction of his hotel. It was past noon when he stepped through the door into the air-conditioned room. After slamming the door, he dropped onto the bed and lay prone, face on the soft comforter, eyes closed.

Feeling the blood rush through his head, he began to gain control of his breathing. *I can't be washed up—I'm in my prime! I know of other corporate soldiers who were well into their fifties before retiring. I'm just too busy, and I let that dream, and what that stupid monk said, get to me. Yes, that's it, I'm just tired.* Antony let his eyes droop and he dozed.

The sky out the window was dark when he opened his eyes. He groaned and rolled over. His need for sleep had obviously influenced last night and this morning's events. Feeling better than he had for days, he told himself he wasn't losing it. But he knew there was something wrong with his mental state right now, a reason he was so scattered and unfocused. He needed to fix it, soon. His only other option was to return home to Canberra, tell Corporate he couldn't do it—that he was washed up—and wait for the stray bullet to come whizzing into his skull.

Come on, Viper, pull yourself together. You're better than this, he told himself. Slowly, as if there were weights attached to his body, he pulled himself to a sitting position. The clock read 9:37. His stomach grumbled—he hadn't eaten all day. Antony reached for the communication console by the bedside table.

"Room service, please," he said. "Your daily special would be fine. Thank you." He hung up. His heavy feet slid off the bed and he stood, bracing himself against the wall. This assignment might take longer than he'd expected. There was no way he could do a hit in this physical or mental condition.

Take a few days, get yourself back where you need to be, he thought as he made his way to the bathroom. He thought of his father, how he would frown at Antony's current state and demand he go back to the dojo and meditate. *That's it,* he thought as the image of his father faded from his mind. He had not fully prepared for this assignment. The fight with Elite, the woman at the airport, the man in the bathroom, the flight here with his mouth pounding from being hit—every event had drained Antony's reserves, and he had not prepared or meditated at all.

Antony thought of the conversation he had with Catelyn at the church. Everything about this hit was odd, and he was neck-deep in the middle of it now.

A knock sounded at the door, and he opened it to find three large, covered bowls on a black lacquered tray, alongside silverware and chopsticks. Antony picked the tray up off the floor and set it on the table, then grabbed his shirt out of his pack and pulled it over his head. The dirty clothes he placed in the complimentary in-room cleaner would be done in thirty minutes. Looking at the beer in the fridge made him want one, but he needed his wits about him. Instead, he chose flavored water and sat at the table with the tray. He opened the bowls. One held white rice, another chicken, and the last, an aromatic soup. He breathed in deeply, picked up a spoon, and sipped the hot soup. It tasted so good after over twenty-four hours of not eating.

A brightly colored brochure that had been partially obscured by his napkin caught his attention, and he pulled it out.

The Gion Matsuri Festival, or Festival of Purification, lasts the entire month of July, Antony read. "Oh, great," he groaned. There was no way he could stay the rest of the month until the crowds died down. *The celebration peaks on the seventeenth with a large parade. It's the second largest event in the city for the year. Everybody in Kyoto attends. We recommend you find your place for the parade early, as the sidewalks fill fast.*

"Date," Antony said into his earpiece.

"July 15, 2087."

Antony smiled. The parade was in two days. Hopefully, Mr. Yuji would attend the celebration. It would be the perfect time to sneak around his shop and see if there was any clue as to where he went during the day, or slept at night. Meanwhile, Antony would pull himself together and be ready by late afternoon on the seventeenth to take up his assignment again.

After he finished eating, he took off his earpiece and silenced the communications unit. Then he assumed his karate ready stance, his arms hanging at his sides, his shoulders back and his feet apart. He began his routine with qigong, an Asian exercise often practiced with tai chi. He closed his eyes and breathed deeply. Then he brought one hand to the front, palm up, then the other. He swept his right hand down and then back to the middle, then the other hand down and up again. Then his right arm went up and around again back to the center, then his left. Each arm movement brought his hands back to the center.

His father had taught him that when he felt scattered, he must activate the center points and align himself to allow the energy to flow. These exercises would pull the energy from the center point at the base of the spine and allow it to flow through his body. His father claimed this practice was religious in nature, but Antony denied it had anything to do with religion. Again and again, his arms moved in a dance that flowed from one movement to another.

As he felt his anxiety abate and his mind stop rushing, he added a step to the side and swept his arms in a circle again. Then he lunged to the side with his other leg. Feeling centered and energized, he sat on the floor between the bed and the table. Placing the soles of his feet together to create a constant circuit, he closed his eyes. He felt himself fall into a state where even the hum of the air conditioner disappeared.

Silence.

11

"HQ, Viper in recon position," Antony said into his earpiece. He sat in the shadows of the building, waiting for the lights to go out in the shop. In front of him, a butterfly sunned itself in one of the remaining patches of sunlight on the gravel behind the store, the wings flapping in and out, the antennae moving in the breeze. It lifted off the ground and flew toward Antony. He sat still as it landed on his knee before flying toward his head, and then out of his line of sight.

"Roger, position noted. Radio silence commenced."

No one, not even Elite, would be able to reach him until he called them. If he didn't contact Corporate for more than a few days while in recon position, they would assume he was dead and send a crew to clean up the corpse.

The crowds in front of the store were growing. On the sidewalks, people stood several bodies thick in anticipation of the parade that would start any minute. It would be dark soon—the light was fading slowly on the hot summer evening. Antony would break into the shop when he was sure it was empty.

He had gone back to the store that morning, hoping to see Mr. Yuji so he could follow him. Antony was paying for two kimonos—one a pale lilac for Elite, the other blue for him—when a man with an envelope came in and walked up to the counter.

"I've got a delivery for Mr. Yuji."

"He isn't here. He'll be down momentarily," the lady behind the counter had said. "I can sign, if it's okay."

The delivery man nodded and handed her the digital notepad. She signed it and took the envelope, and the man left.

Antony had heard heavy footsteps above him and looked up. The ceiling was nothing remarkable—the lights hummed slightly, and the occasional wind chime dangling from hooks moved in the breeze. However, the building itself was at least three stories tall. That's why there was no residential address—Yuji lived above the shop, Antony had realized. Then he'd returned to the hotel to prepare for that night, and now, here he was, his plan in place.

The light in the back of the store went off, and he looked at the door in silence. The young girl who had helped him earlier checked the lock as she stood on the landing. She had changed out of the red kimono she wore in the store—as beautiful as it was, he imagined it was uncomfortable to walk more than a few feet in it. She rushed down the stairs and out to the alley that led to the front of the stores.

Mr. Yuji's store was dark, except for the security lights. The two floors above the store were black. Antony stood and looked both ways, listening for anyone in the near vicinity. With slow, sure steps, he made his way to the door and walked up the steps. He pulled out two thin metal sticks, each about four inches long, and placed them in the card slot on the lock at the same time. They would short the system momentarily. He had five seconds to open the door, get in, and shut it before the security reset itself. To any monitoring system, it would appear as a surge. He shut the door and heard the lock reset. Both times he'd been in the store, Mr. Yuji had not been there. Antony decided to look upstairs before risking a search in the partial lights of the shop.

A stairway to the left led to the upper floors. He pulled his weapon and started up. The landing on the second floor opened into a living room. Light from the street lit the room in a dim glow. A bamboo and rice paper screen, painted with delicate branches of cherry blossoms, almost hid the kitchen. He walked down the hall and opened the first door on the right—bathroom. The second door led to a bedroom with storage boxes lining one wall. The third door hid another bedroom. No office, no books—nothing to indicate any sort of schedule.

Antony sighed. This hit was proving to be as difficult as the last, but for different reasons. Before, he knew who and where the guy was, but he would just disappear. Here in Japan, Antony had little information about the victim, yet he had run into him twice in places where performing the hit was impossible. But he'd had an idea while watching the clerk sign for the envelope that morning. If he could get Yuji alone under the premise of signing for a package, he could kill him and be done. Antony stepped back into the hall, ready to go to the hotel and manufacture a package and uniform.

"Kyo." He heard a female voice speaking Japanese as someone stepped onto the stairs. He stopped breathing and slipped into the spare room, leaving the door ajar. He found a space next to the boxes and crouched in the darkest corner.

A man answered the woman and paused on the stairs. The man took another step—whether up or down, Antony couldn't tell.

The female sighed. Antony heard the door shut, and the footsteps continued up the stairs. They didn't stop, but ascended the second set to the floor above. This was perfect—Mr. Yuji had arrived alone and Antony was already in the house. He climbed the stairs as quietly as possible. The landing opened up into a large room. Moonlight streamed in the windows along the front. In the far corner, a small room had been made with screens and bookshelves.

He could hear Yuji shuffling around. Antony stepped toward the office and stopped as his foot sank into the floor. He looked down—the floor had mats from wall to wall. Along the windows leaned folding chairs in stacks of four or five. He had covered over half the distance when Yuji stepped out of the office. He held a book in his left hand and a katana in the other. The man stopped moving, and it almost looked like his mouth twitched upward.

"I had a vision that I'd meet you again," Yuji said.

"Vision?" Antony smirked. "Did this vision show you why I'm here?"

"I know you're here to kill me."

Antony stepped forward and raised his pistol, just as Yuji threw the book at him. It hit him in the shoulder, knocking him sideways. He grunted and dropped his pistol at the same time Yuji unsheathed his sword. Antony bent down to retrieve the pistol and Yuji was on him in a flash. Antony grabbed the familiar grip and brought the pistol up to block the swing of the blade. It left a large gash in the slide. He cursed and grabbed for the knife strapped to his calf. This time, blade met blade and he was able to stand after throwing the katana to the side with his dagger. He holstered his pistol, needing to use both hands.

"If God existed, wouldn't he save you instead of just warning you?" Antony asked, blocking another downward strike.

"He expects me to do all I can to protect myself." Yuji swung from the side and Antony felt the sting of the blade cutting flesh.

"That doesn't sound ever-present or omnipotent. I hope you studied well."

"God gives us room to do what we choose. Hopefully, we choose the right things most of the time."

"Sounds like a story to placate the masses into feeling they're doing it right." Antony leaped forward and caught flesh with his blade.

His hands bled in a few places. He wished for his bamboo practice sword—it would give him some reach this dagger didn't, even if the dagger had a longer blade. Not that his shenai would stand up to this sharp katana for long.

Antony's blade blocked another blow. Yuji pulled up hard on the katana and Antony's dagger flew out of his hands, clattering against the wall before falling to the floor. He pulled his pistol out of the holster and pointed it at Yuji, only to be met with the razor-sharp end of the katana pricking the skin above his heart. Antony flinched at the pain and pulled the trigger.

"Goodbye," he whispered as Yuji's face blanched and he fell to the ground. Antony fired the two other shots in quick succession, then picked up the dagger and started for the stairs. Just a few feet from his dagger lay the book Yuji threw at him. Antony picked it up. It had a leather cover and onionskin pages, similar to Elite's scriptures. He dropped the book and ran for the stairs. As he reached the top, he saw someone just a few steps from him. He stepped back into the shadows and held his breath, standing perfectly still.

There must be a way to escape. The front windows were out of the question. The crowds would surely notice a six-foot-two-inch Caucasian jumping out the window. The stairs were an option, but he would have to dismantle the alarm again. It would take too long. The figure stopped at the landing, gasped, and ran for the dead body on the mat.

"Kyo?" the woman said. "Kyo!"

Antony bolted for the nearest back window—it was his only choice now. He covered his face with his arms and threw his body through the glass. The pane exploded and he free fell until he hit a metal awning that slanted out from the brick wall. He rolled off the awning and hit the ground in a crouch. He stood, then ran as fast as he could. He heard a scream from the window.

He hadn't noticed the awning as he reconned the place, but he hadn't planned on killing the guy and making his escape today, either. He needed to get out of there. He ran down the almost deserted street, his chest aching from the knife wound. It was bleeding a lot—it would be obvious to anyone he passed. But if there was a day to kill a man in Kyoto, this was that day. The streets off the parade route were almost deserted.

To the left, Antony saw the gravel and manicured grass of a meditation garden. He had walked past this one yesterday. A river with a bridge lay ahead and to the right of him. He dashed forward on the grass and trail, avoiding the gravel—it would hold a footprint. He could hear rushing water, and above that, sirens. This was as close as he had cut it in years, like the time he jumped in the river.

The river shone in the moonlight just ahead of him. He skidded down the embankment, then grabbed the stone of the bridge and swung himself under it. He panted in the darkness, forcing his breath to become regular and even. After shrugging his pack off his shoulders, he laid it next to him and plunged his hands into the water, washing off the blood. He pulled his shirt off, dipped it in the water, and used it to wipe at his chest. The blood oozed thick and red.

The police would do a global DNA with the blood found at the scene. Antony imagined they would be shocked to find that the samples didn't match anyone on the entire planet— his employers had made sure of that. Genetically, Antony Danic did not exist. There were only a few people who knew who he really was—Gage, Elite, Catelyn, and his employers. Everyone else knew him as the HR guy.

Holding the wet shirt on the chest wound, Antony reached in his pack with his other hand to pull out his first-aid kit. He stopped to rinse out the bloodied fabric, then removed a small spray bottle from the kit. He sprayed it on the gash on his arm and held the flaps of skin shut. The spray dried and the wound stuck together. It almost looked normal—it would swell a bit, but not enough to be too noticeable. Next, he sprayed his chest and held the wound closed. It didn't matter what this one looked like, as long as it didn't open and bleed through his other shirt. He sprayed it again and let it dry, and then a third time, just to be sure.

There were three cuts on his left thigh and one on his right. He pulled at the cloth around the largest and ripped it open further—he was not going to be caught under a bridge with his pants down. After all the cuts were sealed, he looked to the right and then the left, then pulled his pants off and the clean ones on as quickly as possible. After the spray was no longer sticky, he put on his clean shirt, then placed his earpiece in his left ear again.

He crested the bank of the river and was about to activate his earpiece when a flashlight lit his face. He covered his eyes with one hand, his other still on the piece.

"You there," the policeman said in English. "What are you doing?"

Antony looked at the officer. "My cell phone," he stuttered. "I was looking at the water, and I dropped it." He made gestures so they could understand. "I found it." He smiled, pulled the piece out of his ear, and held it up. "I wanted to beat the crowds to my hotel, so I left the parade early." He groaned to himself. *Too much information, Mr. Danic.*

The cop nodded and then turned to his partner. The words "katana" and "pistol" were mentioned, and Antony was glad he'd sealed the cuts on his hands. His gut feelings had saved the day again. Then without a word to him, the two officers walked away.

He strolled away from the cops, and when they were out of sight, he picked up his speed and turned toward the street to flag a taxi. He hit his earpiece.

"HQ, this is Viper. Assignment complete. I need a flight out of Kyoto tonight."

"Roger, Viper. There's a flight out of Kyoto to Hong Kong, and then a connection to Canberra three hours later. That's the fastest I can get you out. The flight to Hong Kong leaves the Kyoto airport in ninety minutes. Can you make it?"

"Yes. I'm getting a cab now. When does the flight arrive in Canberra?"

"Seven thirty PM on Friday, sir."

"Tell Catelyn to meet me at the airport with a black tux, size 36 tall, with size 11 shoes and black socks."

"A tux, sir?"

"Yes. Charge it to this account. Oh, and a dozen white roses. Did you get all that?"

"Black tux . . . size 36 tall, shoes . . . white roses. Sure."

"Tell Cate she owes me. Viper out."

12

"I owe you nothing," Catelyn said as she met Antony at baggage claim.

He smiled and took the bag-covered tuxedo from her arms. She offered the roses, and he shook his head. "Hold them for me," he said, ripping the plastic off the tuxedo. "Did you bring a car? I need a ride."

"Ride? What? No! I was told I'd never have to do you any favors. I'm risking too much by being in such a public place with you."

"What? It's not like I saw you last week in a church, of all things."

"Is this payback?" she snarled.

Antony grinned. "No, I'm simply late for an event my wife planned, and you might as well take me, since you have a vehicle." He dropped his other shirt into his pack, then threaded his left arm through the sleeve of the dress shirt, pausing momentarily at the pain. It served him right for not wearing his body armor, though he wasn't sure it would have stopped a katana that sharp. He pulled the shirt on, buttoned it, grabbed the tie off the hanger, and pulled it around his neck. Closing his eyes, he tied it the way his father taught him when he was a teen. "Do I have to drop my pants here, or can I change while you drive?" His hands were on his belt.

"No!" Catelyn hissed and grabbed his arm. "I'm not going to watch you strip to your boxers in public."

"Boxers? What if I go commando?" He laughed.

"That's too much information, Mr. Danic. Fine, come with me."

She turned on her heel and stormed out of the airport. Antony followed her to a sleek black limo. He paused as she opened the door and disappeared into the car. He stuck his head in and smiled. She sat on the seat directly across from the door, her body turned from him slightly, her arms folded and her mouth drawn into a tight line.

"Catelyn," he said slowly, "you've been holding out on me. I didn't know the corporation treated you so well. A limo—really? Tell me, Cate, do you even have a driver's license? Or have you been spoiled by the corporation all these years?" He dropped his pants for the second time in a day and pulled the black tuxedo pants off the hanger.

"That's none of your business—Corporate asked me to tell you . . ." She turned toward him, then threw her hand over her eyes. "Oh, Antony, I said I didn't want to know what you wear under your trousers."

He let out a low chuckle.

"Where to, Miss Hurst?" the driver asked.

"National Museum, city center," Antony replied.

"You've got a guest," the driver said. "Is he invited, or should I get rid of him?"

"He's fine. The museum, please."

"Yes, ma'am," the driver said, and the limo elevated up, next to the line of overhead traffic, until the driver could maneuver into the stream of shuttles.

Antony's mind spun into high gear. Catelyn's last name was Hurst? The head of the corporation was also a Hurst. She rode in a limousine and wore expensive clothes. From the few times he'd seen Mr. Hurst at a distance, Antony knew he was old enough to be Catelyn's father.

Antony's assignments had drastically changed when Catelyn replaced his old handler. He had gone from acting as a courier, bodyguard, and sometimes hit man to almost a full-time assassin. He never saw the inner workings of Hurst Enterprises, but when Hurst had swallowed Corporate whole in a hostile takeover, everything had changed. In his first meeting with Catelyn, he had signed that "till death do us part" contract.

"So tell me, Miss Hurst." He settled back against the seat. "Who are you, really? You dress in boutique clothes and ride in a limo. Certainly you aren't just my handler. What else do you do for the corporation?"

"I'm not obligated to tell you anything. Besides, that's privileged information. I'm your handler. That's all you need to know."

"Did you just dump me, or are you playing hard to get?" Antony pulled on his jacket, then smoothed his hair. The roses lay on the seat beside him.

"Must I remind you of your wife, Mr. Danic?"

"I'm keenly aware of how much I miss her," he said. "Can't you take a joke?"

Catelyn turned from him, her eyes wet. Antony frowned—he was good at making women cry. He looked at the buildings as they drove past. The museum was just a few blocks away.

"Stop the car," he said under his breath.

"What?" she asked as he moved toward the door.

"Just tell him to stop. I'll walk from here."

"There's no trouble. We can drop you off at the door."

"Just stop the car!" he said. His hand was on the door handle now. "Please," he added almost silently. "Don't make me watch you cry." He studied the floor of the car, not daring to look up.

She turned toward the driver. "Stop, please."

Antony felt the sway of the car as it pulled out of traffic and descended. The door opened and he stepped out before the vehicle came to a complete stop. "Goodbye, Catelyn," he said and shut the door. He slipped into the crowd, the roses in his arm and his pack slung on his back. The limo sat idle for a moment before it drove off.

"Yes, Antony, you're a real work of art," he said to himself as he walked toward the museum. He paused. Would Elite even want to see him? Was she still mad at him? Catelyn was. He turned and set off in the opposite direction. Then he thought of Elite's face when she came in tonight and found him there— how hurt she would be if he chose a shower and bed over participating in the culmination of her entire year of work. This event, the charity for the local orphanage, was her pride and joy. He turned and walked to the steps of the museum.

"Good evening," a man said as he reached the door.

Antony nodded and stepped inside. Standing in the shadows, he watched the slide show Elite had put together over the last few months. As the show ended, a spotlight opened on her slender form. She wore a shimmering, dusty rose dress, and the ends of her deep auburn hair framed her face.

"The orphanage houses one thousand children a year." Elite's voice echoed through the room. "Not only that, it serves as a crisis home for abused mothers and children, and as a safe house for children who have been removed from their parents."

Antony thought of the abusive man he'd left dead in the airport restroom, and the family he helped escape. He wondered if the Sanctuary had ever helped the woman who called herself Danielle.

"This work is expensive," Elite continued. "In order to maintain a full staff and keep the children fed and clothed, we need money. Yes, we do accept donations of food and clothing—please don't let your financial donation dissuade you from giving things like that as well.

"However, when a child is placed with a family, they take their belongings with them, as it should be. These clothes, blankets, and other items are often the first objects of permanence in their lives. The things they bring with them eliminate a small amount of financial burden for the foster parents, too."

Antony remembered the backpack, doll, and toys the little girl carried. Were they the types of things Elite meant?

"These children need you, citizens of Australia. They count on your donations to feed and buy the necessities they would otherwise go without." She paused as a group picture of the children from the orphanage, taken on the front steps, appeared on the screen. "Who will donate the first dollar tonight?" she asked.

Silence filled the room. People shifted and whispered between themselves.

"I'll donate ten thousand," Antony said, and the light swung toward him. He pushed himself away from the wall, the roses laid in the crook of his elbow. Elite looked at him, and her smile almost consumed her face. He stepped forward, wanting to pause as every head turned in his direction.

Opposites attract, he thought. She loved the limelight— he hated it. He took a route to the front of the room where he passed Gage and his bronze date.

"Here, hold this," he said. He dropped his pack in Gage's lap while his tablemates laughed. Antony cradled the roses in his arm and paused at the bottom of the stairs. Elite held out her hand to him, and he took it.

"Ladies and gentlemen, this is my husband, Mr. Danic," she said.

Antony climbed the stairs, then kissed her hand before giving her the roses. She laughed, her eyes shining with tears. He pushed the microphone away from them. "I'm sorry," he said as he pulled her close to kiss her rosy lips.

"I know."

"I'll match his ten thousand," Antony heard Gage say.

Elite's well-dressed assistants started moving through the crowd as people held out cash and checks.

"How was your day?" she asked her customary question.

"Boring as ever," Antony answered.

13

The scenery passed by the window as the train took Antony south into the city. His lawyer, Mr. Caldecott, had called the day after the fund-raiser, wanting a meeting about the creation of GA Tech. Antony didn't blame him. When an important client did something like forming a new corporation, Caldecott wanted to make sure everything was above board. They'd agreed to meet the next day. Caldecott's partner, a criminal defense lawyer, had defended Antony years ago when he was arrested not far from the scene of a hit. Antony had covered his trail well, and they couldn't pin it on him.

They'd found nothing wrong with the GA Tech contract, and Antony was headed home now. After a nice lunch and a few glasses of Scotch, he felt warm and relaxed, something he hadn't felt since he had received the assignment in Japan.

He hoped all the stupid mistakes in Kyoto were just circumstance and bad luck, not his head. The train moved too fast for his buzzed brain, and he closed his eyes. Elite was going to have a fit, but it'd been lunch with the boys, with lots of rich food and liquor and a very fine Scotch at that. Never before had he drunk more than a glass in a social setting, but this time that glass kept being refilled and he kept drinking.

Elite was probably still at the office anyway. Every year, she worked more than forty hours a week for a month after the charity. Antony would be asleep before she walked in the door, and she wouldn't have to know. To any other person— well, maybe except Gage—he could tell yarns and lie like the professional he was. But Elite could look into his eyes and he'd spill everything. Such was the power she had on him. Besides the details of his work, everything between them was an open book.

He had to admit, his desire to drink today came from the memories and guilt of his last hit. His bumbling in Kyoto was so out of character for him. He was an assassin—a professional killer. There was no room in his occupation for emotion or mistakes. To mess up was to be caught or killed himself. His and Elite's safety depended on him being a machine when he was working. An assassin wasn't allowed human frailties like emotion. His cold, calculating brain was what had allowed him to survive for ten years as a corporate soldier.

Don't think about it so much, he reminded himself. The train lurched as it approached a station. His stomach betrayed him by turning sick, and he stood to exit the train. He was still miles from home, but the motion was not helping him at all. He stood in the fresh air, cool compared to the stuffy train, and breathed deeply. His head spun as he scanned the signs for one that said Restroom. *I'm better than this,* he thought as he headed for the door and found an empty stall just before his lunch and the alcohol came back up.

He was not getting back on that train—he would walk. He was used to traveling long distances on his feet. He had hiked miles in full battle dress when he was in the military; he could certainly walk ten miles to his home. It was late afternoon, and the winter sun was beginning to set as Antony headed south. The streets were full of cars and shuttles, the sidewalks full of people. His stomach was still sour, but he wasn't sick or dizzy anymore. *That's good, right?* Elite would be happy. His thoughts turned to the first time he saw her.

He arrived at the Special Olympics water station, where he was assigned, with two cases of water bottles. It was a warm spring day and the participants were going to be thirsty. Gage was working at the first-aid station that year.

"Hello," a young woman said, turning from one of the coolers to look at him. She wore her blond-streaked hair short, and her tanned olive skin made her chocolate-colored eyes stand out. Her full lips were painted bright pink and shiny.

"I'm supposed to work here today—I brought more water." Antony *struggled to swallow as he stared into her eyes. He wasn't used to being caught off guard, especially by a woman, but she was so pretty.*

"That's great. Can you break the packages open and put them in one of the coolers?"

"Sure," he said, and began to do as she asked.

"Elite, girl, how was skydiving last weekend?" another woman asked as she brought two more cases of water to the tent.

She skydived? She was pretty, and daring, too.

"It was a blast! I made my instructor wait until the last possible moment to pull the chute. What a rush!" She laughed.

"That sounds cool," the other girl said. She offered her fist and the woman named Elite touched it with her own. "You going to dinner tonight?"

"Of course. I can't stay too long, though. I need to help my mom—we got a new shipment of supplies."

"Talk to you later," the other woman said, then walked away.

Antony closed the cooler and walked toward the beautiful woman. "Elite, right?" he said, thinking it was a unique name.

"That's me. And you are?"

"Antony. I happen to overhear that you went skydiving last weekend. I wondered if you'd like to go rock climbing with me."

He looked up. The sky was darkening, and the Brownstone house that was his five-mile mark when he ran was just ahead. He was almost home. Elite was so beautiful, and he was still enamored with her. There were moments when he looked at her and all other thoughts fled. He remembered her turning to him, crying, the evening of her parents' funeral.

Though her eyes were red and her hair was a mess, she had never looked as beautiful as she did when she clung to him, needing him—the wandering assassin—as her rock. She had tried to get Antony to love her that night, but he refused, knowing how much she would regret it in the morning, even though it would erase her pain in the moment. That night, as she clung to him, he asked her to move up the date of the wedding, and she agreed.

She looked stunning in her white dress, walking alone down the aisle on their wedding day. As she lifted her skirts to walk from the ceremony to the reception hall, he noticed her hot pink toenails.

"Where are your shoes?" he asked.

Elite blushed. "I couldn't find any I liked."

He stopped and took off his shoes and socks.

"What are you doing?" she asked.

He smiled and kissed her forehead. Instead of holding flowers, she wore them in her hair, and she smelled amazing.

111

"If you're doing this barefoot, so am I." Antony loved how short she was when she didn't wear shoes—how he had to lean over to kiss her, how she stood on her toes to kiss him.

Everything she did was different. The cake was bright pink, and a barbeque dinner was served. Elite requested that guests donate money to the orphanage in lieu of wedding gifts.

They danced late into the night and missed their flight to Hawaii. When they came home from their lengthy honeymoon, his belongings were at his tiny one-bedroom apartment. Elite still owned the large home her parents had willed to her. Antony gave his thirty days' notice, she put her house up for sale, and they bought the penthouse apartment they lived in now. It was a new life, filled with promise.

He entered the building, nodded to the doorman, and pressed the lift button. Antony wondered if he still smelled like Scotch. He was not drunk—vomiting at the station had sobered him up fast. Once he reached the top floor, he pulled out his key and unlocked the master lock, a series of three deadbolts in the steel-reinforced door. He opened the door, but a hand touched his before he could flip the light switch. He pulled his Glock immediately.

"It's me," Elite whispered.

He reholstered his gun and sighed. "El, don't scare me like that. I pulled my pistol," he said as she turned on a flashlight. "Is the power out?" As soon as he said it he realized it wasn't, since the lift worked and the lights in the hallway were on.

"I wanted to go camping but it's too cold," she said, "so I thought we'd go camping here."

Two lanterns glowed, and he could see the furniture pushed against the wall, and their tent set up in the middle of the living room. Something simmered in a Dutch oven on a portable electric stove. Folding canvas chairs sat in front of the tent, and their camp table was open and set with enamelware dishes. Antony breathed out slowly and chuckled. He turned and locked the door, setting the security system. The door screen showed that two windows were unlocked.

"Lock windows?" the screen asked, and he pressed the YES button. He turned from the screen when he heard the kitchen window lock.

"El, I'd love to go camping with you."

"Good. I made dinner, and for dessert we can roast marshmallows over the fire."

"Fire?"

Elite laughed and shone her flashlight on the stove. He reached for her hand and felt flannel. She was wearing her camping shirt and her jeans. Antony slipped off his pack and pulled her close.

"Let me get comfortable, and I'll help you find sticks for those marshmallows," he said. He locked his pack and his pistol in the safe, then changed into his pajama pants and a T-shirt. He hurried to the bathroom and brushed his teeth thoroughly and gargled with mouthwash. Hopefully she hadn't smelled anything earlier. He moved to where she was stirring the stew and took her by the hands, pulling her into a slow dance.

"There's no music," she said, an amused smile on her lips.

"We don't need music—just the beating of our hearts."

"That was really corny." Elite laid her head on his chest.

He leaned over and kissed her head, still swinging her from side to side. "It was, wasn't it? I love you," he whispered, and he heard her sigh against him. He understood completely.

She led him to the folding table and served him stew and rolls. "I hope you like it—I used your favorite recipe."

"Anything you cook tastes good." Antony dipped his roll in the stew, sopping up the liquid. "I thought you'd be working late," he said. "You know, charity wrap-up stuff."

"We're done. My office manager hired a new assistant who's excellent with numbers, and she whizzed through it. We earned almost twice as much this time. Now we can get rid of that old, dilapidated swing set and get one of those cool new ones for the play yard. And some game systems for the teens."

"I thought we already got some."

"No, the money had to go to rewire the kitchen after the fire."

The fire had damaged the kitchen and scared the kids, but harmed no one. "Oh, right. You should have reminded me. I'd have gotten them some systems and games," Antony said.

"So you could go there and play for hours?" Elite asked as she cleared the bowls from the table.

"Well, yeah." He loved to play games. It helped with his reflexes and response times.

"You're such a kid," she chided.

"I know. Well, where are the marshmallows?"

She turned around, opened a box, and pulled out marshmallows, graham crackers, and chocolate bars. "I thought you'd like these. I can't remember what you call them."

Antony grinned. "They're s'mores, El, and thank you. I haven't had one in a long time." His mother used to make them for him and his father. The taste always brought back sweet memories.

Elite pulled out two long barbeque forks. Antony laughed at her makeshift roasting sticks and sat on the floor in front of the camp stove, patting the rug next to him. She sat and handed him two marshmallows. He put them on the end of one of the long forks, then held them over the burner and slowly turned them as they browned. Elite leaned against him and closed her eyes as he placed the marshmallows on the cracker and chocolate.

"You want one?"

She shook her head. "I'll just have a bite of yours. I think I ate too much." She leaned forward and turned off the stove.

"Must be the crisp mountain air," he said, and she laughed. He offered his s'more and she took a bite, the melted marshmallow stringing from her mouth. She caught it with her fingers and placed them in her mouth, closing her eyes. He took a bite and then shoved the rest in his mouth.

"You, um . . . got something on your chin." Antony leaned over and kissed off the sweet stuff.

She caught his head with her hands. "You have chocolate on your lips."

14

Antony stood on the thick rug in the living room, his feet shoulder width apart. He stepped forward with his left foot and leaned forward, then kicked and struck backward with his right foot and hand. "Aiya!" He brought his hand and foot back to his body and stood for a moment on one foot, his hands at his side. Next, he stepped backward with his right foot into a middle knife hand block.

He was prepping for another block when his phone rang. He opened his eyes and looked in the direction of the ring. Where was his phone? He had it in his pocket when he moved the coffee table onto the couch so he had room to practice. It rang again and he saw its red metallic corner under the couch. He leaned over and grabbed it. It was Elite's number.

"Hey, honey," he said as he opened it.

"Hello? Who is this?" a male voice asked.

"This is Antony Danic, Elite Danic's husband. Who is this?" He pulled the phone away from his ear and checked the caller-ID display. "Where's Elite?" he asked as a chill ran down his back.

"My name is Elder Calder. I am a pastor at your wife's church. Your number was on her speed dial. I'm afraid your wife is ill and collapsed in the chapel. I have her in my office right now and she's awake, but weak. I was going to call the emergency line, but I thought I'd see if I could get hold of someone first."

"Don't call the emergency line. I'll be there as fast as I can, and I'll take her to the hospital myself." Antony didn't trust anyone anymore.

"Sure, Mr. Danic. I'll be waiting for you. My office is on the east side of the building."

Antony ended the call, grabbed his pistol and his wallet from his office, and locked the office door.

"HQ, this is Viper," he said into the phone as he walked out the front door.

"Acknowledged, Viper. What can I do for you?"

He locked the door and hurried to push the lift button. "Where's the nearest available shuttle? I need one ASAP."

"There is a shuttle sitting unused in front of the German Embassy on Empire Court. It uses a green card to start. Are you in trouble?" the Corporate operator asked.

Antony smiled despite his worry. "No, I'm fine. Thank you." He stepped to the curb and looked for a taxi. They weren't common, but they sometimes worked in the area. Most people in the Deakin District owned cars or shuttles, and paid horrible fees to park them near their homes.

"Anything else?" He contemplated having the operator call a taxi, but it would take at least ten minutes to arrive, and in ten minutes he could be halfway to the Embassy District by train.

"No, thank you. Viper out." He hit the sidewalk running. It wasn't until he noticed his feet felt funny that he realized he had slipped his feet into the pink fuzzy slippers Elite gave him for Christmas a few years ago. What a sight he must be in his black AC/DC shirt, plaid pajama pants, and pink slippers, he thought. He caught the train with two minutes to spare and exited just a block before the Embassy District, where the train route ended. Trains were not allowed into the area.

He turned down Empire Court and easily found the Corporate shuttle. He pulled out his green card and slid it through the scanner, then felt the engine hum as the air cushion pushed the shuttle off the ground. He turned the vehicle and headed north to Elite's church. He pushed the engine, but the speed regulator stopped him before he could break any laws. He set the shuttle down in a stall on the east side of the church building twenty minutes after he hung up the phone with the Calder guy. His friend Samual met him at the door, a man in light blue robes right behind him. Antony had to suppress the shudder that the memory of blue robes gave him.

"She passed out right in the chapel," Samual said. "It freaked us out. Melinda went across the street to get her some food."

"Where is— Melinda is here at church with you?" Antony asked. Samual's wife was as much an atheist as Antony, and he knew she went to church with about the same frequency he did.

"She got a new pair of boots and wanted to show them off," Samual said under his breath.

Antony shook his head. Melinda was so unlike Elite. "Where's Elite?" he asked.

"Mr. Danic? I'm Elder Calder. She's just inside here," said the robed man, opening a door.

Antony walked past him to see Elite resting on a couch in a side room. He knelt by her. "Elite?" The panic in his voice surprised him.

Her eyes fluttered open and she smiled. "Antony." She reached out a hand. "You came."

"Of course I did." He placed an arm under her head and the other under her knees. He lifted her up and adjusted his grip.

"I hope she's feeling well soon," Elder Calder said.

Antony turned and swallowed his bitter remark. Calder had done nothing wrong. It wasn't this man in his blue robes who had caused so much trouble. *Be professional,* Antony reminded himself. "Thank you for calling and for taking care of her. I appreciate it."

He pushed the door open with his back. Elder Calder followed as Antony placed Elite in the shuttle's passenger seat and buckled her in. Samual stood next to Antony.

"Her bag," the elder said suddenly, then dashed back inside the building.

"She's going to be okay, right?" Samual asked.

"I'm taking her to the hospital. We'll find out what's going on there. I'll let you guys know when I know something."

Elder Calder rushed out the door and handed Elite's bag to Antony, who placed it at her feet. He climbed in the driver's seat and used his card to start the shuttle again. The vehicle floated up to the interstate travel height. The hospital they used was across town.

"Hold on, El," he said as she groaned. She hated shuttles. "I'm taking you to the hospital."

"No, Antony, I want to go home. I'm just nauseated."

He glanced over at her tight, sallow skin and realized she was dehydrated again. She had a habit of not eating or drinking anything when she was either busy or stressed. "No, you're going to the hospital. You need an IV."

"Antony, please. If they admit me I'll be in for several days, like last time. I promise I'll drink plenty of fluids and take the anti-nausea medication." She turned her head to look at him. "Besides, we're having the Vants over for dinner in two days."

Antony pulled into the mild Sunday traffic and headed south. "I don't care—you're getting help." The last time she was admitted for dehydration, her veins were so contracted, the nurse had to place the IV in her neck. The doctors kept her for a week and didn't want to let her go home. He didn't want to repeat that again.

"I care," Elite said, her lower lip trembling.

Antony looked at her and cursed under his breath. "Fine, you win, but I am going to force you to drink something."

"Deal." She closed her eyes.

He turned the shuttle toward home. "El, is this just a virus?" he asked after a while. "Or do you need to adjust your meds again?"

"I'm sure it's just a virus," she said.

He could see worry lines across her forehead. They both hated this discussion. "But the last time we needed to lower your meds, it was just like this." The fertility hormone treatments she took caused her body to react in an adverse way, and they'd had to lower her dose three times already.

"Antony, if we lower it much more, the medication will be worthless. Then we'll never get the chance to have a baby of our own."

"I don't care," he said. She opened her eyes and studied his face as if measuring the truthfulness of his words. "I really don't care," he went on. "I hate seeing you so sick, just to get pregnant. It's stupid. Besides, we've turned in the papers for a baby, and it won't be long now, right?"

Elite smiled and shook her head. "No, it won't be long." She closed her eyes and he saw her face relax.

"Call Dr. Werner tomorrow and ask him to taper you off the meds," Antony said. "That is, if you want to get off them." He lowered the shuttle to the curb in front of their apartment building. He lifted her out of the seat after undoing the restraint, then grabbed her bag. "I'll make you some of my famous chicken noodle soup."

She giggled. "Don't cut your finger on the can this time."

"HQ, this is Viper," he said into his earpiece. "The shuttle is now located on Carrington Street. You need to come get it before midnight." He elbowed the lift button and stepped inside when the doors opened.

"New position acknowledged. HQ out."

Antony pulled the silk shirt on and felt the coolness ripple down his back. The color, sandy beige, was not exactly his favorite, although he had plenty of it in his closet. Elite had picked the shirt up a few days ago so he could wear it tonight. She loved the color on him—she thought it made his eyes look more blue.

"Immensely happy" was the only way to describe her since the orphanage benefit dinner, when she had dragged him from table to table to introduce him to her friends and colleagues. She smiled and laughed more often, and he was blissfully unaware of anything else, with the exception of her dehydration for those few days. With no declared time off, he would spend every moment he could with her until Catelyn called. Fatigue wore at his muscles as he buttoned the shirt. He had told no one about his recent nightmares. He couldn't sleep, and he became more tired as the days wore on.

He was a soldier—he knew the symptoms of traumatic stress. However, he also knew that with a little meditation and concentration, he would be as good as new. He hesitated to do anything because he didn't want to spend time away from his wife, and he didn't want to close himself off to her, of all people. *So what if I don't sleep well—there are other things to do at night anyway,* he thought with a grin. He slipped his suede shoes on. Although he and Elite made a habit of not wearing shoes in the house, it seemed silly to host a dinner in stocking feet.

Smells of cayenne and cheese filled the apartment, and he breathed in deeply. It wasn't often Elite spent half the day in the kitchen, even though she loved it. Neither of them had time for that. His own job required more than just hunting his target. He had reports to file and budgets to send to the accountant. Now he had added silent partner of GA Technologies to his to-do list. An envelope from Gage lay on the leather bench at the foot of the bed, stuffed with quarterly reports and minutes from the last board meeting. The company was growing faster than Gage had predicted. In a year or so, Antony's investment would be paid back in full and he would start earning money. All he had to do was keep from being injured or disabled for a few more years, and then, if something happened to him, he and Elite could live off the profits from his investment.

Mat was a genius of a computer. Gage had sent Antony the specs for a new medical program using the arms. It could replace doctors in situations too dangerous for humans—like combat and contamination. The program could either perform on its own when basic care was needed, or by remote in more serious predicaments. Transplant teams at two hospitals were very interested in it for their isolation rooms. GA Tech stood to make millions if the trials went well.

Antony shut the door to the bedroom, made sure his office was locked, and walked to the kitchen. The table was set with terracotta plates and rustic flatware. He touched the hand-blown pitcher that was filled with water. The glass was riddled with bubbles, giving it a rough look, so perfect for Elite's theme for tonight. She had a few weaknesses—collecting dishes was one of them. She had all colors, shapes, and styles. One wall of their dining room was filled with cabinets of her dishes. *Whatever makes her happy,* he thought.

He looked from the table to the clock—their guests should arrive in a few minutes. It had taken Antony a long time to get used to not wearing a watch. However, having something on his wrist that could be caught, ripped off, or tracked was too dangerous. He relied on his earpiece instead. His connection to Corporate, and to Catelyn, was his lifeline. He shook his head—he had promised himself he wouldn't think of her. Knowing she was the CEO's daughter, and that Corporate was unhappy with him—enough to send someone to threaten him—was a good reason for nightmares.

The doorbell buzzed and Elite looked at him, clearly expecting him to answer it. He stepped forward, kicking the little automated floor cleaner. It skidded sideways and then hovered.

"Excuse me," it said.

Antony grunted at the machine and booted it a few more inches with his foot. "What are you doing out? Go to sleep."

Stupid machines, he thought.

"Antony, what?" Elite peered over the counter at him and the little hovering box. "Be nice. He's just doing his job."

"Its job is to always be under my feet, apparently," he said. "It's annoying, and you shouldn't be giving inanimate objects a gender." He moved toward the door as the bell buzzed again.

C. Michelle Jefferies

"Go to sleep," Elite said. The floor cleaner rushed into the kitchen to the storage space in the pantry. "See, if you're nice to it . . ."

Antony shook his head and turned the door handle. "Mrs. Vant," he said as he pulled the door open wide. "You look lovely tonight." He took her hand and grasped it lightly, then shook hands with her husband. "Mr. Vant, welcome. I'm happy to have you in my home."

Antony shut the door and locked it behind them, then led them to the living room. Elite followed, untying her apron and hanging it on a hook with her other aprons.

"I'd offer you a seat on the couch, but your timing is perfect. I just placed dinner on the table," she said.

Mr. Vant smiled. From the size of his belly, Antony could tell he enjoyed eating.

Mrs. Vant turned and held out a bouquet of daisies. "These are for you."

Elite's face lit up. "Daisies—I love them. Thank you." She took the flowers and turned to the kitchen for a vase. Mr. Vant sat at the table as his wife looked around, her eyes settling on a large shell Elite had insisted on sending home from Tahiti.

"The shell, is it new?" Mrs. Vant asked as she sat in the chair Antony held out for her.

Elite nodded. "Isn't it wonderful? I saw it at a street vendor's booth and just had to have it," she gushed. "We spent the next hour finding a postal office to mail it home. Antony carried it for me the whole time."

Antony looked down at his plate. She loved to tell everyone what she thought about him. He didn't mind attention from her, but attention from anyone else made him uncomfortable.

"Well, we should say a prayer before the food gets cold," Elite said.

Mr. Vant looked at Antony, who began to study the pattern on the plate. "I've never heard you say a prayer, young man. Does the cat have your spiritual tongue?"

"Not that I'd have one in the first place," Antony murmured in reply. *Calm down!* he told himself.

"I'm sorry—what did you say?" Mrs. Vant asked.

Her husband looked between his wife and Antony.

"Antony is an atheist. I'll ask for providence," Elite explained. She touched her forehead and lowered her head, and the Vants did the same.

Antony lifted his chin and closed his eyes, suppressing a groan of annoyance. Elite had told the Vants at least twice the last time they were over about his absence of faith. When they opened their eyes, he grabbed the serving spoon and pulled out a steaming cheesy enchilada, eager to change the subject. He served Mrs. Vant first, and then Elite and Mr. Vant. As he set his own plate down, Mrs. Vant cleared her throat.

"Well, Elite, it's good to see you looking normal. You didn't look that great last Sunday," Mr. Vant said.

"I feel much better now, thank you."

"Speaking of church, did anyone tell you?" Mrs. Vant's face flushed as if she was about to expose a piece of juicy gossip.

"Tell me what?" Elite asked.

Mr. Vant frowned, clearly thinking his wife's behavior was inappropriate.

"You missed the last meeting. It was announced over the pulpit," Mrs. Vant continued.

Antony sighed inwardly—more church talk.

"The Speaker is dead."

"Dead . . . how?" Elite questioned.

Antony stuffed a piece of food in his mouth. Another dead guy—big deal. He saw them about every other week.

"They say he was murdered. Someone broke into his house, and he put up a fight with a blade. But they—whoever it was—shot him and escaped."

"That's awful!" Elite's voice raised an octave. "Why would anyone do that?"

"According to his wife, nothing was taken," Mr. Vant put in. "It wasn't a burglary."

"So, do you think it was intentional?" Elite asked.

"His scriptures were thrown on the floor, and his wife says she heard Kyo arguing theology with someone before she heard the gunshots."

Antony gasped and began to choke on the piece of enchilada in his mouth. Elite stood as he coughed repeatedly. He waved her off and grabbed his glass of water.

"Rumors abound in the Quorum of Elders," Mr. Vant said after Antony could breathe again. "Some insist it was an accident or armed robbery. However, I believe the High Elder in training was assassinated. Mr. Kyo Yuji was killed because of his future calling."

Antony pushed his plate away. "I think I've had enough," he announced as he stood. "Perhaps your flu was more contagious than I thought." He looked at Elite. "I apologize for my rudeness, but I'd hate it if I got either of you sick," he said to his guests. "I need to go lie down." He turned away from them and walked down the hall to the bedroom. Once the door shut, he locked it and leaned his head against the wood.

According to Elite's religion, he had just killed a man of God.

15

"That was *so* not nice of you," Elite said as she shut the bedroom door.

Antony looked up from his book and raised an eyebrow. "Nice?"

She pulled the clips out of her hair and slammed them down on the dresser. He put the bookmark in his book and set it down on the table by the chair.

"Nice, leaving me at the dinner table with the Vants." She paused as she began to unbutton her blouse. "You ruined dinner."

"Dinner was smashing. I feel bad I didn't get to eat more of it." He stood and moved to her side, but she turned from him. "I wasn't feeling well," he said. At least that was true.

"What you did was selfish and arrogant!" She threw her shirt on the bench at the foot of the bed. Her skirt followed, and she grabbed her nightgown from the chair next to the bed and pulled it on.

"Selfish? Not feeling well is selfish?" he asked. He reached for her shoulder and she shrugged away from his hand.

She turned from him, folding her arms. "You couldn't handle one minute of church talk?"

"That's not it, El," he countered.

"You couldn't bear to hear about that poor man being killed by an intruder, couldn't listen about the man arguing religion with his attacker, or hear about his scriptures being thrown on the floor—"

"This isn't about religion, Elite," he argued. "Just because I'm an atheist doesn't mean that I haven't been more than tolerant of your religion—even indulgent about it."

"Then what is it?" she asked.

"Why don't you believe me that I started to feel ill? You do it all the time. You eat some food and it doesn't sit well in your stomach, and you excuse yourself, saying you don't feel well."

"Because you choked when Mr. Vant said he believed that Mr. Yuji was killed because of his calling—" She paused and turned around. "You killed him, didn't you?" she whispered.

Antony looked at the floor. "It was a hit."

"You killed him. You shot the Speaker. You were in Kyoto last week—I remember you saying something about it."

"He was a name on a paper. I don't question my assignments, Elite."

"Maybe you should!"

"And do what, become friends with him before I shoot him? Ask him to tea so I can poison him? Feed him dinner while I plant a bomb under his shuttle? There's a reason I don't know anything more about them than necessary."

She stood still, her eyes filling with tears. "He was innocent—a teacher, and a religious man." She gathered a blanket to her chest.

Antony knew where this was leading. He stepped in front of her and pulled at the blanket until she let go. It dropped to the floor. "Maybe he's not as innocent as you think," Antony said as she grabbed a pillow.

"He was the Speaker. It's a position of honor and trust. He had a wife, and you cut his life short," she stammered.

"Life is risky, El—you know that." Antony reached for the pillow, and she began to wrestle it from his hands.

"He was somebody—" she said.

Antony grabbed her shoulders, letting her keep the pillow. "Elite." She had begun to cry, her chest heaving. "Elite, listen to me."

"Let me go," she said, but her sobs prevented her from maneuvering away from his hands. He held on to her as if their marriage depended on it.

"It was a hit—nothing more, nothing less. If I refuse a hit, I'm as good as dead."

Elite looked at him for a moment, her face a map of tear marks. "You're a murderer," she whispered.

He saw emotions flash through her eyes—anger, betrayal, a broken heart. His hands flexed in shock and she took advantage of it, racing for the spare bedroom and locking the door behind her.

"You knew that when you married me," he said to the closed door.

Antony opened his eyes as the door clicked shut and the alarm system reset itself. Sensitive hearing was as much a curse as a blessing—it woke him several times a night. For their safety, he accepted his interrupted rest and learned to fall back to sleep almost immediately. Tonight, Elite wasn't in bed with him, and that meant he slept even lighter than usual. He sat up, pulled his robe over his pajamas, and slipped his feet into his slippers.

He recalled the argument in excruciating detail as he walked through the living room and opened the door. The clock above the kitchen sink glowed 3:21. With his weapon in his waistband and his keys in his pocket, he shut the door and listened for the system to reset. He rode the lift to the main floor.

"Good morning, Mr. Danic. Can I help you?" the doorman asked.

"Did you see which way Elite went?"

"I can honestly say she hasn't been past me this evening, sir."

"She didn't come down here? It would have been in the last few minutes," Antony said as he scanned the lobby of the building.

"No, sir," the doorman replied. "I took my break two hours ago, and I've been here ever since."

Antony searched the couches again before punching the UP button.

"Goodbye, Mr. Danic."

"Goodbye, Charles," Antony said as the elevator door closed.

He almost had the key in the lock when he felt a breeze to his left. Turning, he saw that the door to the roof access was propped open by a small stone. He hurried over and pushed the door open, making sure the rock stayed when the door shut. The door stood behind the elevators and the stairs that led down all eight floors. He and Elite found out by accident that pressing on the door in a certain way would open it. They had been making out in the hallway and when they leaned on the door, it swung open and they fell into the landing. Now, Elite came here often, watching the sunset, enjoying the rain, soaking in the sun.

He walked out onto the roof to see her standing near the ledge, looking up.

"Took you long enough," she said without turning. "I thought you would be here sooner."

"I thought you were downstairs, so I went there first," he said as he stopped next to her. He waited silently, looking for any sign—a move toward him, a casual brush of her fingers—that would tell him she was okay. He leaned his back against the ledge and stared into the sky. The stars were out in force tonight, the sky clear of clouds. The city spread out below. Satellites moved across the sky, slow and steady.

Elite shifted and turned in the direction he faced, closer, but still not touching him. She gasped and pointed. "Look—a falling star!"

He looked where she pointed and saw a green fireball streak across the sky. Spines of light seemed to shoot out from it as it turned like a thorny seedpod. They watched it until it disappeared behind the city lights.

"That was beautiful," she whispered.

"Amazing."

"I'm sorry—I shouldn't have called you that. I was angry," she said, turning to him.

Antony still looked ahead. "Do you really believe I'm a murderer? I need to know how you feel about me."

"You kill people for a living." She reached out and touched his arm.

"You knew what I did before I proposed." He looked at her hand. "It was a hit. I don't ask, they don't tell me. I work for a military contractor, so I'm sure some of my hits are government sanctioned—how's that different?"

"But—"

He turned and pressed his fingers to her lips. "Elite, you said it didn't matter, that you don't care. I've got to know you still believe that." He sighed. "I'm not a monster."

"Of course not. I love you regardless—"

"But you still think I'm a murderer," he said.

She paused, biting at her bottom lip. He closed his eyes and groaned.

She pulled his hand up from his side and kissed his fingers. "I was angry. I said what I thought would hurt you."

"It did." Antony looked down and pulled her hands to his mouth. His intake of breath shuddered in his chest. "Do you believe it?" he asked. Until now, he hadn't realized just how much her opinion of him mattered.

"Believe?"

He knew she was ready to drop the subject, but he needed to know what she thought. "What you said about me."

"I said I was angry."

"I know, but you never said if you really believe I'm a murderer."

"I . . ." Emotions played across her face. He hoped she wasn't going to say something just to end the discussion.

"No, Antony, you're not a murderer. I'm sorry I said it."

He could see her chin tremble and the tears welling in her eyes again. He pulled her close. He felt as if a terrible weight had been lifted from his blackened soul. If there was such a thing as salvation, she was his.

"Forgive me?" she asked tenderly.

"Forgiven."

She gasped again, and he looked up. Above them, the sky was lit with hundreds of falling stars. Laughing, she reached her hands above her head as if she could touch them.

16

It shouldn't matter, Antony told himself after a nightmare woke him from a deep, much needed sleep. He rolled away from Elite and closed his eyes tight. The image of Kyo Yuji dead on the mat, his wife beside him, an inhuman wail coming from her mouth, burned in Antony's memory. Her scream haunted even his daylight hours. He was looking forward to sending Elite to camp so he could spend some time recalibrating his psyche. He knew it would take a few weeks of intense training, both physical and mental, spending hours working out and then even more time meditating and retraining himself mentally.

It hadn't been hard to begin this work—his life as a military sniper had dulled his sense of morality. The death of his mother, Emilie, had drastically changed his family. His father stopped going to church—in fact, he stopped getting out of bed at all. By the time Antony entered the military, his family was barely functioning. Just six months into his training, Jarod, his father, flew to the US for an important meeting and never came home. The plane crashed in the Pacific Ocean somewhere between Hawaii and Fiji. There were no survivors, and suddenly Antony was alone in the world. His heart died that day. Not only did his biological parents not want him, but the parents who raised him were both dead. Rejecting his parents' faith and declaring himself an atheist after his father's funeral was easy. Antony hadn't stepped into a church again—until he met Elite.

Some life, he told himself as he slid out of bed. He padded to his office and opened his new computer. The thing was amazing. It booted immediately—no waiting—and was guaranteed not to crash. "No one could hack this baby," Gage had assured him. It was heavier than Antony's old computer, but not uncomfortably so. He kept the old one, but now only used it for work.

"Good morning, Antony," Mat's voice said. "You're up early."

"Couldn't sleep," he answered.

"What can I do for you? Sing you a lullaby?" the sweet voice asked.

"No, thanks. I need information."

"Sure, Antony. Ask away."

"Who is Kyo Yuji?"

"Yuji, Japanese name?"

"Yes."

"Searching." She paused a moment. The screen lit with several tabs and a large picture on the front. "Kyo Yuji, a merchant in Kyoto, Japan. Thirty-two, married, wife Nami Yuji. Murdered on July 17. Police have declared the case a homicide and are actively searching for the murderer. The picture is from his national ID, by the way. The police files state that they have collected enough blood from the scene to run the DNA on the worldwide registry. No matches have come up. That's odd."

Antony smirked. *Odd for someone who exists.*

"His murder is the only time his name comes up in police reports. He has the standard debt—his home and business.

His wife was the sole beneficiary of his will. There are no children listed. He's the average Joe." Mat paused.

"What about his religion?" Antony asked.

"Religion . . . let me see."

Antony watched the screen flash through many pages before stopping on one. There was a picture of Yuji lying on a wooden pyre. He was dressed in what appeared to be white choir robes, with stitching on the cuffs and hem. A woman in a black dress stood by the pyre. Next to her, a man in red robes held a flaming torch. The photo caption read, "The victim's wife stands at her deceased husband's side as the priest prepares to begin the fire."

"They're going to burn him?" Antony asked in surprise.

"It's tradition among their leaders," Mat replied. "Sending a person's soul to heaven in the smoke."

"Tell me, what's it about this guy, who has no police record, that gets him a bullet in the heart?"

"There is nothing. No records, not even a traffic warning. He was a model citizen."

"Dig deeper—there has to be something. What about the church?"

"The pages I see mention 'The Devoted of Naimaku.' It's a small, obscure religion—no active proselytizing, and some meeting places mentioned in a few countries. There is no tax information on them. They operate on contributions and donations. They own the property their buildings were built on, and then a small area around that. They run a school on each of the sites. Not a religious school—a training school, much like the Royal Military Academy in Duntroon."

"Training school? Like a private school? Are these guys cultists?"

"Not that I can tell. The only thing I found remarkable was a report of the latest conference the church held, on an island called Natani in the Pacific Ocean. Our Mr. Yuji spoke about the dangers of drug use and addiction and about building faith. The boy was so clean, he squeaked."

"Hmm." Antony sat back, looking at the screen. He would have to ask someone about the religion. He didn't dare ask Elite. He wouldn't get her hopes up—he didn't want to look like he was investigating her church.

"Mat, can you search deeper and get everything on this church you can find, and on Mr. Yuji?" Antony counted out three sleeping pills and poured himself a tumbler of Scotch from his secret stash.

"Sure, Antony. I'll compile it and have it ready for you as soon as possible."

"Make sure you send it to this computer only, and encrypt it, please."

"Of course, Antony."

The screen went blank.

17

Antony stared at the fan as it slowly rotated. The noise helped him sleep, except for tonight. Unlike last night, he was exhausted. His muscles screamed in protest and he needed to rest, even if he didn't sleep. He couldn't keep taking sleeping pills mixed with alcohol. That was an overdose waiting to happen.

He was falling apart mentally—and worried what it would do to him physically. *If Corporate knew my mental state, I could kiss my job and probably my life goodbye.*

As he lay in bed, he focused on the fan and let himself fall into meditation. The slip was easy—it usually was. The trick was getting there, or staying there, when he was stressed. The episode with Sori Katsu, Antony's complete mess of a hit in Kyoto, and Elite's revelation and their fight had shaken him to the core. He felt as if he was living in a whirlwind where the out-of-control spinning was increasing in speed. He had never come unglued like that before. Not even as he witnessed his mother's rape and death when he was fourteen. At the funeral he had stood at his father's side, unblinking, to show his dad how strong he was.

Antony focused on controlling his anxiety, so if the panic arose again he could squelch it before the symptoms hit in earnest. He focused on relaxing when they did hit. Over and over, he told himself, *You're going to be okay. Everything is going to be all right. You're better than this.* He stared at the fan until his eyes watered. *It's just a glitch. I'm not washed up.*

His need to feel normal was foremost in his head. He also needed to know Elite loved him. He needed to love Elite with everything he was. He needed to know that if their situation went south, she would be safe and wouldn't be lonely. He needed to be Antony Danic, the man he was ten years ago.

Next to him, Elite shifted and rolled over. He closed his eyes but couldn't hide his furrowed brow.

"Antony?" she said. He pulled himself out of his trance and turned his head. She leaned over and looked into his eyes. "Can't sleep?"

He closed his eyes again. "No," he whispered. She could read him so easily.

"Did you take something?"

"I took something last night, but I can't keep doing that. I can't afford to get addicted." His heart raced and he began to pant. He wanted to jump out of bed and stand in the middle of an empty room so he could breathe normally.

Elite frowned and placed a hand on his forehead. He closed his eyes—her touch soothed him, but the panic did not leave. "You poor thing," she said. "Is there something I can do?"

He bit down hard on his tongue to avoid the fall into a full-blown attack. Pain overrode the instinct to give into the anxiety. He tasted blood. He looked in her eyes, speechless.

She frowned and began to stroke his head, smoothing his wild hair out of his face. "Do you need anything? Your medication?"

He shook his head—he had dumped it in the toilet weeks ago. He breathed deeply, letting the air slowly escape his mouth. One heartbeat passed. He breathed in again. Another heartbeat. He breathed out and could feel the panic fading. *Breathe in.* His heart slowed in its rapid pounding. *Breathe out. There. Think of anything besides how you are falling apart.*

"Let's get bonded. I'll do anything you want, El. I need to know you're mine and you're happy. We can have as small or big of a celebration as you want."

Her eyes grew large. He wondered if he would regret the words that just left his mouth.

"No," she said.

He shifted to look at her. "No? Why?"

"If I agree to bond with you, will you go to church with me every Sunday? Will you stop drinking?"

"I . . ."

"Do you believe in God, Antony?" The question hit him like a fist in his gut. She had a look of compassion on her face, not the contempt he expected. She sighed. "I can't bond with you right now, as much as I'd love to. You see, to act without meaning is to mock God. To bond with you and not have you truly mean it, I'd be throwing away everything I hold dear for a fleeting ordinance. However, if you ever come to really live the gospel like I do, then I'll bond with you without question. Please understand—I mean no malice and I'm happy you would change whatever in your heart has kept you from even thinking about it. But if it is to be forever, it must mean something to you. It must be with your whole soul."

"I don't know if I can ever be what you want," he replied. "I don't know if I should have ever asked you to marry me."

"Don't be silly, Antony. I love you, and even if we aren't bonded at the moment, there is no one else I want to be with."

"What if I never get to that point? What if I'm never what you want?"

"You're not listening to me." She closed her eyes.

He knew that face—the blinding pain in her head must be back. The migraines associated with her hormone treatments were one severe side effect of their ongoing attempts to get pregnant, even if she was tapering off the medication.

"You're what I want, and I wouldn't have it any differently." She pinched the bridge of her nose.

"El?"

She waved him off. "I'm fine—I'll be okay by morning."

"I'm sorry."

"Antony, don't. Let's just leave it at that. I'm not in any position to argue with you tonight."

"Can I get you anything?" he asked softly. The oncoming headache must have been what woke her.

"Some pain medication and some water."

He carefully left the bed, trying not to jar it. Any movement would make Elite's pain worse.

He found the bottle and retrieved the glass of water from her bedside table. He opened her clenched hand and placed the two tablets in it, then touched her hand with the water glass. She placed the pills in her mouth and took the water from him, sloshing it on her chest. She uttered a slight gasp.

He took the glass from her shaking hands and helped her lie down. Then he covered her with the blanket and turned off the fan. As she closed her eyes and breathed in deeply, he left the room, not wanting to disturb her. He fell on the bed in the guest room and closed his eyes.

It seems as if we're both falling apart.

18

"Your phone is buzzing," Elite said.

Antony groaned and rolled over. "Let it go to voicemail." He buried his face farther into his pillow. It was Saturday, and he had no assignments as long as he didn't answer the phone.

"This is the third time they've called," Elite said from where she lay against his body. He slid his arm from under her and pulled himself from the bed.

"I'm coming," he growled, then opened the bedroom door and made his way to his office. He grabbed the door handle just as he realized his pants, with his keys, were in the bathroom. He stumbled his way there and fished his keys out of his pocket. He heard the phone ring again as he jammed the key in the lock and turned it. As he grabbed the phone out of the drawer, the message tone beeped. "Four times," he said with a sigh. He woke his phone and punched in his code.

"This is Catelyn. I've got an assignment for you. There will be a black BMW parked in front of your building in approximately twenty minutes. The keys will be under the seat."

He checked the clock—it was 8:56.

"There is a flight coming in at 10:30. On the seat of the car is a sign and a pass to get through security. Go to Gate 6A and hold up the sign. A passenger will meet you—you're to drive them to the hotel on Blackall Street. This client is very important, and all courtesy is to be afforded. Their safety is imperative. Goodbye."

Antony shut the phone. It would take at least thirty minutes to get there, and he didn't dare be late.

"I've got to go," he said to Elite as he entered the bedroom. She still lay under the warm, soft covers. He really hated that he could be there snuggling with her, but instead had to go to work.

"So it was Catelyn?"

"Yes. I'm just picking someone up at the airport and taking them to a hotel. I won't be long."

He pulled the shower door shut and turned on the water. He scrubbed his hair, thankful he'd had it cut last week. It would dry on the way. A minute later he pulled the towel off the hook, wrapped it around him, and stepped into the closet. Elite had his black corporation suit on the bench and the white shirt in her hands. He pulled the pants on and then the shirt. He tucked it in and fastened the belt. Elite began tying his tie as he put on the jacket. Leaning over, he kissed her and then let her finish the tie. When he went into his office, she headed for the kitchen. Antony donned his Lanzen shades, grabbed his pack, and locked his office door. Elite stood in the doorway with a bagel and juice.

"Goodbye, love. I'll be back soon." He walked out the door, then waited until she shut it and turned the master lock. He frowned as the lift stopped on another floor and three people got on. He nodded to the guy with the golf clubs. They had met years ago at the pool where they both exercised.

"Working on the weekend?" the man asked. "Bummer."

"There is no rest for the wicked," Antony said.

The guy laughed. "No, there isn't. So, are you going out of town?"

"No, this one's local. I should be home this afternoon."

"Haven't seen you around much. Probably a good thing, though."

"Yeah, if I'm getting paid," Antony replied. "The HR branch is hot and cold. I prefer it hot."

"No kidding," the guy said as the doors opened.

Antony saw the BMW and couldn't help but smirk. It wasn't a normal antique car. This was armored and large, not the size of Cate's, but comfortable. He waved at his neighbor, opened the door, and sat in the driver's seat. Surely, his passenger was very important to warrant an armored car. The keys were under the seat and a meticulously lettered sign sat on the seat. The directions to VIP parking at the airport were taped to the dash.

The car started with a hum. Antony put the vehicle in drive and pulled into traffic. The handling was so smooth, he was grinning like a kid as he got on the highway and headed out of town. If he were to purchase a car, it would be expensive like this, though not armored, of course. He didn't need that. The engine would hum and it would drive as if floating. Gage had a new Hummer that Antony had driven in the desert a few months ago. He liked the bells and whistles, but it was too rough. He wanted smooth and sleek. He tapped his finger to the music—the stereo system was excellent, too. He wondered whose car he was borrowing.

The thrill was fleeting as he pulled off the highway at the airport. He followed the directions to VIP section and parked along the curb in a line of black shuttles and limos. As he stepped out, he spied a strange car ahead of him. The shape was reminiscent of a 1930's Ford Roadster, the color a deep purple, almost black. He stopped and looked at it for a moment.

"It's a 1989 Dodge Prowler, to be exact," said the driver standing next to it.

"It's nice. How does it handle?"

"This one is souped up. It handles nice, not like that BMW of yours, but the experience is a good one."

"If I had the resources, I'd get one of those," Antony said.

The driver of the Prowler nodded. "I love driving this one."

"A little cold for the convertible, isn't it?" While they were heading out of winter, it was still a cold day.

"I usually drive an enclosed sedan in the wintertime. However, my boss wants me to use this car every once in a while. I figured since I wasn't picking up a passenger today, I'd take it."

For the second time that day, Antony contemplated buying a car. As much trouble as it would be to own a car in Canberra, this one would be worth it. Shuttles were more city-friendly, but the thought of owning something so antique was appealing.

Antony checked the terminal and found the plane was on time. It would land in ten minutes. Sign in hand, he stopped at security and flashed his new ID, which would allow him to go to the gate.

"I'm here to pick up a passenger," he said.

The guard looked at his card and waved him through. The signs pointed Antony in the direction of the gate he needed. All along the causeway, people sold food and trinkets to the passengers and airport staff. Video screens displayed platters of delicious-looking food that never equaled the images in taste or looks. A young woman walked toward him carrying a phone while a luggage trolley followed her. As she walked, her pant suit changed to a business suit with a skirt. *Holographic clothes,* he thought. *What a waste of good technology.* The woman took another two steps and the suit changed color.

Antony turned to his right and headed down a less crowded hall to terminals where small private jets taxied and parked on the black tarmac. As he arrived at the designated gate, a black plane with silver streaks was coming to a stop just outside the windows. He was right on time. The airport staff rushed around, opening the doors and grabbing things. Antony watched them run as he stood still. Placard under his arm, he pulled down on his jacket, then checked the buttons and straightened his tie. He pulled the sign out just as a young man emerged through the door.

Antony didn't expect the lady escorted out by the pilot to head straight for him after seeing the sign he carried that said "Hurst Enterprises." She was followed by a young man pushing a trolley full of matching luggage.

"Where's my regular driver?" she asked, her red hair pulled tight against her head. Her suit must have been worth ten of Antony's.

"I'm sorry. I was told to drive you to the Imperial Hotel. I wasn't given any additional information," Antony said as he bowed.

"I'll see you later, Mrs. Hurst?" the pilot said.

"Thank you, Gregory," she replied.

Mrs. Hurst? Antony fell into step beside her, his eyes scanning the area around them for any threat. The lady obviously demanded attention, as a berth cleared ahead of them as they walked. Perhaps it was her looks or how she carried herself. Either way, they were given plenty of room. He walked to the farthest of the four lifts and gently coaxed her in that direction. After pressing the call button, he stood scanning the area. When the lift opened, he held the door for her and the trolley, then stepped in. He stretched his arm across the doorway, barring anyone else from getting in.

They rode in silence as Mrs. Hurst checked something on her phone. He eyed it with envy. Probably a Hurst Enterprises invention, it was sleek and simple-looking, but he doubted it held close to the computing power of his GA laptop.

The lift stopped and Antony held the door open for Mrs. Hurst, and then followed her as they made their way to the rotunda. His breath misted in the air and he suppressed a shiver, whether from the temperature or the woman's company, he didn't know. Antony opened the door and offered his arm to help her into the car. She refused and settled into the rear seat as far from the driver's seat as possible, it seemed. He hurried to the other side, started the car, and turned on the heat. After pulling the trunk lever by the door, he got out.

"Sorry about the temperature," he said as he left the car to help the porter with the luggage.

The porter had the two biggest suitcases on the curb and was loading the smaller ones in the trunk. Antony took one of the big bags and groaned. It felt as though it were loaded with cinderblocks.

What in the world is in this thing? He placed the bag in the trunk. The porter picked up the other bag—from the strained look on his face, it was just as heavy.

Antony touched the porter's shoulder. "We need to even out the weight on these." He gestured to the trunk. The car leaned toward the ground on the side with the large bag. The porter looked at him, slid his carefully packed smaller bags to the center, and allowed Antony to place the other heavy suitcase opposite. A dress bag was laid on top of everything, and the porter turned to Antony with his hand out. Antony opened his wallet and handed him a large bill.

"Thank you," the young man said.

Antony shut the trunk and sat in the driver's seat. "Is everything okay back there?" he asked as he signaled and pulled out onto the road that ran beside the airport.

"The water's not as cold as I like it, but I'm fine," his passenger said.

Antony nodded. He turned onto the highway and looked back to see a black Mercedes merge two shuttles behind him. He drove fast, but cautiously, on the highway and changed lanes as the exit he needed approached. Again, the Mercedes changed lanes behind him. He pulled his phone out, set it on the seat next to him, and instinctively touched his pistol in his waistband. He didn't like this at all.

Once on the expressway, he cut across three lanes of traffic and merged into the commuter lane. The Mercedes tried to merge, but the big semi-truck Antony passed with inches to spare was blocking its access. He watched the signs as they drove and decided that a detour was better than leading the Mercedes straight to the hotel. Taking an inside exit, he pulled into a commercial area and took several unnecessary turns, hoping the black Mercedes didn't see where he went.

Why am I being followed? Is it my passenger? Or whatever is in those suitcases? If this was indeed the wife of Mr. Hurst, the CEO of Hurst Enterprises, why would she be put in a situation where her safety was compromised? It was obvious she usually had a different driver. Surely Hurst Enterprises had other people in Canberra to pick her up if her regular driver wasn't available. Why use the company hit man, if she wasn't in danger? Whatever was in those suitcases, it wasn't clothes, unless it was chain mail.

What is she transporting, for whom, and does she know what it is? Is she a willing player, or in the dark about the whole thing?

The hotel was ritzy. There would be plenty of people on the curb, and hopefully nothing would happen to his passenger. Antony turned right and parked in front of the hotel, then hit the button to open the trunk. The Mercedes drove past and continued along the road. *How did they find us, with all the twists and turns I took?* Antony wondered. *Did someone put a tracking device on our car?* Things were not looking so good.

"I'll be at your door in a moment," he said. He turned off the engine, then walked around and opened the door. His passenger placed a pale, delicate hand in his tanned one and stepped from the car. She had let her hair down, making her look much younger. He saw her resemblance to Catelyn now. The golden hazel eyes and the bow of the upper lip were the same, although Catelyn's eyes were Asian in shape and her hair was straight and brown compared to Mrs. Hurst's wavy red. Pretty, but untouchable and reserved.

Antony followed her to the front desk and waited as she checked in. A porter appeared with a trolley of her luggage and stood next to her. The older man looked like he couldn't have lifted the heavy suitcases if he wanted to, but the monstrosities were there on the bottom of the stack.

Mrs. Hurst retrieved the card key, and Antony followed her to the lift.

After she was securely settled in her room, he returned to the car and sat in the driver's seat. His phone rang. "This is Antony."

"Mr. Danic, I trust your subject is at the hotel safe and sound."

"That she is, although the bottled water wasn't cold enough."

"The water . . . never mind. Take the car to the parking terrace on Linnaeus Way and park it on top of the building. And leave the keys under—"

"You know, you look a lot like her," Antony interrupted.

"—the seat. Like whom?"

"Your mother, Mrs. Hurst," he said.

Catelyn breathed out hard. "My mother—that's none of your business, Mr. Danic."

He grinned. Because Catelyn was serious and always composed, he enjoyed frustrating her. "I'm sorry. I suppose it isn't, is it?"

He heard her cover the mouthpiece and whisper, "Why is my mother in Canberra?" to someone, probably that big, burly, Polynesian driver of hers. Then she said to Antony, "Regardless, leave the car there, and I'll contact you when you have another assignment, Mr. Danic. Goodbye."

19

Antony heard someone shout his name. Turning, he saw Samual's wife Melinda working her way through the afternoon foot traffic.

"Antony, wait up," she called as she hurried to catch him. "I thought it was you."

Elite had sent him to the new artisan center in the Turner District, on the other side of Lake Burley Griffin and past the Australian National University. There was a little Italian bistro that sold the fresh noodles and cheese she used for her lasagna. He hadn't been able to stop thinking of Mrs. Hurst and what was in those suitcases, as well as why Catelyn was so surprised that her mother was in Canberra.

"Melinda, hello," he said. "I'm running errands for Elite while she works." Samual and Elite had served on a few church committees together, and Antony and Melinda had gotten to know each other as the nonmember spouses.

"I was just going to get lunch," Melinda said, "Care to join me?"

His stomach growled. He had forgotten breakfast. "Sure. Where were you thinking?"

"I wanted to see if that new place at the hotel was any good. It's just a block from here."

"Sounds ideal. I'll carry your bags."

"Antony, you're such a gentleman," she said, handing some of them to him.

"I was looking for some new clothes," she said as they turned and walked in the direction of the hotel.

"I can see that." He wished something as simple as buying Elite a lot of clothes would make her happy.

"A table for two," Melinda said as they reached the front desk.

The host took them near the back of the room and offered them a booth in the corner. Antony placed the bags on part of the bench while Melinda sat and picked up her menu. He took a seat across from her and laid the linen napkin in his lap. He slid the black digital menu across the glass tabletop. It lit as he picked it up.

"Everything looks so good," Melinda said as he scrolled through the offerings.

"Would you like anything to drink?" the host asked.

"I'll have a bottle of white wine, and two glasses," Melinda said.

"One glass, none for me," Antony added, but the host had already turned and left.

"Not drinking? Antony, what's the matter with you? You do seem different since the bonding in July. Samual said he noticed it when he saw you at the church that Sunday Elite was sick, but I didn't believe him until now."

"Nothing's different. I just don't drink during the day. Besides, I've got errands to run after this, although lunch with a friend is nice."

The server walked up and stood next to the table. "What would you like, ma'am?"

"I want your grilled chicken salad and a side of bread."

"I'll have the steak and potatoes, medium," Antony said. "And put both of these meals on my ticket. Don't let the lady pay for anything."

"Oh, Antony, you're so nice," Melinda gushed.

"My mother would come back from the dead to haunt me if I didn't pay for a lady's lunch." He took a drink of his water.

"If your mother were still alive, I'd tell her myself what a gentleman you are."

Antony winced as he thought of his mother. *She would kill me if she knew I was an assassin. With her bare hands!* he mused, but he said instead, "So, tell me, are you and Samual still looking at buying the McGovern farm?"

Melinda opened her napkin and placed it on her lap. "We made an offer a few days ago, but they haven't gotten back to us yet. What about you and Elite? Is she pregnant yet?"

"Isn't that a question for her?" he said, placing his water glass on the table harder than he intended.

"Did I hit a tender spot? I'm sorry, Antony."

"I really don't want to ruin our lunch by speaking of something so personal."

"I'm sorry. So, how's your work? Is that too personal?"

"No, that's an okay topic. Work is fine. I just got back from Asia a few days ago." He recited his patent answer. "You know, training the corporation's employees is a never-ending job. They're hiring and firing people all the time."

"I saw your new phone," Melinda said. "It's cool."

"Just a small side benefit of the job. The pay and hours are much better incentives. So, how's your job?"

"I was promoted to manager," Melissa explained. "I'm over all the sales floor associates now."

"A promotion. That's nice."

"Yeah. I'm earning as much as Samual now. I've decided I'm buying the farm whether he wants it or not."

Clearly, the wine had loosened her tongue a little. "Are you and Samual doing okay?" Antony asked.

"The same as always. We live together and go our separate ways."

"He seemed affectionate enough the last time I saw you."

"It's a show for his church friends." She drained her third glass. "He wanted a trophy wife and that's what he got. He said it didn't matter that I wasn't a member when we got married, but I wonder now. He seems distant. I hope you, of all our friends, understand that."

The server placed the food on the table. Antony grabbed his knife and fork. "I think I understand." He knew Samual was the one getting itchy, and he felt a sudden sympathy for Melinda. "Life with a member isn't easy, but you have to make compromises."

She nodded.

"I'm sorry," Antony went on. "It's not easy mixing religions, or lack of. But I've done it for ten years now, so it's possible."

They talked for a long time after the plates were removed and the ticket paid. Finally, Antony looked at his watch. It was late afternoon and Melinda was past tipsy.

"Let me take you home." He gathered their bags from the bench.

"I'd like that," she said.

He took her by the arm and led her out of the restaurant. He hailed a cab and helped her sit, then put the bags in the trunk. Their houses were both in this direction, and besides, he wasn't sure she would be able to get home on her own.

"Banner Street," he said and sat by her. When the taxi stopped, he paid the driver, pulled his and Melinda's bags out of the trunk, and helped her up the stairs of her large home. They went inside, and Antony set the bags down in the foyer.

She shut the door, then turned and smiled. "Thanks."

He looked around. The house appeared odd, not at all like he remembered. The floor shone in the light of the lamps. That was it—some of the furniture was missing.

"Mel, what's going on?" he asked, turning to her.

She was staring at the half-empty living room. She gasped and her hands flew to her throat and face, her eyes recounting her terror. "He left me," she whispered. "He left me for some young thing. They're going to be bound next year. He took almost everything. She's . . . expecting. He told me last night." She threw herself into Antony's arms and began to cry.

He frowned. This was not the Samual he had gotten to know over the last seven years. *What should I do?* Antony wondered. Melinda was his friend and she was hurting, but he felt so uncomfortable holding a woman who was not Elite. If only Elite were here with them, she could give Melinda the comfort she needed right now.

Melinda's tears wet the front of his shirt as she leaned against him, her arms clinging to his shoulders as she shook with her weeping. "Melinda, please," he said.

She reached up and pulled his head toward her. He jerked back as their lips met. He unwrapped one arm from around his neck, then the other, and gently pushed her away. He didn't know what was talking—the shock of the news she received last night, or the whole bottle of wine she drank—but he would never kiss someone other than his wife.

"I thought you liked me." Melinda hiccupped. "I could give you the child you want, Antony. I wouldn't make you go to church . . . We could be good together." She unbuttoned the top button of her shirt.

He backed away. "Mel, please don't do this. We're friends, but I'm not interested in you romantically." She dropped her bracelets on the floor and slipped out of her shoes. "Look, I wish you happiness in your future," he went on. "I think what Samual did was despicable, but I have a love in my life, and it's not you."

"Just sleep with me, and the child will carry your name. You can visit anytime."

"Look, you're drunk—you're not making sense," he said as he reached for the door. "I love Elite. Whether she ever gives me a child, I'm devoted to her, and that's that. Goodbye, Melinda." He left the home and ran for the street. Who cared if he left his bags behind? He could hear her scream his name behind the door as he flagged a taxi. He knew if he saw Samual any time soon, he'd have a hard time not breaking his neck.

Antony stopped in the bathroom in the lobby of his building and washed his hands and face. He smelled like Melinda, and he didn't want Elite to have any reason to doubt him. He walked in the door to his apartment and turned to lock it.

"Antony?" Elite came out of the kitchen. "I thought you were going to grab the things I need. I can't make lasagna without mozzarella."

He looked at her and pulled her to him. "Oh, Elite, I love you. I'm so thankful for you," he whispered in her ear.

She wrapped her arms around him. "What happened?" she asked.

He pulled back so he could look at her. "I met Melinda as I came out of the bakery. She asked me to lunch and we went to the new place at the hotel by Reconciliation Place. We talked about being married to a member; she had a lot of wine. In fact, she drank the whole bottle. I went home with her so she would get there safely. I walked into their apartment and almost everything was gone. Samual left her for a young woman, a member who is carrying his child."

"Samual left her?" Elite covered her mouth with her hand.

"Melinda is distraught, to say the least. She threw herself at me and tried to get me to sleep with her."

Elite's face froze in an expression of fear. "What did you do?" she asked quietly.

"I mean, she even told me she would have my baby," he continued as if he hadn't heard her. "I don't think she was in her right mind at all,"

"Antony! What did you do?"

He looked at Elite and kissed her hand. "I left her undressing, screaming my name. I set her lock. So she hopefully can't get out until she's sober." He smiled. "I told her I was devoted to one person, and it was you. Even if we never have children." He looked at his wife and saw tears forming in her big brown eyes.

"Melinda wants a baby really badly," she said. "I can't believe Samual will have a child with a member, but not her."

"Yes, and people like us who want children, in spite of our differences, can't have them." He paused, sensing he had Elite's full attention. "Not to cause an argument, but this is one point on my side to be an atheist. Samual, who has just taken everything he professes to believe and thrown it out the window, can have a baby. But you, who are faithful to the end, and I, who have no rules to break, can't have any. Do you see why the arguments form in my head?"

She paused and looked at him, placing her hands on her hips. "Nothing you can say will change my belief in God, but yes, I see it from your perspective. And I'm grateful for learning it. I want to know all of you, not just bits and pieces."

He kissed her. "I'm sorry I left all my stuff at her house when she lunged at me."

"Like Joseph in Egypt," Elite said.

"Huh?"

She laughed. "Never mind—let's go out. There's that new movie at the mall I really want to see. We can grab some sandwiches on the way, and stop and get more noodles and cheese on the way home. I'll make the lasagna tomorrow."

Antony kissed her again. "Let me shower. I hate her perfume, and now I'm wearing it." He locked his pack in his office and went into the bathroom.

20

"Deliver this package by hand. Wait for your recipient to read it and answer, then bring his reply back to Canberra with you."

"The recipient is . . .?"

"To remain alive, unless you want to die," Catelyn said.

Antony tucked his phone between his shoulder and ear as he held a silver ball gown for Elite. She was adjusting the hem, her mouth full of straight pins. They had talked into the night about his lack of belief and her devotion to her beliefs. The conversation seemed to have formed a deeper bond between them.

"So I'm a mailman now."

"I prefer the word 'courier.' I pay you too much to call you a mailman," Catelyn said.

"Where do I get the package?"

Elite finished and took the dress from his hands. He walked into his office and shut the door, but didn't lock it like he had in the past. He wanted Elite to know she was always welcome in his life, even in the parts where he dealt with Catelyn and his job, although he kept his targets and detailed information from Elite for both their sakes.

"It will be at the Canberra International Airport in locker 15B. The combination is your employee number. I've purchased a ticket for you to Taipei. The flight leaves at two this afternoon."

"Two, right."

"Address and instructions will be with the ticket."

"Anything else?" Antony zipped his pack shut and laid it on his desk.

"No," she said, then ended the call.

He walked out of his office and locked it this time.

"When do you leave?" Elite asked as he came up behind her in the kitchen.

"I should get out of here by noon."

She looked at the clock on the stove. "I was going to make that lasagna tonight, but I'll wait until you come home."

"I shouldn't be long. I'm just going to Taipei and back."

"You said that when you went to Florida. You didn't come home for weeks."

"I couldn't keep an eye on the guy. He was slick." Antony took a dish from her and placed it in the dishwasher.

"You don't have to help me—"

"But I want to. I want you to know how much I love you."

"You're not still feeling guilty about Melinda, are you?" she asked as she handed him a pot.

"A little," he admitted. She touched his chest, and the warm wetness seeped through the fabric. He looked in her eyes. "I'm sorry, El."

"Shh." She pressed her fingers against his lips. "I don't care."

He closed his eyes, her touch calming him in a way he couldn't explain.

Taipei was crowded, no matter what time of day or year a person arrived. Antony stood in line at customs, his passport in hand, his mind on the time he'd spent with Elite that morning before riding the train to the airport. The last few weeks had been hard on their marriage. With the hit on Kyo, and Melinda throwing herself at him, Antony and Elite had decided what was important to them. Last night seemed to have mended some of the damage.

In the days after Elite's accusation, Antony realized she meant so much more to him than his job. His quandary lay in the fact that if he left his job, their lives were in jeopardy. He had become painfully aware in the last few weeks what a dangerous life he had asked Elite to lead with him. He hadn't thought about the ramifications of his occupation when they were young and so passionately in love.

"Sir, your passport?" said a woman behind the security desk.

Brought out of his thoughts, Antony handed her the document.

"Reason for visit?" she asked. She wore the dark blue uniform of air security.

"Business," he said.

The woman stamped the passport and slid it back under the pane of bulletproof glass.

He eyed the glass with curiosity. *I wonder what caliber it would take to get through that glass. I bet Mat would know— I'll have to ask her.* Once past customs, he wormed his way through the crowds toward the front of the airport, where bright yellow taxi shuttles were parked three deep and ten long. He walked to the back of the line and listened as destinations and offers were yelled back and forth. After a few moments of waiting, he finally stood at the head of the line. It looked like chaos, yet it actually ran like a well-oiled machine.

"Where you going?" a Taiwanese driver asked.

Antony pulled the paper from his pocket. The address was an office on the 117th floor of some skyscraper. He read it out loud.

"I take you there," the driver said.

Antony climbed into the back seat of the shuttle. The noise of the crowded city faded as the door closed, and he leaned back, shutting his eyes. It was hot and muggy in Taiwan, worse here than in Sydney. He felt his clothes begin to cling to his body, sweat beading a line down his spine. He ran a hand through his short hair and looked out the window.

I'll love you forever," Elite said. She lay next to him, her hand tracing circles on his chest.

"You mean until I die," he said as she lay next him, her hands tracing circles on his chest.

"No, silly, forever and more." She kissed him and relaxed against his body.

"We're here," the driver said.

Antony opened his eyes and got out of the shuttle. Tall buildings, much like in New York, surrounded him. He pulled two international credits out of his pocket and handed them to the driver, who bowed and backed toward his vehicle. Antony scanned the miniscule space of blue sky above him, feeling very small at the moment, and then entered the building.

The scanner clicked green as he walked through the security gates, despite the pistol in his waistband—an embedded chip from his employer made it invisible to security equipment. Catelyn updated the codes from time to time when they met. The lifts stood in rows straight ahead of him, and he made his way through the crowds of people to the first one, then pressed the button.

"What is your destination?" the lift asked him.

"Mr. Kurosaki, on floor 117."

"Step inside," the voice said.

The doors opened, then closed behind him. While he wasn't afraid of heights, he disliked the sensation of going up or down in lifts in any skyscraper. It made his stomach twist.

Soon, the elevator toned, "Floor number 117." The doors opened into an elegant lobby, with dark brown leather couches on plush, cream-colored carpet. A dark mahogany table with a large flower arrangement matched the armoire in the corner. Antony stepped into the lobby and stopped.

"May I help you?" a young woman asked. She wore a tight black skirt and a starched white blouse. She offered him a tall glass of ice water.

He took it and drank several long swallows, then said, "I'm here to see Mr. Kurosaki. Catelyn sent me."

"Yes, Mr. Danic. We're waiting for you. Come this way."

She led him through frosted French doors into an office more elegant than the lobby. The man behind the enormous desk waved his hand at them and continued to speak into his phone. The man was Asian, although his eyes were more amber than brown and his skin a little more pale. He was probably half Asian, half Caucasian, Antony decided.

"He'll be right with you," the woman said.

She took Antony's empty glass and bowed, leaving him in the office. The glass doors clicked shut behind her.

"So, you're the infamous Mr. Danic," the man behind the desk said, gesturing toward him. "Catelyn speaks of you often."

Antony shrugged off his pack and pulled out the envelope. As he placed it on the desk, he saw the man look at him as if trying to catalog him or unnerve him. "I hope Catelyn spoke well of me," Antony said.

Mr. Kurosaki opened the envelope and unfolded the papers. He read the first one and then the second. Antony still stood, not having been asked to sit. Mr. Kurosaki grunted, then turned to his computer and began to type. Antony could see something dark on the skin under the short hair behind Mr. Kurosaki's ear. Looking intently without making it obvious, he stared at the spot until it became clear. The man had a barcode tattooed on his head.

Why on earth would he want something like that? Antony thought. The man was very formal in appearance, and didn't seem like the type to have some secret life where that kind of tattoo would be acceptable. His visible skin was otherwise ink-free and his ears weren't pierced. Perhaps it was a throwback to his rebellious teen years.

When Mr. Kurosaki finished, he clicked something on the screen and picked up two pages from under his desk. He wrote something on one of them, folded them, then put the pages in a new envelope and sealed it.

"Give this to Catelyn as soon as you get back to Canberra." Mr. Kurosaki slid the envelope across the desk. "You're dismissed." He turned away.

Antony nodded, even though Mr. Kurosaki didn't see it, and walked to the door. The assistant opened it and smiled.

"Have a good evening, Mr. Danic." She bowed again.

"Toshia! Come here!" Antony heard as the lift doors opened and he stepped in. *He's certainly not winning any personality contests,* he thought as he moved to the back of the lift. "Lobby, please."

Catelyn stood in the luggage area, her hands on her hips. "Where is it?" She thrust out her hand.

"What? No 'Hello, how was your trip?'" Antony shrugged off his pack and opened it.

"It wasn't a trip, it was a job. Hand it over."

He pulled the envelope out and held it above her. "Who is Mr. Kurosaki, Catelyn? From the sounds of it, you two are pretty close."

Her driver and sometimes bodyguard stiffened at the mention of the name. Antony smiled—he shouldn't take such pleasure in seeing people squirm. He lowered his hand to her eye level.

She snatched the envelope out of his hands and smiled smugly. "Too much information, Mr. Danic."

21

"Meet me at the diner on Darling Street in fifteen minutes."

"It's . . . three in the morning," Antony said as he took the phone off speaker. Elite rolled to her side of the bed.

"They're open all night."

"I'm not," he growled into the phone. "I was sleeping."

"You're lying. Dress for your assignment. Boss wants this thing by morning."

"Crap. By morning? Are they out of their minds?"

"Apparently. Time's ticking—you have fourteen minutes."

"Crap!" Antony leaped out of bed and dashed for the bathroom.

Elite followed. "You have an assignment?"

"Yeah," he said through his toothbrush.

"Now?"

"Yeah. Look, Elite, I'm sorry. I should be done by morning." He rinsed his mouth.

"But it's the middle of the night."

"I know, but I . . . Every time I leave lately, we have this argument. What's wrong?"

"Nothing. I just miss you," she said, looking down at her bare feet peeking from under the long nightgown she had pulled back on.

Antony stopped and took her by the shoulders, raising her face to look him in the eyes. "You're a terrible liar. What is it?"

"I said it was nothing. Now get dressed—you'll be late."

"Forget about Catelyn. I care about you. Elite . . ."

"Okay . . . I had a dream. A horrible dream. You were hurt and I couldn't do anything to help you."

"Elite, I'm just fine. Nothing is going to happen to me, okay? The corporation didn't hire me because I was incompetent."

"Just go. We'll talk about this tomorrow," she said as she pushed him toward the shower. When he was done, she was there holding a pair of pants and a shirt. He grabbed a towel and gave himself a once-over, then threw the pants and the shirt on as she pulled a brush through his hair. He whirled around and kissed her, placing both hands on the sides of her head. She smiled and closed her eyes, and he dashed out of the room.

"You're late," Catelyn said.

Antony waved the waitress over. "I was busy."

"I should deduct from your bonus—"

"So, I was a little late. Who cares?" The waitress sauntered up to the table, and Antony smiled. "I'll have number 4 on her tab, with juice. She'll have the fruit plate, with coffee—decaf."

"Antony, you don't have time."

"I've been up all night. I'm tired, and if I'm going to work, I'm eating. And since I don't like eating alone, you're going to join me. Besides, you're paying anyway. So, tell me what's so important that I'm working at three in the morning."

She slid an envelope across the table. Antony smiled. Manila envelopes must be at the top of her work shopping list. He opened it and a single piece of paper and a memory chip fell to the table. The paper had one word—Crawford—and a .doc address on it.

"We've tried for days to hack into this system, and we can't. You need to get past security and go to the computer in room 245. The password and address are there." She nodded toward the paper. "Save the document to the memory chip."

"Sure. Where is this place?"

"Patience, dear Mr. Danic."

After a long silent moment, he put the chip and paper in his pocket. Catelyn sat back as the waitress returned to fill their glasses and set their plates down.

Antony drizzled syrup on his waffle while chewing on a piece of bacon. "Eat up," he mumbled around his food. She sighed as she picked up a piece of melon and popped it in her mouth.

He finished his plate in a matter of minutes. She stared at him as he pushed it away. She had eaten maybe a few pieces of her fruit. He looked at her plate, snatched a strawberry off it, and grinned. "You'd think you weren't hungry," he said and stood. "Well, are we going?"

She laid a bill on the table. "You'd think you were a teenager again. My brothers use to eat like that. It's disgusting." She walked out the door and headed for her black limo.

Following, he smiled. "So, you're not an only child."

"Too much information, Mr. Danic." She opened the car door.

"You've gone back to calling me Mr. Danic. I liked it when you called me Antony."

"I've never called you Antony. Now, shall we, Mr. Danic? Time's wasting. I'm not sure you've got enough time to

167

complete your assignment." She gestured, and he raised his eyebrows and climbed in the limo.

"I'm sure I'll be just fine," he said as the car pulled away.

Soon, the vehicle slowed and stopped in a grove of trees in a local park. Catelyn looked away from Antony.

"Through there is the building. It's high security, so don't assume you'll be able to get in easily."

He looked in the direction she pointed. There was a small trail in the darkness of the trees.

"I'll be here waiting for you," she said. "Please hurry."

"Wait for me? Tell me, do you have a crush on me? Can't let me go?" He shouldered his pack, grinning.

"Too much information, Mr. Danic," she said and shut the door.

He turned and dashed through the trees. From his pack, he pulled a thin, translucent mask. He placed it on his face, and it sealed immediately. It would blur his face to any security cameras that recorded his image. The last time he went to Sydney, Gage had loaded him up with new gadgets to test. Next, he pulled out a small round disk, peeled the cover off the sticky side, and fastened the disk to his chest, in the place where Gage had showed him.

"Okay, Gage—prove your mettle to me," he said as he pressed the button. The device emitted a small electromagnetic pulse that would temporarily scramble his presence to any monitors. He ran for the building, stopping in the shadows while a guard turned and looked around. When the man disappeared past the corner, Antony ran for a door at the side of the building. He placed the two lock picks in the card slot, then opened the door and slipped inside. He opened the door to the stairs and started up, taking two at a time. He stopped on the second-floor landing. This door had a key entry also, and he had to use his lock picks again. The door clicked and he opened it, slipped through, and pulled it shut. He heard a faint click that didn't sound like the lock resetting. He looked back and saw two sensors hidden in the door frame, one on each side. Each emitted a red light.

Antony paused, wondering why they would need a scanner at head height. Perhaps it was just a movement register or a reader for employee ID cards. But a motion detector or an ID reader could be at any height, so these were probably iris or retina scanners. Hopefully the EMP button would scramble them enough that they couldn't get a good read on Antony's eyes.

He ran down a hallway, but when he rounded the corner, he faced another stairwell. *Dang it! Wrong way. Typical.* He turned and ran the other way. At the end of the hallway was a room. The number on the door was 200. He had forty-five to go.

The clock on the wall in the hallway briefly said 4:12 before it went blank. He had less than an hour before people started arriving. He would have to turn off Gage's device, he realized, before he gained access to the room, or it would temporarily fry the computer. His speed would be his only advantage when he got to the right room. There were things Gage's inventions couldn't fix.

As Antony reached room 235, he pressed the EMP button in his pocket, turning it off, then pulled out the two lock picks. He raced for the door marked 245 and jammed the sticks in the card slot. It clicked. He opened the door and quietly shut it behind him.

Without the EMP device, he needed to work fast. The mask would blur his face to any monitoring cameras, but his presence would be sensed. He inserted the memory chip and typed in the password. The screen flashed and then went blank with a cursor in the corner. Antony typed the .doc address, and soon the bright blue was replaced by lines and lines of code. He hoped the memory chip was large—the code was hundreds of megabytes long. He pulled down a menu, then clicked on SAVE and directed the code to the chip.

The computer was slow, much slower than Mat. The clock on the wall hit 4:22 as the card ejected. He secured it in the case and placed it under his tongue, then hit the button on the EMP device again. The computer emitted a screech and the monitor went off. Antony shut the door and bolted down the hall and into the stairwell, down the flight of stairs and into the west hallway by the side door. He opened the door with the picks and raced to the trees, turning off the EMP device as he ran. As he reached the small trail, he slowed and pulled at the mask—it came off with a popping noise.

He strode into the clearing where Cate sat in her limo. The door opened and she looked at her watch as he climbed in and sat on the bench seat.

"Are you done? You did that in under an hour. Did something happen? Were you almost caught?" The words streamed out of her mouth.

Antony leaned over and placed a finger on her lips. At his touch, her eyes dilated and her cheeks flushed.

"Shh." He opened his mouth, pulled out the case, and opened her fist. He hesitated and wiped the case on his pants, then placed it in her hand and closed her fingers over it.

She sat stunned for a moment before saying, "Ainslie Station."

The car slowly turned around and pulled out onto the main street in front of the park. Antony sat back against the extra-plush cushions and closed his eyes.

"Nice wheels, Miss Cate," he said and began to hum the melody of a song from his player.

Elite was pouring tea when he walked in the door. He smiled at her as he made his way to the office. After locking his weapons in the safe, he removed the earpiece, EMP button, and lock picks. *Thanks, Gage,* he thought.

Elite sat at the table with her herbal tea and croissant. Antony took her wrist and pulled her up.

"What? I was just sitting down to eat."

"If you remember," he said, kissing her neck, "we were interrupted this morning."

22

"Are you ready for your next assignment?" Catelyn asked, each word punctuated like its own sentence.

Antony could tell she was angry. He wondered if his performance the other night was still bothering her. Then again, she almost always seemed curt with him.

"Yes."

"Good. Subject is—"

"What, no envelope?" he joked.

She ignored his comment. "At the Renaissance Hotel in Adelaide. Room 759. He's due to check out at 11:00 AM."

"Adelaide, room 759. Got it."

"Good, because you're giving me reason to question your loyalty, Mr. Danic." She hung up.

Doubt me? Why? He knew his last assignment had been a success. He wondered if they were still upset about the mess-up in Kyoto. The police had dropped the case—with the lack of DNA evidence, there was nothing to go on. Maybe Corporate was still steamed about his vacation.

Antony entered his office and shut the door behind him. He placed his earpiece in his ear. "HQ, this is Viper."

"Viper, this is HQ. What can I do for you?" asked a familiar voice.

"I need a flight to Adelaide today," he said. Then he added, "Please." He had angered enough women that week.

"Sure. I can get you out of Canberra on a small charter at six this evening."

"Great, thank you."

"You're welcome, Viper. HQ out."

He pulled out the earpiece and sighed.

Am I washed up? The thought startled him as it came. Sure, he had begun to believe it when he was in Kyoto, but he'd given the corporation no reason to doubt him lately. It made him think.

He noticed a green light flashing on the GA Technologies laptop. He opened it. The screen was on and white lettering flashed on a blue background. "Press ESC to play message." He sat back and pressed the ESC button.

"Don't panic," the text from Mat read, "but I think your office is bugged. There is an odd electronic signature I can't identify in the room. Gage and I'll be there as soon as possible. Until then, I'll remain in silent mode."

Antony smiled. Mat it seemed, had created her own identity, and often referred to herself as a person. "The church has very little information available, either on the web or in the media," she went on. "They keep to themselves. Mr. Yuji was, it seems, the wrong guy in the wrong place. I'm sorry I have so little information for you."

Another dead end, Antony thought. Sighing, he leaned forward. "Can I speak with you this way?" he typed on the screen.

"I knew you would figure it out. Gage doubted you. But I knew . . ." Mat wrote, finishing with a smiley face.

"Gage . . . has fleas," Antony typed. A smile cracked his hard expression.

"HAHAHAHAHAHA!" Mat replied.

"There is a building to the east of the Dixon District Playing Fields, here in Canberra. What is it?" he typed.

A map appeared on the screen. "Hit the position with your finger." The words flashed over the top in red. Antony studied the map for a moment, then touched the tall building in a complex of buildings. The map disappeared. He sat back, wondering at the computer in front of him. The assignment he had done yesterday was so unusual, it had been on his mind ever since.

"Bradford Development. They manufacture small technology. Digital cameras, music players, cell phones. They are at the forefront of their field. The corporation has many branches, but that's the largest. Don't you work for Hurst Enterprises?"

"Yes," he typed.

"Bradford is a subsidiary of Hurst."

"Tell me more." He had broken into his own company. Why?

"Bryant Hurst, 57, lives in Perth, runs his company by remote. Canberra has better tax benefits than Perth. He's a self-made multi-billionaire. He came on the scene about thirty years ago and began to design cameras better than anyone else's. He was able to beat the Asians many times and became the best camera manufacturer in less than five years. He branched out and began to make things like music players and phones. The entire complex you pointed out is Hurst property."

"Anything else?" Antony asked.

"Nothing apparent on the outside—they stay squeaky clean like most businesses. Keeps the government from looking at them too closely. I'll take a look at their private papers and we'll see from there."

"Wish I could take you with me—you'd be a great help," he typed.

"Would be nice, wouldn't it?" Mat wrote. "Anything else?"

"No," he typed. "See you soon?"

"Of course, Antony."

After kissing Elite goodbye, Antony took off to the east—his regular running route. He ran around the park by his apartment building, then turned south to put him on the circle that brought him home. Past the park, he stopped at the corner and jogged in place until the light changed. As he stepped out into the road, a black car ran the light and grazed him.

"Hey, watch it!" he said as he slammed his fist onto the hood. The man driving said nothing, but stared at him. Antony stared back for a moment, then backed up and turned right, running along the sidewalk.

This route was twelve miles, instead of his regular ten. His lungs began to burn and his muscles felt like they were melting from heat as he hit the seven-mile mark. He had turned west again and was heading for home. When he looked across the street, searching for the dry cleaner's sign that marked eight miles, he saw him.

The man leaned against the black sedan that Antony could now identify a BMW. As Antony ran, the man watched him, not even trying to hiding the fact. Wearing a suit as dark as the car, he stared from behind black-lensed Lanzen glasses, his arms folded. The glasses were a specialized, expensive brand, the kind Antony used when he needed to work in daylight. He would have recognized the man without the glasses and car, though—he was good at details. That's what kept him alive.

Antony turned his face away and picked up his pace. *This can't be a coincidence,* he thought. *Have I become the hunted?* He had been ordered to steal information from his employer. Why? Who owned the computer? Hopefully, Mat would be able to dig deeper and get more information.

He didn't see the man in the black BMW again and filed it into the back of his mind as he walked into the apartment. Elite came out of her office, her headpiece on.

"Hey, I'll call you back. My husband just got home," she said and clicked the button on her waist.

"Hey, I know you." He leaned over and kissed her on the cheek. He made his way to the shower, pulling his sweaty shirt off and dropping it on the bathroom floor.

"Renaissance Hotel, please," Antony said to the driver at the curb. He sat back and closed his eyes for a moment. The day had flown by in a whirl. His morning run, his afternoon with Elite, an early dinner and the train ride to the airport. He opened his eyes a moment later, calm and collected, something he hadn't felt when he went to Kyoto. He'd gone to Japan dwelling on the argument he'd had with Elite, and hadn't taken time to find his center of calm. He knew his lack of preparation had caused the problems with the hit. This time, all was well between Antony and his wife, and he found it much easier to focus—even after seeing the guy in black glasses.

It was dark, and Antony watched the lights of the city rush past the window. He had until morning to come up with a strategy. Usually, it was easy to make a hit in a hotel. However, each hotel was different and individual security was never the same or predictable. He stayed alive because he always assumed everything would be different. Complacency was his enemy.

The taxi stopped a few minutes later. Antony stepped out, handed the driver his fare plus a tip, and turned to the front doors of the building. He checked his reflection in the glass doors. His clothes looked nice—khaki pants and a long-sleeve green shirt in a similar style. His blond-streaked hair ended just above his shoulders, and he adjusted the fake eyeglasses he had borrowed from Elite. The square lenses definitely made him look different. The two of them often played with his hair and accessories to change his looks.

He approached the front desk. He chose the busiest clerk and stood to the side of the man she was helping. She looked at him and he smiled.

"Any messages for room 759?" he asked as the man in front of him dug in his bag for something.

The clerk turned and looked at the large grid behind her. She pulled out a small stack of papers and handed them to Antony. He looked through them. Two of the messages were from him—he had called before he arrived, as it would seem more suspicious if he asked and there was nothing for him. The third note was from someone named Dave Weaver. He read the note quickly. *Meet me for breakfast before you check out. I'll be at the little diner on the main floor.* He pocketed that one.

The man had searched his bag and began to argue with the clerk.

Lucky, Antony thought, moving to his right. There was a clipboard with a signature pad on the counter. He slipped it off the counter and placed it in his pack. He could use that later. The next clerk looked at him as he stepped forward after waiting his turn.

"I . . . I'm sorry. I asked her" —he jerked his head to the side toward the harried clerk— "for messages for room number 759. I made a mistake. I'm supposed to be in room 438. Room 759 was the room I had last week. I travel so much, I get them mixed up." He smiled the smile that always made Elite forget what she was saying, and the clerk smiled back. Antony pushed the slips of paper back across the counter. "I'm sorry. I hope whoever is in that room is okay with me accidentally getting his messages."

"I'm sure it'll be okay—mistakes happen," she said. "Now, room 438, right?"

"Right. I made the reservation this morning."

"Um . . ." she said, looking at the screen and then at him. "That room is registered to a Mrs. Davenport."

"Well, I'm certainly not a Mrs." He looked down at his chest.

The clerk laughed. "Just tell me your name and I'll get this figured out."

"Mr. Adams, James Adams." It was the name on the passport and ID card he'd grabbed from the stack in his safe. He slid the Corporate diamond charge card across the counter.

She typed a few words and then sighed. "You're in room 834, sir. I'll get you registered right now. Just one night?"

"Yes, ma'am. I'm so bad with numbers, it's a wonder I don't get lost."

She smiled and handed him back his charge card and a door key. "Have a nice stay, sir."

The man had stopped yelling, but still stood at the desk. Antony shot the other clerk a sympathetic smile and turned to the lift banks. He had to get to the target, kill him, and be gone before breakfast.

"Sir?" he heard and turned. "I do have a message for you." The clerk held out a folded piece of paper. He took it and smiled. He opened it as he walked back to the lifts.

Nice glasses, it read. No signature. He stopped and scanned the room from left to right. One man slept on a sofa with his head back, soft snores coming from his throat. People got on and off of the lifts, and two hotel workers pushed carts across the back of the lobby. A line was forming at the café, and several people sat on the plush couches reading, talking, or working on laptops. Nothing out of the ordinary. However, Antony was certain he wouldn't sleep tonight. How did someone other than his employer know he was here, or which room he was in?

Antony opened his phone and dialed the operator. "Did I remember to give you a wake-up call time?" he asked.

"What room?" a female voice asked.

"Seven fifty-nine."

"Yes, 6:30, sir."

"Thank you. I couldn't remember if I called you or just thought about calling you."

"You're welcome."

He ended the call and scanned the hotel lobby through the glass walls of the lift. He gasped when he saw the man in the dark suit and black sunglasses. Antony looked away quickly and moved his body in front of another man who had just gotten on the lift. Antony touched his pistol in its holster. Clearly, he was being followed, and the man was making no secret of it.

Antony wished he had Mat with him, but that laptop was far too heavy to carry everywhere. Perhaps he would call Gage when he was secure in his room. What would he say? "This guy is following me, and I don't have his license plate, but he wears these expensive sunglasses"? *The glasses.* They were custom made, almost indestructible, and cost a pretty penny. He might be able to trace the man that way.

When he reached his room, Antony hurried inside and shut the door. The lock slid home and he tested it from the inside. After placing the lamp, phone, and clock on the floor, he dragged the nightstand in front of the door and wedged it against the wood. Sure, it wouldn't stop a bullet, but it might slow someone down. Disappointed that his plan to go to the café on Ninth Street was blown by the man in the sunglasses, he opened the fridge and pulled out a box lunch and a bottle of water. He sat at the desk and opened the box. *Roast beef on white bread,* he read on the paper wrapper. He drizzled Dijon mustard on the meat and opened the container of pasta salad, then put his phone on speaker and dialed.

"This is Gage. Antony?"

"It's me. I need Mat to do something for me."

"Hold on. You got her last message, right?"

"Right," Antony said.

"I'm sending you a new message right now." The hotel phone on the floor started to ring.

"A message?" he said. *But I don't have Mat here.*

"Yeah. Would you answer your phone?"

"But I . . ."

"Answer the phone. I'm not going anywhere."

Antony stood and grabbed the handset.

"Hello?"

"Good. Now end the call on your cell and turn it off. Got that?" Gage said over the landline. "Your earpiece—where is it? Don't answer yet—is the phone off?"

"Yes. It's in my pack."

"Place the pack in the bathroom and turn the shower and the fan on."

"Okay." Antony did as Gage said and came back to the headset. "Done."

"Good. Now sit on your phone."

"Have you been drinking?"

"Your cell phone, idiot. Sit on it, please." Antony placed it under his thigh and rolled his eyes. "Done."

"Good. Mat is on the line with us. What do you need?"

"I managed to link the signal to one of your devices," Mat said before Antony could respond. "It left with you this morning. Don't worry—we'll take care of it when we get there. When are you leaving Adelaide?"

"Tomorrow sometime," Antony replied.

"Gage and I'll be in Canberra in a few days. Now, what do you need?"

"I saw a guy this morning as I went running. Twice, actually. He's about six foot, Caucasian, brown hair. Black tailored suit."

"You think you're being followed?"

"That or hunted. He drives a black BMW and wears black Lanzen sunglasses."

"Lanzen. Are you sure about that?" Mat said.

"Sure. They look just like mine."

"You own some Lanzens?" Gage asked.

"Are you jealous? My company bought them for me for assignments. Anyway, I saw the guy here in Adelaide. He followed me from home, but he's letting me see him. I don't have anything to offer, other than that."

"No worries. I'll compare the client list at Lanzen to people who have traveled from Canberra to Adelaide and who own or lease a black BMW," Mat said. "Did you get the style of car?"

"No. Luxury class, large, four door, dark tint. That's all I saw as I about rolled across the hood."

"That's enough," Mat said. "I'll call you if there's anything in the next twelve hours. Otherwise, when we get there."

"Mate, you need help? Some backup?" Gage asked.

"I'm sure I'll be fine. If this guy is hunting me, I won't be an easy target. It will be good to see you."

"I'm not convinced you're okay. I should be there with you."

"To do what—show them your white butt as a distraction?" Antony laughed. "I'll be fine. Remember, I'm bullet-proof." He winced at the teenage joke. Teflon, they called him. He never got in trouble—everything slid right off him onto someone else.

"Right . . . old Teflon."

"Who are you calling old? Look, Gage, if anything does happen to me, I want you to take Elite somewhere safe. Take care of her. Don't let her get hurt."

"Now look who's being serious. Nothing is going to happen to you. Everything will be fine."

"Sure, Gage. Fine. I'm updating my will when you get here."

"We'll look at it then."

"I should go. I've got an early day tomorrow," Antony said and hung up the phone. He finished his dinner and hopped in the shower while it was still running. Adelaide was a coastal town, more humid than Canberra, and he felt sticky. Once he was dry and dressed, he turned his cell phone back on and called room service again.

"Yes," he said when someone answered. "I need a message delivered to room 834."

"Yes, sir. The message?"

"Please tell Mr. Adams his early morning meeting has been moved up to 5:30 tomorrow."

"Yes, sir. Who shall I tell him sent the message?" she asked. Antony looked around, scanning the room for ideas. "Sir?" she said after several seconds.

"I'm sorry, I was talking to someone else. Sign the message 'Mr. Eau.'"

"Row?"

"Eau, like the French word for water. E–a–u."

"Yes, sir."

After he ended the call, he placed everything back in his pack and threw the lunch box away. He had dragged the nightstand away from the door and was pushing it against the wall when someone knocked on the door.

"Room service," a voice called.

Antony unlocked the door and opened it, keeping the other hand on his pistol.

"I have a message for Mr. Adams," the young man said.

"That's me." Antony opened the door a little more.

"I need you to sign here."

Antony took the clipboard and the stylus. "How much for the uniform?"

"I'm sorry, it isn't for sale," the young man said.

"Really? I've got a thousand dollars that says it is."

"I could lose my job," the messenger said after a moment.

"So the uniform *is* for sale, for the right price?" Antony looked at the young man. He was tall and broader than Antony, but it looked like the uniform would good fit.

The messenger said nothing.

"Two thousand for the uniform, and a thousand for your silence," Antony said. "You have a spare uniform here at the hotel, don't you? I can't imagine a guy as intelligent as you wouldn't have one."

"I do. I'll go get it. How do I know you aren't going to rip me off or get me in trouble?"

"I'm a man of my word." Antony opened his wallet. He was going to tip the boy for the message anyway. He handed him a hundred-dollar bill and showed him the rest of the cash. "This is yours if you bring me back your spare uniform. And I'll give you an extra hundred if you come back in five minutes." The boy took the hundred and put it in his pocket, smiling.

"Five minutes, sure. Um, why do you want it, anyway?"

"You have a girlfriend?" Antony asked.

"Yeah." The young man smiled.

"My wife—she likes uniforms, if you get what I mean."

The messenger chuckled, then turned and hurried away.

Antony shut the door and looked at the clock in the bathroom. Three minutes and twenty-one seconds later, the young man was back with a neatly folded uniform, complete with tie and name tag. Antony let him in the room, took the uniform, and handed him the cash.

"Don't spend it all in one place," Antony said with a smile.

"Yes, sir," the messenger said just before Antony shut the door.

The uniform was perfect. He would get the hit done and be on a flight home tomorrow afternoon. After pushing the heavy nightstand back against the door, he sat on the floor in lotus position. He closed his eyes and meditated. He was not going to be caught off guard again. When he felt completely relaxed, he made his way to the bed and climbed in.

Antony's phone beeped at 5:00 AM. If he checked out at 5:15, the note would pull suspicion away from him. He opened his eyes and yawned, surprised he had slept. Mat had not called—either what she found wasn't important, or she hadn't found anything yet. At 5:10, Antony slid the card into the checkout slot and left the room. With the uniform and clipboard in his pack, he rode the lift to the main floor and entered the café. After the hostess seated him, he scanned the menu, his back against the wall as he faced the entrance of the café.

He looked at the clock. The operator should be making the target's wake-up call soon. Antony ate and left the café by 6:00. He stopped in the gift shop and bought a magazine.

Standing in the lobby, he flipped through the magazine until 6:20. Then he rode the lift to the seventh floor and entered a restroom by the lifts. He donned the uniform over his clothes, then went to stand just outside room 759. Soon, he heard the phone ring. He waited about two minutes and knocked. The door opened and he looked into the bleary eyes of a nearly naked middle-aged man.

"Yeah?"

"I'm sorry, sir, for the early wake-up, but I've got a message from a David Weaver." Antony paused, holding the clipboard. The guy reached out. "Um, sir, perhaps it would be better if I stepped in the room, given your present state of undress." Antony could hear a woman's voice in the hallway behind him. The guy looked up and coughed, probably from embarrassment.

"Um, yeah, come in. I'll pull something on."

The guy went into the bathroom. Antony shut the room door, slid the gun from his holster, and placed it under the clipboard. The man returned with pants on, and when he reached for the board, Antony pulled the trigger. The man grunted and clutched at his chest. Antony shot him again in the head and stepped back as he collapsed, then fired his signature shot into the femoral artery. The man lay there as Antony secured his pistol and holstered it.

Music startled him as he reached for the doorknob. He jerked his hand back as he recognized it as the alarm on a cell phone. The tune was the same one he'd programmed onto his own cell, but it was off and safely in his pack. He looked around for the glow of the other phone's display screen and saw nothing. He opened and rifled through the guy's suitcase after checking the nightstand. No phone. Someone was bound to call and complain because the volume was turned way up, so Antony needed to stop the alarm.

The guy must either sleep like he's dead, or he's deaf, he thought. He walked to the door, ready to bolt, when he noticed the music was loudest as he stepped over the corpse. He rolled his eyes and groaned as he stood over the dead man's body—his victim had wet himself. Antony placed one hand in the pocket—it was empty. He grimaced and checked the other one. He pulled out the phone and wiped it on the man's pant leg, then touched the screen. He pressed MENU, ALARM, and STOP. The phone asked for a password.

"What the . . ." After wiping the phone on his uniform jacket to remove the fingerprints, he threw the phone on the man's chest, pulled out his pistol, and shot at it. The music stopped as the bullet ripped through the buttons. He sighed. Times like this, he was thankful his pistol sounded no louder than a click of a shutting door.

"You're to go to the Renaissance Hotel in Adelaide and wait for a package to be delivered," a voice said from the phone. "Your ticket and hotel reservation will be waiting for you at the main desk in the Bradford building. Don't di . . ."

The words faded as a shower of sparks erupted from the phone and the screen went black.

Antony knew that voice well. Catelyn.

He searched the man's pockets and pulled out a wallet. He opened it and pocketed the cash. He would drop it in the plexi-glass box in the hotel lobby asking for donations to help local youth programs. It would look like a robbery instead of a hit. He found the card section of the wallet and pulled the cards out, dropping them on the floor. Insurance card, library card, Corporate credit card—looking just like his . . . Daniel Crawford. Crawford . . . that was the password he'd used to steal information from the computer. He looked at the next cards. A door key to room 245 in the Bradford Development building, and finally the man's driver's license. Antony dropped the wallet and shuddered.

Why on earth am I killing someone from my corporation? Did I just become like the guy on Huahine? Is Catelyn, or Mr. Hurst, for that matter, using me as an enforcer now? Antony fought the urge to vomit. What had Mr. Crawford done to get himself killed? Was the letter Antony had carried by hand to Mr. Kurosaki related to this assignment? It seemed too close in the timeline not to be considered.

Antony knew that every second of delay increased the risk of being caught, but he had to know. He tipped the guy's head to the side and jerked his hand back when he saw, just under the man's blond hair, the black lines of a barcode tattoo.

Antony washed his hands and the grip on his pistol, and left the room holding the clipboard. Willing his nerves to calm and his stomach to be still, he pulled off the uniform pants and shirt in a bathroom stall and dropped them in the trash, on top of the clipboard. A minute later, he walked through the lobby and out the front door of the hotel. He walked a few hundred feet before flagging a taxi.

"Where to, mate?" the driver asked.

"Airport, please."

There was no sign of the Lanzen guy. *That's a good thing,* Antony thought. *Occupy your mind with him—then you won't have to think about why Catelyn just sent Mr. Crawford to his death.*

23

"What?" Antony said into his phone. He walked down the street toward the market—Elite had sent him with a list of things she needed. There was a hint of spring in the air, and it was warm enough to get away with just a jacket. The hit at the hotel felt so wrong to him, and he'd hardly slept since returning from Adelaide a few days ago.

"I don't have patience for antics right now, Danic. I need—"

"Spit it out, Catelyn."

"I need you."

This wasn't the normal Cate. He slowed to a stop. "What do you need?" he asked.

"Pick me up."

"Pick you . . . what, where? I don't have a car."

"Use mine. It's parked at Ormond Street, Turner District, keys under the seat."

"Awfully trusting, aren't you?" Antony asked.

"It's not easy to steal a limousine. You've got a license?" she said, a hint of her old humor back.

"Of course I do. Where are you?"

"Get on Canberra Avenue, go south to the highway until you get to Tuggeranong, then head west on Isabella Drive. There's an abandoned pit mine."

"I'm on my way." Antony crossed the street and bolted to the train station. Adrenaline rushed though his body, and he could feel his heart beat faster. He didn't like the way Cate sounded, as if she was in pain. "Stay on the line," he told her. "I'm boarding the train now." He stepped on and stood at the back of the compartment.

"Just hurry," she said.

It didn't take long to get to the parking garage, take the elevator to the fifth level, and find her car.

"Okay, I'm in the car. Where is your driver, anyway?" Antony asked as he pulled the car out and drove it down the ramp.

"Busy," she said. He could hear her panting.

"What happened? Are you okay?" As much as she angered him sometimes, she was his handler, and they had a history together.

"Fine . . . hold on," she said, and clicked over to another line. Antony turned onto Canberra Avenue and drove away from the city. She didn't come back for a long time. When she clicked back on, she said, "I see you . . . pull to the . . . building on the left. Get out . . . open the passenger door." She panted harder now. "Get back in the car."

After putting the car in park, he opened his door and stepped out. Buildings lined the left side of the access road to the pit, the fence around the mine itself twisted and in some places flattened. He walked around the back of the car, his feet crunching on the gravel road, kicking up clouds of dust. He held the phone in his right hand.

"Catelyn?" he said into the phone. He scanned the buildings and saw her through a broken window.

"Just get back in the car!" she yelled.

He shook his head and stepped forward. "Not on your life. This time, I'm calling the shots."

He pushed open the corrugated metal door. She leaned against the wall by the entryway, her arm against her gut, her clothes torn and her skin bruised.

"Danic!" she yelled into the air and the phone. "I can . . . do this myself."

"You say my name as if it was a cuss word," he chided as he stopped in front of her, placing his phone in his pocket.

"I told . . . you."

"No more talking," he said and laid his arm against her shoulders. She winced, but he pulled her into his chest, put his other arm under her knees, and picked her up. She didn't struggle—he assumed she had no strength to. She whimpered as he walked from the dark building into the light outside. The bright sun of day revealed more cuts and bruises than he'd seen in the shadows.

"Who did this to you?" he asked.

"None of . . . your business."

"It seems you've made it my business, Catelyn. Calling me involves me."

"It's nothing," she gasped as he laid her on the back seat of the limousine.

"Does it involve me? Is this retaliation for a hit I made?" he asked as he knelt on the floor in the back. She didn't have any deep wounds, but the way she gasped and held her sides, he assumed she had broken ribs.

"Hardly." She smiled but then grimaced in pain. "Do you think . . . I eat, live, breathe . . . Antony Danic?"

Catelyn closed her eyes, her breathing still shallow and rapid. Her face was starting to bruise. The mark was large and half-moon shaped, like the toe of a boot. Her ear was bloody and it looked like her earring had been ripped from her lobe, along with at least a handful of her black hair. On a closer examination, he could see that behind her ear, just like Mr. Kurosaki and Mr. Crawford, was a black barcode tattoo.

Not good, Antony thought. "Is it Corporate?" he asked.

Catelyn looked at him, then turned away. Something in her eyes told him he might be on the right track.

"Take me . . . to the parking garage . . . someone's waiting," she said.

Antony didn't wait for the master lock to set as he made his way to the bathroom. Elite called his name, but he ignored her. He stood over the sink and heaved.

Mr. Kurosaki, Mr. Crawford, and Catelyn each had a barcode tattoo behind their ear. It was too odd to be coincidence. Furthermore, two of the three people with this mark were either dead or wounded.

Antony's gut told him that he had ventured into something dangerous, something deeper than just corporate espionage. He had killed Kyo—someone, who by all research, both his and Mat's, was innocent, a religious teacher with no links to Hurst Enterprises. Antony had broken into his own company and hacked a computer, then later killed Daniel Crawford, the employee who used that computer. Now Catelyn had been beaten for some reason she was not willing to explain.

The life-long contract Antony signed when he was young and stupid now mocked him. He couldn't get out, especially after the threat on Huahine. Elite's life was in danger.

Why a barcode tattoo? he wondered. *Is it like a brand of ownership? Did the corporation do it?* His mind flashed back to the head-height scanners in the building he'd broken into. They weren't for retinal scans, he realized—they were barcode readers, as if every employee of Hurst Enterprises was a piece of property and nothing more, even Hurst's own daughter.

Looking in the mirror, Antony strained to see the skin under the hair behind his right ear.

"Antony?" Elite said. She opened the door and came in. "What is it?"

Was it right or left? he asked himself. With both hands on his head, he checked his right side. He pulled at his hair, strands coming off in his fingers. His breathing was almost a pant, and his heart raced.

"Please, don't let it be there," he said.

"Antony? Let what be there?" She frowned as he continued to pull out hair and dig at the skin behind his ears.

"A stupid tattoo—a barcode, of all things. Like humans are something to own."

"Antony, let me look. There's no reason to hurt yourself."

She reached for his head and he forced himself to hold still and not flinch away from her touch. Whatever nerves he had left were completely shot, and the train ride home, alone in his thoughts, had just escalated his paranoia. He gripped the counter until the edge cut the skin on his palms.

"I don't see anything," Elite said as she fingered through his hair. "Wait. There it is, just like you said—a faint barcode in the hairline, like you'd see on a package. Why on earth would you have a barcode on your head?"

I'm dead.

He felt the bile rise in his throat again. He pushed past Elite to the toilet and collapsed to his knees, retching.

24

"Wake up, sleepyhead."

Antony could never ignore her voice. He opened his eyes, his face almost buried in his pillow. Elite leaned over and looked at him upside down. He rolled to his side, and she sat back and ran her hand through her hair.

"Couldn't sleep?" he asked. He'd been asleep for once. He had lain awake for almost two days, images of Catelyn and the tattoo haunting his thoughts.

"No, I want to play," Elite said.

He looked at his clock. It was 12:49 AM. "El, it's the middle of the night." He yawned.

"I know. Come on." She pulled at him.

He sat up and stretched. "Okay, okay, I'm coming." He didn't have to go anywhere in the morning, so he could sleep when they finished.

Antony wondered when, if ever, he'd hear from Catelyn again. He had sent Gage and Mat a long letter spelling out what had happened in the last few weeks, and his thoughts about it.

"What should I wear?" he asked Elite, used to this by now.

"Oh, jeans and a T-shirt should be fine," she said as she pulled on a pair of pants. "Wear your running shoes," she added, donning a shirt.

Antony shook his head as he began dressing. *She is amazing.*

"Gage left a message. He and Mat are still tied up at work for a new client, and he said he'll be here as soon as he's done," Elite said, then walked into the kitchen.

Antony shut their bedroom door, made sure his office door was locked, and joined her.

Elite cocked her head to the side. "Why is Gage coming here?"

"He wanted to personally check something on my new computer." Antony cringed as he opened the front door for her—he hated lying to her. But she didn't need to know how bad the situation was getting. He was simply protecting her.

He set the alarm and she pushed the lift button. He held her hand tightly as they rode the lift down to the lobby.

"Evening, Mr. and Mrs. Danic," the doorman said.

"Hello, Charles," Elite said.

"Off for a midnight walk?" he asked.

Antony smiled. The things this man must be thinking.

"Of course," she said. "Have a good evening."

"You too, Mrs. Danic."

"Come on, this way." She led Antony toward the train station. "I found this place yesterday and I can't stop thinking about it."

They sat in the back of the train—Antony wouldn't sit anywhere else. He felt better knowing that inches of steel and plastic were between his back and any projectile from the outside. Sitting here, he only had to worry about attacks from the side or front. It was hard, though, especially when the train was crowded. Not only did it give him claustrophobia, but the mass of people made it hard to keep Elite and himself safe.

After they rode a few miles, Elite pulled Antony off the train and then east three blocks. As she turned a corner, her breath caught like a little child's. In front of them was a gigantic playground. She bounced on her toes.

"Isn't it perfect?" she said as she ran for the jungle gym. She climbed a ladder and stood on the platform. "Come on, Antony! Or are you chicken?"

"I'm not a chicken." He stepped forward, leaped up, and caught the monkey bars. Elite squealed as he climbed up and sat on the bars instead of hanging under them.

"Come on," he said.

She descended the ladder, then climbed the rungs to where Antony sat. She stood on the bars, her hand resting on his shoulder. The entire park was bathed in the light of the full moon.

"Did Gage say anything about the tattoo?" she asked.

Antony swallowed hard. This was definitely not what he wanted to talk about, especially when he was so battle weary. He sat silent for a moment. Gage had said plenty, peppered with lots of curse words that made Antony smile. Mat had a lot of theories, but they were just that—speculation. Gage knew about the contract Antony had signed with his employer, and had warned him years ago that such wording was going to come back to haunt him.

What did Elite need to know? Did she need to know he was updating his will? Did he need to be completely honest with her, even tell her about the threat on Huahine? Yes, she deserved to know the truth. Just not now. He didn't want her to worry—she had enough on her mind as it was.

"Nothing," he mumbled. Then he gripped the bars and dropped down to the ground. "Last one to the swings gets to push!" He took off, hoping the change of location would distract her.

She gasped. "Not fair." She climbed down and followed him. When she got there, he held the swing out for her.

"I changed my mind. Have a seat," he said.

She sat and he pushed her into the air, then ran underneath her swing. Her laugh split the silence and he laughed, too. He sat on the swing next to hers and began to push himself with his feet.

When he grew tired, he pulled her back to the jungle gym. She touched him and said "tag," then ran away along the walkway made of metal links. He turned and followed her, chasing her down the slide and across the wood chips to another ladder. She climbed the metal rungs, and instead of stopping on the platform to go down the slide, she climbed on the outside of the slide and crossed to another section of the jungle gym.

Antony followed her, thinking she was going to go down. She laughed at his confusion, but stopped as he came dangerously close to touching her toes. She scrambled away and almost made it to the ground as he brushed her shoulder and then reversed himself, climbing back up on the ladder. He ran from bar to tower to slide. Once on the ground, he raced to the swing and climbed to the top. As he sat there looking down, he laughed at the irony that his own wife was helping him train, challenging his reflexes and skills. She thought it was play, but he appreciated the practice.

"Not fair," she said again, frowning.

"All's fair in love and war."

She stood on a swing and leaned forward to get it to move. After a minute, Antony scooted to the far side pole and shimmied down. He walked to her and stopped the swing.

"Tag," she whispered as he kissed her lips.

"I'm it," he said.

The sky had begun to lighten in the east as Elite looked at him from her spot on the slide. Antony sat at the top.

"We should probably go home," she said.

"Tired?"

"No, not yet."

Antony smiled and kissed her. "Didn't think so. I'm exhausted."

She reached out and pulled him down the slide, and hand in hand they walked to the train station.

"If we have a baby, I want to paint the room a pale green and add stars to the ceiling," she said after they sat in the back of the train.

"Where'd this come from?" he asked.

"Look at the sunrise. Isn't it pretty?"

He turned to the window and saw stars blinking out one by one in a pale blue-green sky. He kissed the top of Elite's head. "Green would be perfect."

25

Antony yanked the towel off his shoulders and hung it on the locker door. He pulled his pants out of his bag and shook them out, a habit he picked up living in the desert when he was in the ADF. Scorpions and other poisonous creatures loved to find dark spaces to hide when you were looking the other way. He pulled his pants up and grabbed at the drawstrings.

"Hey!" he heard from the next row.

"Out of my way," a familiar female voice said.

Antony tied the drawstrings and reached in his bag for his shirt.

"Whoa!" came a man's voice.

"There you are," Catelyn said as she rounded the corner. She'd covered the bruises in heavy makeup, but she looked just as weary as a few days ago.

"You're in a men's locker room," Antony said as he heard guys behind him scatter. He knew at least a few of them were still in the room, probably naked, too. Antony put on his shirt.

"I know." She stood there, her hands on her hips, her posture screaming anger. "Why didn't you answer my call?"

"Call?"

"I've been calling you all night."

"I was playing. My phone was at home." Antony turned and pulled his socks out.

"You're supposed to have that phone with you at all times. You know that. It's part of your contract."

The blasted contract . . . He pulled the socks on after throwing his shoes on the floor.

"I left it at home by accident," he said slowly.

She frowned. "Where were you?"

"At the park."

"You were playing at the park in the middle of the night?"

"Yeah."

"Must have been with that psycho wife of yours," Catelyn muttered under her breath.

Antony grabbed her by the front of her suit and pinned her against the lockers. "Don't you ever talk about Elite like that again. You may hold me in a life-long contract, but you don't own me. I have a life outside of work, Catelyn. I'm not at your beck and call every second."

At that moment, Catelyn's driver appeared and barreled toward them. "Call him off, Cate," Antony said, "or you will find me impossible to deal with in the future."

Catelyn waved a hand at her driver and he stopped as she turned to glare at Antony. "Let me go," she hissed.

"Or what—you'll call your daddy?"

"I'll have you fired." She pulled at his hands. The locker room had pretty much emptied by now.

"Fired? Come on, Cate, you know that someone with my accuracy record is not easy to replace."

"Don't be so confident, Mr. Danic. There are thousands of people just like you."

"If there were, you would have replaced me already. Am I right?"

She glanced at the driver, who stood with clenched fists and neck veins bulging.

"Right?" Antony said, staring at her until she looked him in the eye again.

She turned her head away after a second. "That's too much information, Mr. Danic."

"And you're getting redundant," he said as he lowered her to the ground and let go of her suit. She smoothed it and pulled a manila envelope out of her bag.

"This assignment is imperative. You only get one chance," she said quietly.

Antony took the envelope and placed it in his pack. He slung the pack on his back and grabbed his gym bag, then turned on his heel and left the locker room.

"What are you looking at?" he heard Catelyn holler at someone before the door slammed shut behind him.

"That's not your wife, is it?" a man asked as Antony entered the lobby.

"Hardly—she's my boss." He pulled his bag over his shoulders and hopped on his bike.

The private jet was scheduled to land on a seldom-used runway behind the main terminal. The target would be escorted across the tarmac to a waiting helicopter and then be gone. Corporate said he was thirty-three, but Antony thought he looked about seventeen in the picture.

"I need information on Daniel Grant," he said to Mat.

"Daniel Grant. There are 5,872 mentions of the name Daniel Grant in the news lately. Can you narrow it down?"

"He's thirty-three and is being transferred from a plane to a chopper this Saturday morning in Canberra under heavy guard."

"Daniel K. Grant. Arrested five years ago, not far from the scene of a terrorist bombing. He was charged and convicted when he refused to give any information or accept representation in the local courts. He spent the last few years on death row in the high-security penitentiary. He's being transferred to the federal prison on Saturday to await execution. Rumor has it, the territory governor in Perth was sympathetic to the boy's cause and was going to reverse the sentence. They are supposedly changing territories so his sentence can be carried out."

"If the governor was sympathetic, does that mean Daniel's not guilty?" Antony asked.

"He was found not far from the scene with explosives residue on his clothes."

"Not our call to judge, is it?" he mumbled to himself.

"That bombing killed 642 people," Mat said after a long pause, "including twenty-seven children."

Antony fell silent. *Why is Daniel marked for assassination?* he wondered. *Is he guilty? If so, why does it matter to Hurst Enterprises?* The man was a terrorist and definitely not a threat to the corporation, like the hacker Antony had chased through Pakistan.

"Thank you, Mat."

"No worries, Antony."

He shut the computer and sat back in his chair. If Daniel was guilty of killing over six hundred people, including children, he deserved execution. If not, he was a gigantic scapegoat.

Why did he refuse representation? Antony wondered. *Wouldn't you defend yourself if you weren't guilty? Besides, if he's going to be executed, why am I supposed to kill him?* But regardless of Antony's curiosity, he had a job to do. He pulled up the airport blueprints and photos on his Corporate laptop and studied them for hours. There were three buildings he could use for the hit. With two of them, he could easily access the roof, get the target, and make his escape. The third, which would definitely be the best in respect to position, would be hard to get onto. He had a few days to decide and formulate a plan.

Early Saturday morning, Antony sat on the rooftop of the third building, in the darkness of predawn. Over his running clothes, he wore coveralls stolen from the maintenance office. The flight was supposed to land at 5:15 AM, transfer a few minutes later, and be gone as if nothing happened. It was a cold morning, and no one questioned a man with a piece of corrugated sheet metal and a riveter crossing the parking lot and climbing the roof of the executive hangar, especially when a piece of roofing had come loose the night before.

He left the sheet metal and toolbox on the ground before climbing to the gable. The wind had died down overnight, which was good—he wouldn't need to adjust his shots as much. He pulled at the loose piece and looked down into the hole. There was no noise or light below him. He draped a rope, also stolen from the maintenance shed, over the strut and coiled both ends up, wedging it between the roof and the metal.

The open titanium rifle case lay to the side. Antony made sure his pack, worn in front this time, was open. He pulled out his sniper rifle, a British .338, inserted the barrel, and slid the magazine in with a comforting click.

"Time," he whispered.

"It is 5:01, sir."

"Viper in recon position."

"Position noted. Radio silence commenced." The earpiece went dead.

To Antony's left, a small jet landed and taxied toward the hangar. Below him, a helicopter's rotors began to turn. No need for a silencer—the report of the rifle would be drowned out by both engines. He lay down next to his case and aimed his rifle toward the space by the chopper, watching the scene through his high-powered scope.

The plane pulled close to the chopper and the door opened. Two big men got out and stood facing away from the plane while another man half dragged Daniel, in prison blue, out the door. Two more men followed. Catelyn was right—he was heavily guarded. Antony needed to get out of there as soon as the bullet hit flesh.

He found the man in his crosshairs, aimed for his head, and pulled the trigger. Daniel's head rocked back. Just to be sure, Antony aimed at his chest and pulled the trigger again. By the time Antony was taking the barrel off the stock and laying it in the titanium case, Daniel had crumpled to the ground.

Antony slammed the case in his pack, took the rope in his hand, and dropped into the hole under the loose panel. Gripping the rope with his legs and hands, he rappelled down, the rope zipping past him. As his feet hit the ground behind a large jet, he pulled at the rope and it came snaking toward him over the strut. He stripped off the coveralls and shoved them, along with the rope, into the wheel well beneath the jet. Then he ducked into the shadows toward a side door on the opposite side of the hangar from where the plane had landed. He pulled his pack on, then hugged the shadows of the buildings as he ran west away from the airport toward the city center. He ran down an embankment to the river bottoms by the parking garage and sped along the trail as fast as he could. It was many minutes before he heard the sound of a siren in the distance, and he was on a train passing Duntroon before he saw more flashing lights approaching the airport.

He watched the passengers with little interest, his mind on the young man he had just killed. He didn't know why, but he felt Daniel was innocent, like Kyo Yoji. Antony shook his head—he shouldn't be examining the hit. Daniel should be filed in the back of his head, just like all the other hits. Still, something bugged Antony. He didn't know if it was the hit itself, or what Mat had revealed about the target.

He forced his eyes closed. "It shouldn't matter," he whispered.

Somehow, he had to make himself believe it.

26

"I don't like it," Elite said.

Antony pulled the tape around his hand again and brought it to his mouth. He bit at the tape and tore it, then set the roll down on the bench and pressed the loose end against his palm. "You say that every time I do this," he said as he picked up the tape and pulled the roll around his other hand. The tape supported the bones in his hands so they wouldn't break. "It's just a spar—I do this every Friday with my master instructor. This is no different."

"Your Sa Bo Nim isn't out for blood or money. This guy is." Elite looked away from Antony to the other locker room, where his opponent was getting ready.

Antony bit at the tape and pressed it into his right palm. He always wrapped his left hand first—it was his strongest hand.

"Elite, this is an official spar. There will be a ref on the mat, and all precautions have been taken. I'll be fine." He paused as he pulled his white uniform top over his shoulders. "You liked the idea when I suggested it to earn some money for the orphanage."

"You must have been talking to some other Elite, because I don't like the idea at all."

Antony grinned. "I'll be fine." He kissed her forehead, then tied the strings at his side.

"You'll get hurt. That man is huge."

"He's only ten pounds heavier, and he's shorter then I am." Antony pulled out his black belt and tied it around his waist. "Besides, Sa Bo Nim said this would count for my Dan test." He would be a fifth-degree black belt in a month.

Elite pouted and folded her arms. Antony laughed as he pulled out his sparring gear and laid it on the bench. He and Elite were flanked by bright red lockers that ran down the room in long lines. He could hear voices from the mat area. This was his second home—his dojang and training gym.

"El, honey?" He pulled on the padded chest piece and turned. She tightened the straps, securing them on the Velcro patches. She had done this so many times, she could probably do it in her sleep. She pulled his forearm pads on and then his hand guards; he already wore his shin guards under his black pants. She held his foot pads as he slipped his feet into them. Then she slid his helmet on and fastened the strap on it.

"I love you," he said.

She grabbed a small white box from the bag, opened it, and pulled out his mouth guard. He leaned toward her, expecting a kiss, and instead met with the protective gear in her outstretched hand. Antony sighed and opened his mouth. She placed it inside and patted his cheek.

"Love you too, sweetie," she said.

"Are you ready?" a voice asked from the door.

"He's ready!" Elite called, then turned back to Antony. "The orphanage can use some exposure and money. But that isn't why I'm letting you do this. For some reason, you enjoy fighting and getting hurt, and I'll tolerate it for you." She touched her forehead and then his. He closed his eyes—it was time to think of the spar, not her religion.

I am Viper, he thought.

Antony kept his gaze forward as he walked to the edge of the mat. It was better not to see the crowd. He and his opponent would fight five rounds of five minutes each, and the one with the most strike points or who was left standing would be declared the winner. If Antony won, all the proceeds would go to the orphanage. If he lost, the money would go to a day camp for troubled youth. Either way, the earnings were going to a good cause. He looked straight ahead until his master instructor entered his line of sight.

"Antony, are you ready for this?" Rick asked. "Brian is good. I don't want you injured."

"I'm as good as I'm going to get," Antony answered. "I'm in top shape, even if I haven't sparred enough. It's not like I am a white belt, with only three months of training behind me." Even though he wasn't sleeping well, Antony had been in the dojang a lot recently, training like he did when he was a teen, sometimes four to five hours a day.

Rick nodded and bowed to him. "Go get him," the master instructor said, then stepped aside.

Antony stood at the edge of the mat and bowed. The other fighter was on the mat, bouncing on the balls of his feet. He had only three white stripes on his black belt. *Only a third degree?* Antony thought.

Brian approached him and bowed, offering his protected hands to touch. Antony bowed in return, and then touched his gloves to Brian's.

"Fighters ready?" the referee asked. Antony nodded, and the ref stood back. "Fighting stance."

Antony stepped into hugul jase—fighting stance, with one foot sideways—and pulled up his guards. He could feel sweat gathering under his chest pads. The crowd was loud, the excitement palpable.

"Shi jock!" Antony stepped forward and threw a strike. Brian blocked with a front kick, and Antony had to move back to avoid being kicked again as he threw a strike at his opponent's neck. The man was a kick-boxer—same basic training but different execution. No wonder they said he was hard to defeat. They trained and sparred in two different worlds. Antony focused on the man's legs and began to answer kick for kick, punch for punch, getting in a good strike here and there as Brian got close enough.

Twenty-eight seconds before round three ended, Brian leaped into the air and connected with Antony's head in a spinning back kick. Antony felt his legs turn to jelly as his vision faded. He heard Elite gasp before he fell to the floor.

"Antony, are you okay?" He could hear Rick's voice.

Great. Someone had removed his mouthpiece and headgear. Antony cursed under his breath as he realized he was on the mat, flat on his back.

"You didn't tell me he was a kick-boxer," he said to Rick. He could hear Elite's whimpers somewhere to his right.

Rick laughed. "You've sparred with them before. I figured you'd be fine."

Antony opened his eyes to see a fellow fighter, who was also a doctor, kneeling next to him. He tried to sit, but Rick held him down with a firm hand. "Nope—you're down for the night."

"Crap, Rick, I'll be fine. Just let me finish this," Antony said.

"You passed out," the doctor explained. "You might have a concussion."

"I've been hit harder than that before," Antony snapped. "Let me up. I'm not finished."

"Antony," Elite said. "Please listen to them."

He looked at his doctor friend. "See, you're making her panic. So, I passed out. I'm not disoriented, and I can talk without slurring. Let me finish this. Those kids are counting on me."

The doctor glanced at Rick, then used a penlight to look in Antony's eyes. He felt great, except for the blooming headache, but he wasn't going to tell anyone about that.

"He seems okay. He doesn't have a concussion," the doctor admitted.

"See?" Antony said. "I'm normal. I promise."

Elite frowned. "I was so scared when you hit the floor."

Antony turned to her. "El, honey, everything's all right."

"But . . ."

"Nope."

"You . . ."

"El."

"You . . ."

"I'm fine."

"Antony."

"Think of the kids, El."

"Antony—" she began.

He stood and held out his hand to Rick for his headgear, then took the mouthpiece from him, too. Standing made Antony's headache worse, but he would deal with it. The ref looked him in the eye as he stepped onto the mat.

"You're okay?" he asked. Antony nodded. "Fighters take your positions, fighting stance, and shi jock."

This time, Antony started the fight with a different mindset. If Brian was going to approach this as a kick-boxer, Antony was not going to obey the traditional rules of sparring. As the two met, Antony attacked with ferocity, using strikes and kicks on Brian as though he were a hit instead of a sparing opponent.

As the fourth session ended, Antony made his way to the corner, pulled his mouthpiece out, and grabbed for his water bottle.

"Definitely not your traditional fight," Rick said. "But considering what you're facing, who can blame you?"

Antony looked at him and grimaced. "I hate this 'mixed martial arts' thing. They aren't disciplined enough in one style to make it worth their time—it's all designed to draw the opponents' blood." A lot of the traditional fighters felt it was cheating, compared to their years of training in one style to perfect their skills.

"Hang in there. You only have five more minutes," Rick said.

Antony put his mouthpiece back in and adjusted his hand guards. "This won't count as my testing spar."

"Don't worry about that right now. Go in there and win this thing."

"Shi jock!" the ref said.

Antony jumped toward Brian and attacked him, hitting like he used to do when sparring with his dad. But this time he didn't stop his power when he connected with flesh. He kicked at the man's knee and heard a tendon rip. The crowd gasped. As Brian doubled over, Antony drove a knife strike into his neck and hit him hard. Brian's eyes rolled back and he turned in a slow circle as he crumpled to the ground.

The ref stepped forward. "Return to your corner," he said as he stood over Brian.

Antony nodded and made his way to Rick and Elite. He pulled off his headgear and stripped the guards from his hands. His body wore a coat of sweat, and he was so tired. The headache behind his eyes pounded. Elite rushed forward and brushed his hair from his face.

"See, I'm okay," he said.

She shook her head but said nothing, her mouth drawn into a tight line as if she was holding something back. Rick stood, arms folded. Outside, through the glass doors and windows, the sky had turned black as night.

The referee raised his arms as the doctor who had treated Antony attended Brian. The crowd went silent.

"The winner tonight of the sparring for charity match is the Canberra Children's Orphanage."

Elite squealed and hugged Antony. He closed his eyes. It was for the kids, he told himself. The headache was bearable if he thought of it that way. He could hear the crowd standing and leaving, the din of conversation in his ears. He opened his eyes and looked at his master instructor over Elite's shoulder.

Suddenly, Antony's eyes focused on a man behind Rick, in the back of the dojang. Long black hair tied away from his face, Lanzen glasses over his eyes. He turned and headed for the door. Antony pushed himself to the side and stepped toward him—the man was almost at the door.

"Antony?" Elite said.

"Do you have your phone?"

She rummaged in her bag and pulled out the sleek pink device. He grabbed it and stepped onto the mat, heading for the door.

The man was almost half a block ahead when Antony rushed through the doors. He bolted toward him as fast as his pads would allow. Now the man was reaching for the door of a black Mercedes. The door opened and Antony moved the phone in front of him and placed his finger on the photo button.

"Hey!" he yelled.

The man looked up but put a hand across his face as Antony clicked the picture. The flash pulsed in the darkness. In a second, the man was in the car, speeding away. Antony stood panting, his hands on his knees as Elite caught up with him. Rick was right behind her.

"What was that about?" She placed a hand on Antony's shoulder.

"Did you see him?" He looked in the direction the Mercedes had gone.

"See who?"

"The guy in the black glasses."

"What guy?"

"Never mind." At least he had the picture—maybe Mat could find a match. Hopefully he got the picture before the guy's hand crossed his face.

"Sorry about running away," Antony said. "I thought I recognized someone." He looked at Rick, who stood there stoically. Antony had crossed the mat without bowing, breaking one of the first rules of respect learned in the dojang. He had also ignored his Sa Bo Nim—another rule broken.

"You did well," Rick said, unfolding his arms. "Go home and meditate. It isn't good for your heart if you sleep this wound up." Rick turned and walked back toward the dojang.

27

Antony logged out of his online banking account and opened his email. He clicked on a new message.

To: Antony Danic
From: Mat

I've searched the Lanzen client lists and have found something interesting. Because of the uniqueness of the product, the number of sunglasses sold per year usually sits just under five hundred. However, a few years ago I found an inventory of approximately 3,500 sunglasses with adjustable tint. The buyer is a company based in the United States. The accounts billable is addressed to a company called "The Academy," and paid in cash in advance of the order. Further searches have revealed The Academy is connected to "The Devoted of Naimaku," to which Kyo Yuji belonged. The Academy is a huge military complex with bases all over the world. The money to run The Academy comes from businesses operated on these complexes, plus investments and inventions, therefore funding The Devoted of Naimaku, which is why I can find no tax information on the religion. Further searching has proven difficult at best. They are even better than I am at covering their paper trail and internet presence. They have a series of websites and a network, but it's more encrypted than I've ever seen. It will take time. I hope you understand and are patient with me. Gage and I will be in Canberra on Friday evening.

Antony sat back, staring at his screen. The Devoted of Naimaku was part of a worldwide military operation. Not only that, but they had bases all over the world. What was The Academy? Why had he not heard of them? Did Elite even know that her church was part of something bigger? He sat forward and typed.

To: Mat
From: Antony

I appreciate your effort and what you've been able to dig up. Please keep me informed of anything you find. I look forward to seeing you this weekend. BTW, I'm sending you a picture of the guy who's been following me. I apologize—it's grainy and a little blurry. Can you see if you can match this guy's face to anyone?

For the second time in a few months, he felt the need to talk to someone in the hierarchy of the church, yet his adventure with Sori Katsu had gone sour in a moment. How did the guy know so much about Antony? Only a few people knew what his real job entailed, and he was sure Katsu hadn't simply guessed. Antony knew Elite wasn't telling people things; she knew his survival depended on his anonymity.

He stood and shut the computer. He had sat at his desk for hours, finishing monthly paperwork and reports, and he needed to get up and move around. Locking his door, he made his way to the living room and stood in front of his stereo system, the one Gage helped him assemble when he and Elite moved to this apartment almost ten years ago. The system had all the bells and whistles, and yet in the center of all the modern technology sat an old turntable. A "record player," Antony called it.

When Elite was home, she usually had something going, whether it was an appliance or the radio. She liked sound, where he preferred silence. Today was different. The house had been silent and empty when he woke, not that he expected her to be there when she didn't even know when he'd emerge from their room. He was exhausted from the spar last night and usually slept long hours after such a fight. Today, however, the silence seemed crushing. He pulled out a record, cleaned it with a soft cloth, and placed the center hole over the post on the turntable. Then he lifted the arm, blew the dust off the needle, and placed it on the outermost ring of the disk. Silence was replaced with the sounds of Ultravox. Antony closed his eyes and let the old sound flow over him. Synthesizers and electronic drums filled the room, and he felt some tension leave his body.

As one song scratched to the next, he turned to find the living room a cluttered mess. He had intended to locate the mail and look through it. He was surprised at the state of the room, since Elite was such an immaculate housekeeper. Papers were scattered on the table, along with a plate of half-eaten food. The pillows had been kicked to the floor, and the throw blanket lay crumpled in a corner of the couch. It looked like Elite left in a rush.

He grabbed the plate and took it to the kitchen. Then he pulled a rag from the drawer, wiped the glass top of the table, and rearranged the decorations. He threw the pillows on the couch and shook out the blanket, then laid it over the arm of the chair. Next, he gathered all the papers, dropped the garbage in the trash bin, and placed the mail on the counter by the fridge.

An overstuffed envelope slid off the stack and fell to the floor. He picked it up and flipped it over. It was addressed to him, from GA Tech. He opened it to find pages of the usual statistics for the business. He would look over it later, although it was hard to ignore the fluorescent yellow note stuck to the front page.

Mercy Health System bought the program for their hospitals. We have broken even and will be a profit-earning business by next month. Another company called Trinity Investments is looking at just the AI program. They want an exclusive program and are willing to pay handsomely for it. I'm waiting for their reaction to the sample. Gage.

Antony smiled as he set the envelope back down on the counter. His gut had been right—his investment was about to start paying off, and it made him feel more secure in his world of uncertainty. If GA Technologies did well, he and Elite could eventually retire on the profits of the company. Even more importantly, if something happened to him and the supposed pension promised to him in his employment contract suddenly disappeared, or the orphanage failed to make a profit, Elite would have something for her future.

Antony had set the papers down and started back into the living room to flip the record when he heard the door slam.

Elite stood on the entryway tile, making jeans and one of his old sweaters look good.

"You're home," she said, dropping her purse and a number of shopping bags on the floor.

He moved close and kissed her. "Are you okay?" he asked.

"I'm okay now." Her eyes had a faraway look in them. "I mean, I wasn't. I felt horrible. But I'm okay now."

"Elite?"

She looked at him, her brown eyes shining. "We're pregnant. We're going to have a baby."

25

"A baby? You're pregnant? How? I mean, I know how. I mean
. . . I don't know what I mean. That's amazing, and you're
amazing. This is a—"

"It's a miracle," Elite said. "Even the doctor agreed."

Antony didn't deny it. "I can't believe how lucky we are."
He took her in his arms and held her tight. "Elite, I love you. I
can't believe it! A baby—you and I are going to have a baby."
Her silence startled him. "Elite, are you okay? Is the baby all
right? What did the doctor say?" He held her by the shoulders
and at once noticed her pale skin and hollow cheeks. "What's
wrong?"

When her eyes finally found his, he saw her tears. "What
if something happens? What if there's something seriously
wrong with it? What if I lose it?" she blurted out in rapid
succession.

"Elite, honey, you're young and healthy, so there's no
reason for anything to go wrong. Besides, if there is something
wrong with the baby, we'll still love it. I'll protect you. Nothing
is going to happen to the two of you. I promise."

He felt her sink against his chest and closed his eyes.
How long has she been sick? Why didn't I see it? He meant
what he said—nothing would happen to them. She would

deliver a healthy child, and they would be the perfect happy family.

"When are you due?" Antony couldn't help the grin on his face.

"April sometime. I'm thirteen weeks now. Another five weeks, and we'll be able to find out if it's a boy or a girl. Or we can opt for the gender blood test earlier."

"Really? That fast?" He shifted to move Elite toward the couch and accidentally kicked one of the many bags on the floor. "What's in the bags?"

"Oh . . . baby stuff. I went shopping until I got too tired," she admitted, her cheeks coloring a little.

He laughed. "Well, sit down. Put your feet up. Are you hungry?"

She looked at him. "Antony, I'm not dying—I'm pregnant."

"I know, and I'm going to spoil you. Sit down, please."

She sat. "I'm fine—just tired. Besides, save it for when I'm huge and can't move."

"Why wait?" He placed her purchases by her and headed to the kitchen to get her a glass of water.

"Antony."

"El," he said, turning to her, "please allow me this moment. We'll probably never get another chance. Just let me show you how much I love you."

"Okay." Her voice faded as she looked at him. He smiled back at her, then leaned forward and kissed her on the lips, the soft touch full of passion.

What Antony did not expect when Gage knocked on his door Friday afternoon was the amount of luggage behind him.

"Wha', you're lookin' at me like you've never seen me before," Gage said as he dragged two Pullman suitcases into the apartment. Then he went back into the hall to retrieve a metal trunk.

"How long are you staying?" Antony asked.

"Long enough."

"Gage, come in. Antony's just being temperamental," Elite said from the couch.

This morning had been rough for her, and he had insisted on her taking the day off. They had discussed appointing her a second-in-command at the charities until she didn't feel like throwing up every minute. Antony had offered to paint the nursery however she wanted if she'd do as he asked.

"Don't listen to her," he joked. "She's being stubborn." Elite started to stand as Antony reached for the trunk. "El, please sit. I'll take care of Gage. You can still be the gracious host from a sitting position."

"Antony, I'm fine," she said.

He shut the door and turned to his friend.

"What're you doing, Antony?" Gage asked. "Elite, what's gotten into 'im? Why the kid gloves? Are you sick?"

Antony turned off his phone, threw it into a basket, and replaced the lid. "Elite is pregnant." On top of everything else, the number of people he needed to protect, and his family's risk, had just gone up by one.

"Well, congratulations to both of you." Gage slugged Antony in the arm, then pulled Elite into an embrace. "Antony, turn your phone back on and we'll just have a normal conversation," he whispered as he opened his trunk and pulled out a mini-computer. He scanned the phone, and the light turned red.

Antony frowned. He pulled his earpiece out of his pocket, and again the light went red. Gage took the phone and earpiece and placed them in his metal trunk. "I'll get those later," he mouthed, and then tossed the scanner to Antony and looked at him with raised eyebrows.

Antony nodded. He had seen how Gage scanned the phone—it was simple enough to figure out. From the trunk, Gage pulled out another scanner, just like the one in Antony's hand.

"So, Gage, how was the trip?" Elite asked as Gage brushed the device along the wall. He stopped at the light switch and made a note in the book in his front pocket.

"Not bad. The weather from Sydney to here was beautiful. Perfect day for a flight."

"A flight? You don't like to fly," she said.

"I don't like being a passenger in a plane, but I don't mind it much when I'm the pilot."

"You rented a plane?" Antony asked. "What's wrong with the Hummer?"

"Nothing's wrong with my car. The plane was just faster. I flew the Starlight One, GA Technologies' private jet."

"We have a jet?" Antony asked.

"Yeah, I sent you all the specs with the last business statement. Didn't you read it?"

"You know I don't read all that number mumbo-jumbo."

"Too bad—you should keep up with it. Then you'd know that half the plane belongs to you."

Antony laughed under his breath. Even if he owned over half of the company, he let Gage make all the decisions. Business wasn't his specialty.

The light turned red as Antony waved his scanner over the switch in the dining room. He motioned to Gage, who nodded and wrote it down in the notebook. Antony worked his way down the hall.

"Don't worry about me, El," Gage said. "I'll just move my luggage to the guest room. I know the way."

"Sure, help yourself," she said.

Antony came out of his office and smiled. He shook his head as Gage and Elite looked at him. Gage finished the guest room and the master bedroom, while Antony scanned the bathrooms and Elite's office. They met in the baby's room. Gage whistled at the crib full of bags.

"You've been shopping, Elite," he said.

Antony turned to see her standing in the doorway as he touched the sleeve of the tiny shirt that had fallen out of the bag. He couldn't believe babies started out so small.

Gage sighed. "Mathilde always wanted kids. She wanted a large family, like hers. She was the youngest of ten, you know."

"You need to start dating again," Antony said.

"Don't you believe in true love, that there is one person who can capture your heart?" Gage asked.

"Yes, and I've got her right here." Antony embraced Elite from behind.

"I do too, and I had her with Mathilde. There is no other one for me." Gage frowned. "I hope you guys, of all my friends, understand that. I gave her my heart, and she didn't give it back when she died." He gestured for Elite to come into the room. "Shut the door."

"Gage, I'm sorry," Antony said.

His friend shook his head. "No worries, this room is clean. There are three bugs—one in the living room, one in the dining room, and one in your bathroom. Why don't you two go watch a movie on the couch and I'll get to work. Turn the volume way up, though."

Before escorting Elite to the living room, Antony watched Gage open another section of the metal case and strap a tool belt around his waist.

Elite and Antony settled on the couch, where she laid her head on his chest and closed her eyes. He pulled up a battle movie with a lot of cannon fire. He absently stroked Elite's hair as he tried to pay attention to the movie. Every few minutes she raised her head to see where Gage was. Antony knew from the tenseness in her body that this wasn't easy for her.

The movie was almost finished when Gage came back into the living room. He sat on the floor and placed Antony's phone and earpiece on the table. Antony watched with interest as Gage opened the phone and pointed to two chips inside. He added a third and spliced it into the wires connected to the other chips. He did the same with the earpiece. Antony's old laptop was clean, showing green on the scanner. His new GA Tech model was clean as well.

Gage handed Antony his phone and earpiece. Antony found the remote and muted the movie.

"These detectors are the latest technology. They should have found everything. However, those were some advanced bugs," Gage explained. "I've installed my own surveillance device that will record anything that isn't your or Elite's voice. It will alert Mat when someone besides, or in addition to you, is in your home."

"The bugs are gone?" Elite asked. Antony helped her sit up.

"No, they are all still in place. I did to them what I did to the phones." He nodded to the phone in Antony's hand. "I added a bug of my own, spliced into theirs. It will record all the conversations you have here or on the phone, and relay them to Mat at lightning speed. She will analyze the conversations and alter them to keep you safe. For example, this conversation will probably still be the movie noise. Mat will be triangulating where the signal is being sent, and we should know where the bugs are from soon enough. I also linked my bug to the homing beacon in the phones, so if needed, your location can be altered by Mat, too."

"Homing . . . beacons, and bugs? In my phone and earpiece?" Antony said.

Elite closed her eyes, and the worry on her face made his heart ache. "Sounds like your company doesn't trust you as much as they say they do," she said.

If they trust me at all, Antony thought, but he said, "Obviously not. Probably why the Lanzen guy stands where I can see him." Antony looked at the red metallic phone in his hand. He turned and placed both his phone and earpiece in the basket again. "Wouldn't want to lose them," he muttered and turned back to Gage. His laptop was open, and Mat stood on the mouse pad.

"Antony, I'm sorry it has come to this," Mat said. "Your employers seem to have changed their tune from simple corporate espionage to a global agenda. Mr. Crawford is somehow linked to The Academy, as was Kyo Yuji, by way of The Devoted of Naimaku. Your Mr. Crawford was sending information to an address not in the Hurst Corporation. Who has a vendetta against The Academy and the church, we don't know yet. But it's obvious someone in Hurst Enterprises doesn't like them, and is using—"

"Me as their own personal assassin," Antony finished. He felt Elite's hand tighten on his. Mat didn't know the extent of Elite's connection to the church. It had never really come up since Gage had introduced Mat to Antony and Elite. They hadn't talked about Kyo since that night. Antony didn't dare bring it up, and she hadn't talked to him about his assignments since then.

Her face went pale, and she ran into the bathroom. Antony stood to follow her and closed his eyes against a memory of the guy on Huahine—how he'd looked at Elite like a predator—and turned back to Gage. He grimaced. As much as she needed him right now, his nightmares reminded him that he had serious matters to discuss with his friend.

"My will."

"Who cares about your will?" Gage said. "Go to her."

"You don't understand. A bullet could come through a window in this apartment and hit me in the head at any second. Besides, she needs to be alone for a moment."

"Fine. What do you want changed?"

"Elite inherits everything, even my shares in GA Tech. If something happens to me, I want her to leave Canberra. You will be executor of the will. I want you to take care of her. I promised her that she and the baby would be safe. Make sure my son . . . or daughter . . . knows I loved them and wanted them dearly."

"You're talking nonsense."

"Am I?"

"Nothing is going to happen to you."

"I'm involved in something much deeper than I thought. I will not walk out of this alive, Gage. If the head of the corporation can have his own daughter beaten for who knows what, I'm as good as dead—if they decide they don't like me anymore, or that I'm too much of a risk."

"What if something happens to Elite?"

"Not gonna happen."

"Still, what if?"

"Fine." Antony turned to look at the door of the bedroom, closing his eyes against the images in his head. "If something happens to Elite, all her property and assets go to the baby.

If the baby dies too, Elite's assets go to the orphanage and a committee will be set up to manage the money."

"And if both of you die?"

"Elite's assets still go to her charities. The proceeds from the sale of our home and belongings, too. My assets and percentage in GA Tech go to you, to further the company. Unless the baby lives. Then it all goes to the baby. If you're able, please make sure that Elite's body is treated with the respect it deserves."

"What about your body?" Gage asked, his face solemn.

"I don't care about me. Just make sure Elite is safe or that she's taken care of properly."

"Guardianship of the baby, if it survives?"

"I don't know. I haven't thought that far. Elite will take care of the baby."

"Well, you need to think about it."

"I don't want to."

"I know. Antony, my mom is still alive and healthy. She'll live at least another twenty years. She loves you as if you were her son, and she'd love the baby. If her health turns, she will find someone else."

Gage's mother was an option Antony hadn't considered, probably because he wasn't thinking straight. He knew her well and had thought of her many times as his own mother.

"List your mother as permanent guardian," he said. "Ask her to either take care of the baby or find a good family—one that goes to church, Gage. Elite will need a proper Church burial if it goes that far."

"But you're an atheist."

"Yeah, but Elite is not. This baby is hers more than mine. It will grow in her body—she will nourish it from her body. She would want it this way."

"Whatever you say, Antony." Gage turned to Mat. "What he said."

Antony turned and walked down the hall. He hesitated as he reached out to the bedroom doorknob. Elite had every right to hate him. He had known who Kyo was as soon as he put the facts together at dinner that night, but he'd been too chicken to be honest with her. He tried the knob. To his surprise, the door wasn't locked.

"Elite?" he said. She lay on the bed wrapped in a quilt, her body shaking with sobs. He knelt on the floor. "El, I'm sorry. I didn't—"

She reached out and pressed her hand to his mouth. "I don't want to talk about it, Antony. I'd prefer to stay in the dark about your targets."

"Mat is a computer. I think we forget that and assume she has some tact," he said. Elite said nothing, but snuggled into his chest. He touched her head tenderly. "Everything is going to be okay," he whispered.

"It's called an appearance chip." Gage held up an anti-static bag. The chip was small, barely two centimeters square. "It sits near the cortical part of the brain and can change the appearance of the wearer. It influences the DNA strand and moves fat and skin and melanin to change everything but height and large amounts of weight."

"How?" Antony asked as he looked at the chip and the surgical instruments.

"A cuttle fish has many layers of skin, and it can change the flow of blood, the thickness of skin and melanin in its body to control color. This is similar to that."

"You've created a DNA manipulator, and you're using it for appearance?" Antony asked. *Just for me and Elite?*

"I've plans to sell my research to some interested parties, but for now, your safety is more important," Mat said.

Antony smiled. "I appreciate it."

Elite still lay on their bed, fast asleep. He and Gage had been up for hours, discussing Elite and Antony's safety and future. The will had been witnessed and notarized, and copies were filed with the state and their attorneys.

"I brought two, one for you and one for Elite," Mat explained.

"Not Elite. Nothing to jeopardize the pregnancy," Antony said.

Gage frowned.

"I will do nothing to risk it." Antony's face was drawn tight.

"We can install yours and monitor your systems, and leave the second one with a scalpel-surturer, just in case. It might be a last-moment decision, and I won't be here," Mat said. "I'll show you where the chip goes. I've preprogrammed a few identities in the chip—you just need to trigger the switch by selecting one on the controller." Gage held up the little square. "There are ten female and ten male, including a fallback of yourself and Elite. Just in case."

"Sure," Antony said. Could he and Elite just slip into other identities and convince the corporation they were gone*? No, my employer would have to think I was dead.*

"I've got ideas and things I'm working on, but none of it's ready." Gage said. "The best thing I can offer you right now besides the bugs and the chip is a hand-held version of your laptop."

"It's better than nothing." Antony said.

"Well, good. Because it's all I have. For now."

29

Early morning darkness covered the land as Antony chained his bike to the lamp post. He looked east. The sky was still dark blue, but the stars were starting to fade. *Beautiful,* he thought as he pulled open the door to the pool. Moisture and the smell of the water hit his senses and he breathed in deep. In his ever-changing world, this was one constant. He stripped to his suit and stood on the edge of the pool in an unoccupied lane.

He stretched up toward the ceiling, then crouched and pushed himself into the water. Silence enveloped him and he started to swim. With no gun, no phone, no earpiece, he was just Antony. He relished the thought as he kicked off the wall and started his second lap. He was just a human, nothing different or special from those in the other lanes in the pool.

In fact, he was more like them now. He was going to be a father. Elite's pregnancy had taken them by surprise. Her symptoms—the headaches, sleeplessness, and nausea—were things she suffered with anyway. When she started throwing up every morning, her friend suggested it might be something serious and that she go to the clinic. The doctor at the clinic ran a pregnancy test, along with the other standard blood tests. After Elite received a shot of anti-nausea medicine, she was sent home to rest. With the amazing news, she went shopping instead.

Stroke after stroke Antony swam, immersed in his world, eventually losing count of the laps. This was his new routine— exercise or practice in the dojang in the morning when Elite was working, and spending a lazy afternoon with her when she got home, then out to do something fun for the evening. He hadn't heard anything from Catelyn since the hit at the airport. He was beginning to wonder if the corporation didn't know what to do with either of them. It made him nervous, but he wasn't going to let it ruin this time with Elite. Gage and Mat were working on a way to get him and Elite out of Canberra if needed.

When Antony's arm and back muscles screamed in rebellion, he stopped at the wall, pulled his goggles off, and breathed deeply. The sun was starting to lighten the sky as he stepped out of the pool and walked to the showers. Normally, he ran after swimming, but he had errands to do while Elite was at the orphanage.

He showered and dressed, then caught the train to the artistic center of the city. He walked past the shops, finally stopping in front of one. Infant clothing adorned the windows, and he smelled the sweet scent of baby as he walked in.

Hands loaded with bags, Antony walked to the station. An older woman smiled at him as he sat on the bench with the bags in his hands. He must have bought at least one of every gender-neutral item in the store, along with a beautiful quilt that reminded him of Tahiti.

He couldn't wait until Elite came home. He would make dinner and have the table set with her favorite dishes. He could pick up anything he needed at the corner market after he put the boxes on the couch and signed the card he found a few days ago. This was going to be an amazing six months, full of wonder.

He unlocked the door to find that only the deadbolt was set. He placed the packages on the floor, pulled his pistol from the holster, and cocked it. He set the master lock and the alarm. He wasn't going to take any chances. He tried his office door—it was locked. The bedroom was empty. He stepped toward the door to the nursery and placed his palm on the door, his gun ready in his other hand. He swung the door open to find Elite standing in the middle of the room, paint chips in both hands.

"Hi," she said.

Antony placed the pistol on safe and put it in his pocket. "You need to set the alarm and the master lock when you're home, especially when I'm gone."

"I locked the dead bolt. Besides, I knew you'd be home soon from running.

"I thought you were at work."

"I finished early today, and they made me go home. I guess the pregnancy isn't a secret," she said, holding up one chip and then the other.

He kissed her cheek. "Stay here—I've got something for you." He retrieved the bags and carried them to the nursery. They had bought the furniture a little at a time in hopes of using it someday. The antique rocker was from England. Antony had seen it and shipped it to Canberra a few years ago.

"Close your eyes," he said. He set the bags down and guided Elite to the rocker. "Okay, open."

She opened her eyes and breathed in as she saw the bags. She opened the biggest box with the quilt, and then the smaller boxes with the other things. She held each tenderly and touched the tiny clothes in awe, then giggled when she pulled out the socks.

"I can't believe they start so small and need so many things," he said.

She placed the boxes on the floor by the rocker and jumped out of the chair into his arms. "Thank you," she sobbed.

"Did I do something wrong?" Antony asked.

Elite laughed as tears streamed down her face. "No you did it just right. It's these hormones. I'm an emotional mess. I cry over tying my shoes, for heavens' sake."

He chuckled and held her tighter. He looked over her shoulder into the crib and saw that the mattress was littered with paint chips in blues and greens.

"El, what are all these?"

She stiffened slightly and blushed. "I wanted to surprise you. I wanted to paint the nursery, but I can't find the color we saw that morning in the park. They just don't make that shade of green." Elite frowned. "The salesperson told me about this new paint full of color-changing nanobites that can adjust to the exact tint you want. In fact, he was pushing it really heavily. But I don't know if I'd want something so invasive in the baby's room."

"Me either. Is there anything close?" Antony asked as he scanned the chips. He picked up three of the chips on the mattress. "These look good. Do you like any of these?"

She looked from the chips in her hands to those in his and gasped. She grabbed the one on the left and held it up. "This one is much better. Thank you." She taped it to the wall, then scooped up all the others and threw them in the trash.

He laughed. She was eccentric and energized, and she was his. He couldn't be happier.

30

"Those of you with tickets marked A through C, please follow our hostess Karen," the young woman said as she stood on the platform, pointing to another young woman wearing a matching blue jacket trimmed with gold braid. "Those with D through G, please follow Mark." A man in black pants and a blue sweater waved his hand.

Antony stood on plush burgundy carpet. Chandeliers of polished nickel and glass lit the lobby area, and lush plants and expensive furniture decorated the sitting areas. He could smell coffee and pastries from one of the concession bars around the room. He almost felt as if he had stepped into another world.

"Thank you for choosing AWA Trans-World Flight for your traveling needs."

Antony looked at his ticket and followed Karen.

As they reached the lifts on the right, she turned. "These elevators lead to the first-class suites, as well as the ballrooms and restaurants. The elevators on the left to take you to the coach and recreation areas. Your luggage should have already been delivered to your rooms. If you come across a problem, please don't hesitate to ask me or any of the staff for assistance. These three elevators lead to Level C, these two lead to Level B, and the last two lead to Level A. Have a nice flight."

As Karen turned to the front desk, people started to gather in front of the lifts. Antony held back, not wanting to be in the middle of the crowd of people.

"There will be instructions waiting for you in your room." He remembered Catelyn's voice from yesterday. "You're to speak of this assignment to no one. Complete security is of the utmost importance. Do you understand?"

"Of course," he'd said just before she hung up.

When the level A lifts were empty, Antony stood and walked to the last set of chrome doors.

"Sir, are you lost?" Karen approached him.

"No, I was waiting for the room to clear. I'm a bit claustrophobic," he said, feeling a little sheepish.

She smiled and looked at his ticket. "Your room is at the end of the hall. Just turn left when you get to A. Have a nice flight, Mr. Thompson."

Nodding, he raised his hand and stepped into the lift car. He leaned back against the mirrored walls. He had wanted to take Elite on a cruise for years—now he was on this elegant spaceship alone.

When Antony reached his room, he brushed the card against the key pad. The lock clicked and the door opened with a hiss.

"Wow," he said as he walked in. The suite was large, probably half the size of his and Elite's apartment. Metal cases filled the sitting room and every other spare inch of space, stacked from floor to ceiling. An envelope lay on the bed, his false name on the front. Inside, a piece of paper read,

Mr. Danic,

You're protecting a large amount of valuable cargo. A crew identifying themselves as D3 will unload it when you reach Belize in three days. Their ID will look exactly like this:

Antony looked closely at the picture of an official-looking card.

Memorize it. Once exposed to oxygen, this ink will dissolve in three minutes.

C

Antony stared at the ID until the ink faded into nothing. Then he put the blank piece of paper in his pack and laid it on the bed.

He felt the acceleration through his feet as the ship started to move away from the docking station. This was an amazing aircraft—as huge as a cruise liner, and more luxurious. There were three of them in service and they traveled high in the atmosphere, stopping at orbiting stations like the one where he had boarded. Shuttles ran from the orbiting stations to corresponding Earth stations. As with an ocean cruise, the main point of the trip was spending time on the ship with its many amenities; the docking station stops were a minor diversion.

After slipping off his shoes, Antony curled his toes in the plush carpet and stood in mountain pose. He moved through his yoga routine until his body burned with energy and his muscles felt warm with movement. He had three uninterrupted days to meditate and work out, and he knew he'd be a fool to ignore the opportunity. He sat on the floor, closed his eyes, and felt himself fall into the black silence of meditation.

Click, hiss.

Antony opened his eyes and reached for his pistol under the pillow. His feet hit the floor and he backed against the wall as he pulled the slide on his Glock. He settled his pack on his back and placed his two extra magazines in his pajama pants pocket. Although the noisy door was definitely not a selling point, he was glad he was awake as a lone figure entered his suite. He wasn't surprised—the wording and the tone of Catelyn's correspondence told him that whatever the cargo was, it was important, and that meant other people might be after it.

He could see the beam of the trespasser's flashlight scan the cases and stop. Antony wondered if the man's reaction was like his—shock. He had stopped counting the cases himself after he got to a hundred.

"Command, this is Agent Hansen," the man whispered. "I've gained access to the suite reserved by Hurst Enterprises. Our information is right—there are cases of it. Over half the room is full . . ." His light swept over the unmade bed.

Antony stood next to him, the barrel of the gun pointed at the man's head. "Don't move," Antony said.

Agent Hansen froze for one second as if deciding what to do, then turned. With a sweep of his arm, he knocked Antony's gun to the side and punched at him, his fist grazing Antony's gut. Antony pulled his pistol hand back and reverse-punched Hansen in the face with his free hand. The man tumbled back a few steps before finding his footing, then swung at Antony, who deflected the strike with a simple block across the chest. The agent swung again, but this time Antony brought up his gun hand a little too slowly, so Hansen's fist glanced off his arm and hit him in the head. He blinked at the stars and hit the agent in the chest.

Punch after punch, they fought back and forth. Antony grabbed the agent by the collar of his uniform and pushed him backward against the stack of cases, causing it to tumble. Antony jumped back as the top case hit the ground and broke open, followed by others. He could hear things dropping to the floor from inside the cases. Agent Hansen rolled as the cases came tumbling down, one barely missing his head. He scrambled to a stand and attacked Antony full force. Antony backpedaled as the agent hit him in the face and chest.

When Hansen's fist came at his face again, Antony grabbed it and stopped the strike, then head-butted his opponent's face. The agent's eyes rolled back in his head as Antony pulled him forward and went to knee him in the gut, but the agent twisted and Antony hit something hard on the man's belt instead of soft flesh. Hansen grabbed at his belt and gasped as Antony struck at his neck with the side of his hand. Hansen crumpled to the floor, a black box in his hand.

Antony stood over the unconscious agent and panted. He noticed the box immediately—green numbers were counting backwards from 9:32. He was a munitions expert, so he knew what those numbers meant.

"Crap!" he said and turned from the agent. He stepped on something cold with his bare feet and looked down—he stood on one of many glass tubes with silver caps on both ends. There was a yellow, almost clear liquid inside them. He grabbed one of the tubes, rushed out the door, and turned for the lifts.

He stopped. There were hundreds of people on the spaceship. *If they die, it's my fault.* He looked around—there had to be something he could do to save the passengers. He saw a fire alarm on the wall about one hundred feet away, the red box standing out against the elegant surroundings. He raced for the box and slammed his elbow into the glass, then reached into the box and pulled the bar down, sounding the alarm.

"Emergency. This is not a drill. Please evacuate now. All passengers must evacuate," a voice boomed over the loudspeaker. Bright lights flooded the hallways. People left their rooms, looking groggy and disoriented. Green arrows appeared from the ceiling and pointed down the hall.

"Please follow the green arrows to the evacuation shuttles," the voice said.

Antony placed his pistol in his waistband and raced down the hall. People surged around him, and he heard a gasp and a child's cry as he felt someone hit the floor. A young mother hugged her baby to her chest and tried to stand. Antony turned, grabbed the baby, and helped the woman up. He handed her the baby and pushed her along. An elderly man fell, and Antony turned to a young man, placing a hand on his shoulder.

"Pick him up and take him to the shuttles," he said. The young man startled, but did what he was told.

A mother tried to pull her three children down the hall, two of the little ones crying in the confusion. "You," Antony said, pointing at another young man. "Take her to the shuttles."

Within a few seconds, the chaos settled into rushed cooperation and the hall emptied as the shuttles filled. Antony hurried to one of the shuttle entrances and realized the transport was packed. He pulled the door shut and hit the manual release. The shuttle rocketed away from the main ship.

Elite, if I don't get out, please forgive me. Go to Sydney and let Gage take care of you. Antony ran to another shuttle to find it too was full. He shut the door, hit the EJECT button, and raced to the last shuttle. There was maybe two feet of space left. He stepped in, slammed the door shut, and hit the EJECT button. He fell against the wall as the shuttle blasted away from the ship. The small vessel was filled with panting and coughing, the wails of frightened children, and the comforting voices of mothers.

Antony closed his eyes. His whole body hurt from the fight, and his lungs burned from the frantic evacuation. The shuttle rocked as the exploding ship lit the sky.

Something in the back of his mind confirmed what Mat had already suggested—that he was part of a much larger plan than corporate espionage, that his actions this morning were far more global than the hit of a turncoat computer programmer.

31

As he passed the green laptop on his way through the kitchen, Antony noticed a message from Mat. He placed his lunch plate on the counter and tapped the computer screen to open the message.

To: Antony Danic
From: Mat

I checked both the passenger list and the cargo manifest on the flight. Besides you, there was no other person on board that seemed suspicious. That's not saying someone wasn't there under a different name. Maybe you were being "hired out" to some other company for a Corporate favor. I'm still working on it.

I'm going through the passengers and crew and checking names and photos against other public records and doing background checks. Hopefully, something will come up. As for D3, there is no reference that I can find. The ID you described is nonexistent in the world databases.

Do you know how expensive it is to carry freight on a Trans-World Flight? Whoever shipped the boxes must be independently wealthy. I'm still trying to chase the paper trail on it.

The vial you sent me is definitely a narcotic. It resembles an older street drug, but it's chemically different in a few places. I'll be running more tests in the next few weeks. Please be patient with me.

Also, I found some mug shots that closely match your picture of the man in Lanzen sunglasses. I have attached fifteen pictures. Do you recognize any of these men?

Antony stared at the photographs. While none of them were the man at the hotel or in the car, both Daniel Grant and Agent Hansen stared back at Antony. He suppressed a shudder. Why would Mat have pictures of one of his previous kills and the agent who was after the cargo on the ship?

To: Mat
From: Antony

None of them are the "man." However, I do recognize some of them. Where'd you get these pictures?

To: Antony Danic
From: Mat

I dug up a memo from The Academy site that listed recently retired agents. It was just a long shot—grabbing pics that closely matched the guy at the karate competition. Because the man who is following you wears Lanzen glasses, he might be from The Academy and be watching people from your corporation. Seeing that The Academy seems to be working opposite of Hurst, I thought it was worth the try.

Antony swallowed. Two more pieces of evidence that Hurst was involved with something sinister.

32

"I never figured you for a Frosted Flakes guy."

Antony turned to see Catelyn standing next to him at the grocery store. She wore jeans and a T-shirt, and her dark hair hung over her shoulders in loose curls. It was a radical change from her business suits and slicked-back hair. Her bruises must be fading—her makeup had been applied with a much lighter touch today. His hand reflexively reached for the barcode tattoo behind his ear. He tried not to think of it, but seeing Catelyn always reminded him that there was more to the situation than he'd previously thought.

"I didn't figure you for a do-your-own-shopping gal. Or are you here to give me another envelope?" He could see her large driver-turned-bodyguard standing a short distance off. How a man that big fit into any of his clothes without shredding them at the seams, Antony didn't know. He dropped the box of cereal into his basket. "Have a nice day, Cate."

"That's a stupid assumption. Why wouldn't I do my own shopping?"

"You ride in a limo and your father is probably the richest man in Australia. I guess I assumed you sent Mr. Driver there to do your errands."

"Hardly." Catelyn slipped an envelope from her bag and slid it in between the boxes of cereal in Antony's basket. "There are detailed instructions on this one. Be sure to read every word." She looked down into his basket. It was full of unique foods Elite insisted she had to have. "Nice nutritional values there, Mr. Danic."

"So?" He placed the envelope in his pack.

"So . . ." Catelyn said, her face smug. "How's the wife? Still sick? Or are these foods for her hormonal cravings?"

"How did you know?" he asked, then remembered his house and phone were bugged. He shut his mouth, glaring at Catelyn.

"I have my ways. I was rather excited when I found out about her pregnancy. I mean, it's been almost ten years now, hasn't it?"

"That's none of your business." Antony mindlessly grabbed something off the shelf and pushed his cart away from her. He was sure she was trying to throw him off.

"Oh, but that's where you're wrong, Mr. Danic. It's my business to know everything about you," she said, following him. Antony knew her driver wasn't too far behind her. "Since I am your handler, you are my job," she went on, emphasizing the last four words.

When Antony stopped and turned to look at her, she smiled innocently. "Have a nice day, Antony," she said, then walked off, her driver following her.

Antony held the bags in his arms as he returned to the apartment. That had to be his weirdest meeting with Cate ever. He didn't like her tone, either. He had a private life—that's why it was called private. Was she carrying the envelope in her bag as she shopped, or had she followed him?

He put the groceries on the counter, then unlocked his office door and went inside. He sat in his black leather chair and slit the envelope open with his knife. As he unfolded the travel itinerary, a picture fell onto the desk. Antony picked it up. The man looked important in his dark blue suit and red tie, his temples salted with gray. His plane would arrive at Heathrow in two days. He would attend meetings in various places for four days, then fly back to New York. The second paper was a grainy copy of the security details of his trip. He must be *very* important—Interpol was handling his safety.

"HQ," Antony said after hitting his earpiece. He wore it almost all the time now, after Catelyn's outrage in the gym.

"This is HQ. What can I do for you?"

"This is Viper. I need a flight to London tomorrow, and a hotel near Parliament."

"I've booked you on a flight tomorrow at 10:15 AM," the operator said after a moment. It hadn't taken long to figure out that there were four HQ operators. Each woman worked a specific shift, and Antony could now tell them apart by their voices. "The hotel I can't guarantee—there's a big meeting of world leaders in two days."

"Then just get me something in London," Antony said. "I'll manage."

"There's a suite at the airport. Do you want that?"

"Sure, I'll take it. Viper out." He clicked his earpiece off, leaned back in his chair, and began to memorize the itinerary. He needed to figure out how to execute a hit with such high security. This man would be heavily guarded, just like the prisoner at the airport. Antony wondered why. Maybe this guy was one of those world leaders HQ had mentioned.

A soft knock interrupted Antony's work.

"Hey," Elite said, "thanks for getting the groceries. But what's this?" She held a bag of dog food. He laughed as he looked at it. He must have grabbed it as he was trying to get away from his handler.

"I saw Catelyn at the store and got kinda distracted," he said. "Sorry. I'll return it tomorrow."

"You've got another assignment," Elite said, glancing at the papers on his desk.

He covered the picture of his target with his arm. "I'll be gone four to five days, max. I'll help you paint the nursery when I get back."

Elite frowned. "You saw Catelyn at the store?"

"Yeah, weird, huh?" He slid the papers into his drawer and turned the key.

"Weird," she agreed.

Antony stood and wrapped his arms around her. "Did they have paint in the color you wanted?" he asked, happy to have an excuse to forget Catelyn.

"I ordered it, and they'll deliver it in a few days." Elite's stomach growled. "I guess I'm hungry."

"Let's get you some lunch then." He took her hand. "You sit and tell me about your plans for the nursery, and I'll fix you some food."

Rain drizzled from ceaselessly gray skies. Antony looked for a touch of blue, only to find that clouds stretched from one horizon to the other. He was beginning to hate London. After days of no sun, he was craving the warm summers of Canberra. In the shadow of an awning, he stayed dry for a moment. Still, he felt soaked to the bone, and the cold chilled his entire body. The scent of fresh bread and pastries wafted through the alley door, making him hungry.

He slid the black motorcycle helmet on his head and fastened the chin strap. He touched his earpiece and said, "Viper in recon position." He lowered the helmet's face shield.

"Position noted. Radio silence commenced." The cold unfeeling of an assignment slid over his body. He liked the absence of emotions in contrast to the last few weeks of intense stress and worry.

The bike humming under his legs, he checked the road ahead as well as the alley behind him. The motorcade would pass in a few minutes. The traffic had trickled to a stop, just as the driver told him it would. Antony had lost almost a thousand British pounds in a vicious game of poker last night, but he considered it money well spent, considering the information he had conned out of the other players.

A siren turned his attention back to his assignment. Two police shuttles passed, and then the black armored car, followed by two more police cars. He waited a few moments, released the clutch and brakes on the bike, and pulled out onto the street. He could see the flashing blue light of the police vehicle and aimed his bike for it. The bike performed as promised and accelerated with ease, racing along the road at seventy miles an hour.

He passed the second shuttle and slowed to match the speed of the motorcade. Holding onto the handlebar with his right hand, he pulled the grenade pistol out of his jacket and aimed it at the back window. The pistol fired in a flash of flame, the grenade arcing toward the black car. The window shattered as the diamond-tipped projectile hit it.

He heard the high-pitched scream of a young child and the shout of an older man as he accelerated and shot ahead of the cluster of shuttles. Three seconds later, he felt the explosion of the black armored car, and saw the ball of flame in one of his side mirrors.

One of the police cars appeared out of the flames and began to follow him. The vehicle's black-and-white paint seemed to smoke. Antony turned the motorcycle and managed to dodge a large delivery truck and then drove along the shoulder of the road as the cop car sped past him. He skidded into a roundabout and cut off a shuttle, whose driver immediately leaned on the horn. Placing his foot on the ground, Antony turned east. The smoking cop car found him again and he pulled on the throttle, cutting across an intersection.

He accelerated ahead of the police shuttle and saw a mid-sized truck ahead of him. He raced forward, almost lying on the petrol tank as the bike's engine screamed. The road was narrow, only two lanes. If the truck were to block the road, the police car would be stuck. When Antony cleared the truck, he yanked hard on the handles, almost laying the bike over. The truck slammed on its brakes and slid sideways, then came to a stop.

Behind Antony, the sound of crunching metal filled the air. He righted his bike and sped off along the streets of London. To the left, he saw a mall parking garage. He maneuvered around the turnstile and raced up the ramp to the second level. He stopped the bike between two shuttles, left the keys in the ignition, and pulled off his helmet. He skirted the wall and looked over the edge to see if it was possible to jump. It was, but there was another option. Below him was a Dumpster. He dropped the helmet in it, as well as the leather jacket and chaps. Dressed in a button-down shirt and khaki pants, he tightened his ever-present pack and walked into the mall. It was cold and rainy this time of year. He would buy a jacket and some lunch before getting on the train to Heathrow Airport.

Sitting back as the train rumbled down the tracks, Antony closed his eyes. He couldn't stop thinking of the screams he heard before the car bucked off the ground in a fireball. *Who was the man I just killed?* he wondered. *No one told me his family would be with him.*

Opening his eyes, he turned his phone on. "Viper has delivered the package and is heading home now," he texted.

"Acknowledged. I'll notify those who need to know. Your return ticket has been activated," the operator typed back.

He ended the call, selected the music application, and pulled the headphones out of his bag. He chose his harshest, loudest song and turned up the volume. Only then could he erase the scream of the child as the grenade sliced through the car window.

33

"Aren't you being a bit silly about all this?" Elite asked.

Antony sat on the floor of the living room, suitcase and backpack by his side, supplies scattered over the floor. "I call it being cautious, El."

"You're overreacting." She sat on the floor by him. It took more effort for her now, with her belly growing every day.

"Did you get two spare sets of clothing?" he asked.

She pointed to a pile by his foot. "I'm humoring you."

He smiled and turned his attention back to the suitcase. "And for that I'm thankful."

"Nothing's going to happen."

"Then we're ready for nothing," he said. He picked up the first-aid kit and placed it in the suitcase. "I don't want you to feel like I'm restricting you, but will you please tell me where you're going, even if it's to the corner market?"

"If it will make you happy."

"It will. If I call you and tell you to go to Gage's, or if something happens to me, what do you do?"

"I get on the train to Sydney. Gage will meet me and take care of me," she recited, mimicking their friend's inflection and tone. "Antony, this is silly."

"Humor me, please?"

"Of course, my love," she said and kissed him on the lips.

He closed his eyes and let out a long breath, then looked down and started packing again.

Elite frowned. "Why won't you let me distract you?"

"I'm almost done—then you can distract me all you want." He zipped the pack shut. "If I'm meeting you, you can take both bags. But if you don't know for sure, just take your bag. I got you one with wheels so you don't have to lift it." He added her clothes and a first-aid kit. "There's cash and an untraceable charge card that draws from GA Tech, and cards for the train. And the phone. It only calls Gage, and my matching one." He pointed to his bag.

"You're so cute when you're serious," Elite said.

He looked up and smiled at her. "I promised you that you'd be safe." He stood and placed both bags in the closet.

"When nothing happens, can I say I told you so?"

He turned around. She was standing right behind him, and he took her in his arms. "What time is your appointment tomorrow?" he asked.

"Nine," she answered, resting her head against his chest.

He looked at his watch. "We better get to bed. We don't want to be late." She nodded and led him to their room.

Antony opened his eyes as he rolled over. The sun streamed into the room. It got lighter every morning—soon the days would be warm all the time and summer would be upon them. This Christmas holiday would be memorable. And today they would know whether the baby was a boy or a girl. They were paying cash for the optional gender blood test, as well as getting the routine ultrasound. He hoped for a boy, since currently there was no one to carry on the Danic name. Antony had some distant cousins who were male, but he had never met them. His mother, Emilie, spoke of them sometimes. But that wasn't the only reason. He wanted to teach his son to do all the things his own father had taught him. Elite didn't care—she just wanted a baby to hold.

He rolled over and touched her face. Her eyes fluttered and opened. She smiled and sighed.

"Good morning, Daddy."

"Good morning. The appointment's in two hours. We should get up." He pushed himself up on his arm.

Elite closed her eyes. "Just a few more minutes," she whispered.

He laughed and stood. She groaned, and he laughed harder. A pillow hit him from behind, and he turned to see her sitting up. Smiling, he ducked another and walked into the bathroom to take a shower. He loved her so much.

A short time later, dressed in his blue button-down shirt and jeans, he pulled out bread, butter, milk, and preserves. Elite walked in the kitchen as he placed two pieces of toast on her plate. Her belly was just a little too big for her clothes, so she wore one of his shirts over a stretchy white T-shirt. She looked beautiful, he thought, and happy.

She sat next to him and pushed her plate away.

"You don't want toast?" he asked.

She shook her head. "I don't want anything."

Antony frowned. Eating always had been an issue with Elite. She never consumed enough. Now with the pregnancy, she found it easy not to eat because of nausea, heartburn, or other stomach upsets.

"You've got to eat. You're going to be lying on your back for a long time this morning. It will make you sick." She shook her head, looking down so he couldn't look into her eyes. "Some crackers, at least?" he asked.

She closed her eyes, picked up a piece of toast, and took a bite, then stole a swig from his juice, avoiding the milk. He didn't mind. At least she was eating. Hopefully the nausea would go away soon—then she could gain weight.

After snatching her second piece of toast and shoving it in his mouth, Antony took the dishes to the sink. She scrunched her brows at him, but he just shrugged. He pulled her toward him and swept her hair, no longer streaked with blue, away from her eyes. "I didn't want us to be late, so I called a company shuttle. We'll be there in plenty of time." He turned and led her to the door.

Elite's eyes widened. "Company shuttle? They'll hear us talking."

"I know, but we can't give them the impression we know anything. We must present a picture of normal. You have to trust me on this one. Gage is working on solutions for us." Antony locked the door and set the alarm.

"What if I mess up? What if I say something stupid?" Elite asked as he pressed the button to call the lift.

"If we talk about the baby, there won't be anything to mess up." He kissed her forehead.

She looked down, her lower lip between her teeth.

"What?" he asked.

She shook her head. He touched her chin and lifted it so he could see her face. She closed her eyes, and a tear streaked down her cheek. "I'm scared," she whispered.

"So am I," he whispered back. He wrapped his arm around her and pulled her close. He shut his eyes and hoped the lift would take them to the lobby without stopping on other floors.

The lobby was crowded with tenants leaving for work. Antony escorted Elite through the crowd. After pushing open the door and letting her through first, he followed with almost no distance between them. *This is stupid. I'm acting like I'm guarding her,* he thought. *I don't like this.*

He stopped short and pulled Elite around so she faced him. He put his glasses on and stepped back toward the door.

"Antony, what?"

He looked left and then right. The shuttle wasn't there yet. "Slowly turn around and casually look across the street. There's a man leaning against the building, wearing a black suit and glasses. Have you seen him before?" Antony stood near the wall, his phone in his hand.

Elite turned and looked. "The guy with long black hair?"

"You see him?"

"Yeah. Who is he?"

"My hunter." The words dropped cold from his mouth.

"He's . . . oh." Her realization was evident in her eyes. "Can you do something about it?"

"If I knew anything about him, I could do plenty. If I kill him without knowing who sent him, or without dealing with who sent him, they'll just send another."

The company shuttle, shiny and black, came around the corner. "Let's go," Antony said. He took Elite's arm and opened the door. After they climbed in the vehicle, he placed his arm around her shoulders. She was shivering. He looked for the air vents and angled them away from her. Still, he knew the cause of her fear. The Lanzen man haunted his every dream and waking hour.

The driver turned the shuttle away from the curb and into traffic. Elite reached into her bag and pulled out a notebook and pen. "Let's move," she wrote, her hand shaking.

"I'm working on it," was Antony's written reply. He pulled her close to him. "Think happy thoughts," he whispered.

Soon, the shuttle pulled out of traffic and into a business complex. It stopped in front of a building only three stories high. Antony opened the door and stepped out, then reached in to grasp Elite's arm. She grunted as she maneuvered herself out of the shuttle. He suppressed a smile, but she saw his smirk and swatted him with her hand.

"My middle name is Grace, all right?"

"Sure," he said, trying not to laugh. He turned to the driver. "I'll call you when we need you."

The driver nodded and drove off.

"Mrs. Danic?" the nurse said as Elite opened her book.

"That was fast," she said.

"I'm not complaining," Antony commented. The waiting room was crowded, and he felt hot just sitting there among all the patients.

"I still find it hard to believe you're claustrophobic," Elite said as they walked back to the exam room.

"I just don't like a lot of people around me."

"So, is this your husband?" the nurse asked.

"Yes, this is Antony," Elite said, smiling.

He stuck his hand out, and the nurse shook it.

"Nice to finally meet you."

"Same here," he said.

They walked into a windowless room with an exam table and an ultrasound machine. Except for the wall of cupboards and a few chairs, there was no other furniture.

"Have a seat and we'll get started."

The nurse took Elite's chart and had just begun scanning in her information when the door opened and an older man entered.

"Mrs. Danic, how are you feeling? And this must be the elusive Mr. Danic. I'm Dr. Young."

Antony offered his hand again. "I travel a lot."

The doctor looked at him and smiled. "I was always in school when my wife was pregnant. I can sympathize. Well, should we see this little one?"

Elite lay back and Antony stood at her head, holding her hand. She shivered when the doctor spread the transducer gel on her stomach.

"That's cold."

"Sorry. We try to warm it up, but sometimes in the morning it's still cold."

"Is it normal for her to be so sick this far into the pregnancy?" Antony asked.

"Define normal," the doctor said. "Each pregnancy is so individual. For some women, yes, it's normal. And although Elite isn't gaining as much weight as I'd like, she isn't losing, so I call it sixes. There are shots and medicines to stop the nausea. But if it's bearable, I'd prefer her to be as drug-free as possible."

"It's safer for the baby?"

"Yes. Now, we have an image. If you see here, this is the femur, the leg bone. And there are the toes. Looks like ten of them. There is the heart—you see there are four chambers. Looks healthy." He kept pointing things out, and Antony tried to see what the doctor was seeing.

"Why can't you tell the gender on an ultrasound this early?" Antony asked. "Especially when the blood test can."

Doctor Young checked the chart, then placed the wand in the holder and offered his hand to Elite so she could sit up.

"Regardless of advances in technology, we can't ask Mother Nature to keep up with us. You see, until about eighteen to twenty weeks, boys and girls look the same," he explained. "There's no real way of visualizing the gender on a screen. However, we are advanced enough to pick out miniscule DNA messages in the blood or amniotic fluid." The doctor paused to make a notation in Elite's chart. "But I received the results of the blood test, and you are definitely having a boy."

Elite pulled her shirt down and reached for Antony's arm.

"A boy? Really?" Antony said, looking at Elite. Her tears had started falling as soon as she saw the baby.

"A boy," she said. Antony leaned over and kissed her.

"Sounds like that's what you wanted," the doctor said.

It's exactly what I want, Antony thought. *I can't believe it.*

"Antony is the last of his family," Elite offered.

The doctor pulled a strip of pictures from the machine and handed it to her. "Well, there you go—your baby's first pictures."

Elite took the pictures and handed them to Antony. He stared at the tiny feet. *Amazing,* he thought.

"Whether you're ill or not, Elite, you need to eat. I don't want you losing weight," the doctor said.

"I'm trying, honestly."

"She did eat a piece of toast this morning," Antony said.

"That's good. I'll see you in two weeks." The doctor handed her the paper he'd signed.

"Let's celebrate," Antony said to Elite. "A trip to the National Botanical Gardens, and some shopping?"

34

Commonwealth Park was deserted at this time of the morning. Antony usually ran through Reconciliation Place in the summer, but today his advanced bike route took him past Capitol Hill. Because of the pregnancy, instead of sending Elite to geology summer camp, they had planned short day trips in the afternoons when he wasn't working. Every morning, he worked through an advanced exercise and meditation program he'd mapped out weeks before. As his concentration increased, his anxiety decreased.

After he finished in the park, he would run to Parres Way and take that road to Kings Avenue, retrieve his bicycle, and head home. Sweat poured from his body as he ran the last circuit before he connected to Parres. Canberra was an architect's dream and a navigator's nightmare. Gardens and parks littered the city, making it a beautiful place to live. Streets circled outward from central points, twisting and winding through the landscape. There were no street numbers, only names—and interesting ones at that, like Dunkoona and Coolabah.

The trail took him past a body of water surrounded by trees. Park benches lined the walkway. The day was warming, so Antony took off his shirt and tucked it in his shorts. Heading northeast, he would connect with Parres in a few minutes.

He heard the whiz of a bullet just before it grazed his shoulder. He stumbled at the searing pain. The muscles around the wound cramped, and a burning sensation flared across his chest. He clenched his teeth. *Crap.*

His feet faltered and he almost ran into a bench. He scanned the open area where the bullet came from. Nothing looked out of the ordinary. Dashing for the cover of the trees, he pulled his pistol out of the holster.

Antony needed a way out. Behind him was Lake Burley Griffin, where he would be out in the open. In front of him were the highway and a residential area. Overall, the residential area would provide better hiding places, even if it was the opposite direction from home. *I shouldn't have left my earpiece at home, even if I don't trust Corporate anymore. I could have called for a company shuttle, or a taxi.*

The main road through the park ran under the highway and into the residential area. He ran from his hiding spot to another grove of trees—he was a harder target if he was moving. Bark exploded in front of him, and he ducked and bolted to the next large tree. His speed might be his salvation. He was exhausted, but adrenalin coursed through his veins, giving him energy. To his left, he could see the road, and he followed the curve through the trees. The highway was just ahead of him, and the roads were getting busy as people started to go to work. Antony thought of flagging someone down and getting a ride home, but he would never put an innocent person in harm's way. He had *some* morals, he reminded himself.

The underpass was just ahead. Now it was sink or swim. In the underpass, he was a running duck rather than a sitting one, and there would be less chance to secure a shot. Yet if he climbed the hill and crossed the road, he could get a bullet in the back and be hit by a shuttle. He looked around—he could see no one following him. He decided the underpass was the lesser of two evils. He burst out of the tree line and hit the road at breakneck speed, the way he used to sprint in military training. He looked behind him and ran in front of a shuttle, causing it to swerve as the driver hit the brakes, the horn blaring. He crossed again, slowing a shuttle in the opposite direction, and then bolted ahead before crossing the lane again.

Another bullet whizzed overhead. Was this guy a bad shot, or was he not used to a moving target? *Maybe they're missing on purpose. Anyone shooting at me had to be a good shot—it would be stupid to have anyone other than a professional try to take me down.* Antony cleared the underpass, and with his T-shirt covering his pistol, he ran up the road to another intersection, where he vaulted over one hood of a car by planting his hand and jumping. Horns blared and he heard a few curse words.

Ahead of him was a small business district. Unless he found a store open at this time of morning, his goal was to make it to the houses just beyond the district. He saw a brown building, made of stone, with the door open. Looking back, he didn't see his pursuer, so he bounded up the steps and dashed into the building. It was dark inside. He raced to his right and dove into a corner hidden by a partial wall. He heard a set of footsteps and closed his eyes, concentrating on slowing his breathing so he wouldn't be heard. The door slammed against the wall, and he heard the heavy panting of someone who had been running.

"What are you doing? And with a gun?" a voice bellowed. "This is a church! Be gone, sinner, or I'll call the authorities."

"I'm looking for a man," a gravelly voice said.

"Well, he isn't here. There is no one in this church but you and me."

"I saw—"

"You didn't hear me. I said go."

Antony could hear phone buttons being pushed.

"Okay, okay. Don't call the cops—I'll go. But if I find you're harboring him, I'll burn your place to the ground." The door slammed again.

"Good riddance."

Antony heard the man move from the door. He sat in the corner, his gun pointed in front of him. A shadow filled the open space, blocking what little light there was in the building.

"Put that thing away. Do you seek sanctuary?" said the man who had just sent Antony's pursuer away.

Antony looked at him. The man was on the portly side of broad. He wore pajama pants and gray wool slippers, with a robe draped over a white T-shirt. His almost bald head sported a few gray hairs.

"Do you seek sanctuary? I can't do anything for you if you don't declare it."

"What, sanctuary?"

"There you go. Please come out so I can bandage your shoulder. You're bleeding." Antony looked down—he had forgotten that the first bullet had grazed him. He holstered his pistol and stood. The man was taller than him by a few inches.

"Thanks."

"Eh, no worries. I'm Reverend Miller." He jerked his head to his left. "I was about to sit and eat breakfast. Something told me to unlock the doors early. Looks like I was inspired." He led Antony through a side door into a living area.

"You were lucky, that's all," Antony said, watching as Miller pulled out a chair and retrieved a first-aid kit from a cupboard in the little kitchen.

"Don't you believe in inspiration?"

"No."

"Why?" Miller asked.

He poured antiseptic on a piece of gauze, then pressed it gently to Antony's wound. The sting made him jump. His nerves were frayed to the point of breaking. He had a million arguments, but he couldn't form a coherent thought.

"I . . . I'm an atheist," Antony said, looking down at the floor.

"An atheist? Well, you're not the first one to pass through these doors."

"Really?"

The pastor began to swab an antibiotic gel on the wound. "Sure. Even people who go to church their whole lives don't necessarily believe in God. When we face trials, there's a streak of atheist in all of us." He used thin strips of tape to bind the sides of the wound together.

"The world is too wicked for a God to be watching us," Antony remarked.

"There is nothing good in your life? Not one thing?"

"I was being chased by a guy with a gun." Antony said, stating one obvious bad thing.

"You've got a gun of your own."

"Touché."

"So back to your question. If God doesn't exist because the world is too wicked, then there is nothing good in the world at all."

"You're twisting my words."

"Nothing good. You can't think of one thing?" The man raised his eyebrows.

Antony growled and looked at his shoes. "I have a wife. She's beautiful. And she's pregnant, due in April."

"Boy or girl?" Miller asked as he placed the last piece of tape on the wound.

"Boy."

"So . . . there is nothing good in this world at all." Miller paused. "You have a beautiful wife, and you will soon have a son. God gave them to you."

"I was lucky."

"Luck had nothing to do with it. God blessed you."

"How can you be so sure?" Antony asked as the man taped gauze in place over the wound.

"Because, Son, I feel it here." Miller touched Antony on his sternum just below his collarbones.

It was the second time a religious man had touched him there. He felt nothing spectacular, but his agitation seemed to go away. *Chance,* he thought, *and the guy probably has heartburn.*

"Well, it's as good as I can get it," Miller said. "Let's eat."

"I've already been an inconvenience to you. I certainly can't eat your food, too."

"Nonsense. I love company." The pastor set a plate in front of Antony, then removed two plates piled with food from the oven. It smelled delicious.

"Why'd you make all this food?" Antony asked.

"Inspiration," Miller said, serving him huge spoonfuls.

Antony's arguments were sound, even if they went unspoken. He knew there was no God. These men with their mumbo-jumbo weren't inspired—it was just a trick, something to make the weak want to believe.

"Your silence makes me think you're pondering our conversation," the reverend said after a few minutes.

"So?"

"So, it means you felt something."

"Yeah, fatigue after being chased. I appreciate it, but I need to go home. My wife will be wondering where I am."

"I'll call a cab for you."

"I'm fine. I can call—"

"What if the shooter's still out there?"

"I'll take my chances."

"You can go out the back door and no one will know any different," Miller said. "Besides if he sees you leave my church, he'll burn it down."

Antony fell silent. He didn't want that. Even if he didn't believe, he wished no harm on those who did. "Sure," he said finally.

Early morning sun had conceded to early afternoon rain. Even in the throw-away coat and second-hand clothes Miller had given him, Antony was soaked by the time the cab arrived. He'd insisted on standing out back, away from the reverend.

"Where to?" the driver asked.

"Deakin. Carrington Street."

He looked down and covered his face with the collar of the coat until they were way past the brown church off Constitution Avenue. The gauze was soggy and the wound wet—he would spray it with skin sealant when he got home. Then he could take a hot shower. Between the cold rain and the sweat and dirt from running, he felt like he had a crunchy layer of skin.

So much for training, he thought.

After dumping the overcoat and second-hand clothing in the trash, Antony arrived at home—three hours later than usual. The wound had opened in the rain, the gauze acting like a sponge, and red blood had spread across the shoulder of his white shirt.

"Where were you? I was worried," Elite said as he walked into the apartment.

"Someone shot at me in the park."

"You're hit." She reached for his shoulder, then paused, her eyes wide. She brought her hand back to her mouth, fingers trembling.

"It's really nothing—it just grazed my shoulder. I slowed down to tuck my shirt in my shorts and the bullet missed . . . that was luck."

"It's bleeding really badly," Elite said. "I'll get the kit."

She disappeared as Antony pulled his shirt off. He winced at the pain—his shoulder would be sore for days. He dropped his shirt on the tile and began to pull the gauze from his shoulder. He jumped as Elite draped a hot, wet towel over his shoulders.

"Come sit. I'll take care of this, and you can get warm."

"Thanks, El."

She softly wiped at the wound and pulled the tape off. He clenched his jaw—no chance of summoning any form of self-control now.

"Was it him? The guy across the street?"

"I don't know—I never really saw him. I heard his voice when I got away."

"How did you get away?" she asked.

"Oh, I got lucky." Antony didn't want to tell her had spent the morning arguing with a minister.

"Mat said there was a traffic disturbance in the Duntroon area. Was that you?"

Antony chuckled. "Probably."

She sprayed the wound after cleaning it again.

"I left my bike," he said. "It's probably gone by now."

"We can get you another bike. You're safe, and that's what's important."

"No, you're what's important. How's junior?" he asked, placing a hand on her ever-growing belly.

"Just fine."

Antony smiled, and she leaned over and kissed him hard. "I was so worried about you. You didn't come home and you didn't take your phone. I couldn't get hold of you, and I was—"

"Shh," he said. "I'm here, and nothing's going to happen to us."

He gently guided her to the living room and put on a record, then held out his hand and pulled her close. They began to dance as the sounds of music filled the room.

35

Catelyn sat on a pale purple yoga mat. Her heather gray pants and tank looked new—the fold lines still showed. Her dark hair was pulled up in a bun. A bag and water bottle sat at her side next to two foam blocks and a white strap. She was in perfect shape—thin, muscled, and athletic. She wasn't married and didn't have any boyfriends Antony knew about. Her ring finger remained empty, and she'd never been pregnant in the last eight years, as far as he could tell.

His first handler had been an older man named Garret. He was a fidgety, worried character, definitely not the type of person suited to manage the life of a corporate soldier. One day Catelyn met Antony at his and Garret's usual meeting spot, after a call in the middle of the night, and explained she was his new handler. For security, they'd meet only when and where she deemed necessary. Antony's life changed that day. Not only was his handler different, but his assignments went from an occasional hit and lots of theft and guarding, to almost all hits. Antony had assumed Garret died of natural causes, but now he wondered.

"I'm surprised you came. I figured you would meet me after class," Catelyn said, interrupting Antony's thoughts.

"You thought I was a chicken" He rolled out his mat. The forest green was swirled with black. He had no strap or blocks.

"I didn't—"

"Admit it, Miss Catelyn—you thought I'd see the sign on the door and turn away."

"That's Ms. Catelyn to you, Mr. Danic. I thought no such thing. I know guys do yoga."

"Then why are you so surprised to see me?"

"I didn't figure you to be a yoga guy."

"There are lots of things you don't know about me."

"I know you were shot at three days ago. That your shoulder was grazed."

Antony looked at her for a long second. Of course, Mat wouldn't change everything the bugs picked up, and he had been out in public since the injury.

"Okay, class, welcome to hot yoga. Today we're going to start with mountain pose," the teacher said.

The doors were closed and the heat turned on. Antony stood straight, feet parallel, arms at his side. They moved to eagle pose; he twisted his legs together, then his arms, and bent into a sit. After about twenty minutes of warm-up poses, the instructor directed the class in sun salutations. Catelyn had sweat streaming off her body. Antony wiped at his face and stood in exalted warrior, his legs in a lunge, his hands stretched toward the sky.

This is perfect, he thought, *just the kind of workout I needed today.*

"Now we move the hand here and raise the top leg parallel to the floor," the teacher said. "This is gate pose."

Antony moved his hand and raised his top leg. He remained in the pose, thinking about what Cate had said. He wished he could remove the bugs in his and Elite's apartment, but he was sure if he did, they would be replaced within days.

A woman to his left collapsed to the floor and grabbed her water bottle. Catelyn sat in lotus when her body couldn't hold the pose any longer. Antony heard grunts and moans as he slowly became aware of his surroundings. He released the pose, sat in lotus like the teacher, and began to breathe his cool-down.

"Now lie in corpse pose as we begin our meditation," the teacher said.

Antony felt the envelope hit his chest just as he started to relax, and he sat up to see Catelyn packing her bag. He stood and rolled up his mat, then walked out the door. He ripped open the envelope, ignoring the floating TV screen that blared commercials to passersby, as Cate stepped to the curb. Her limo came around the corner as he pulled the paper out.

"Sori Katsu, Natani," it read.

Antony froze. This couldn't be real.

36

Do something! his mind screamed at his body. *Move! Tell her no.* He dropped his yoga mat on the sidewalk. In a second, his hand was on the door of the limo before it could swing shut. He wrenched it open, jumped in the car, and slammed the door shut. The car pulled away from the curb.

"No!" he said and threw the envelope at her. "I refuse."

"You don't have a choice, Mr. Danic."

"I do, and I just made it."

"Must I remind you, you've got a lifetime contract?"

"I don't care, Cate. Fire me."

"Fire you? You don't understand. If you refuse, you're dead."

"Didn't you hear me? I refuse. I'll not kill another innocent man."

"Innocent? You don't know the man from Adam. I don't even know him—I get my orders from someone and give them to you."

"Listen carefully. That man is a High Elder—he isn't a criminal."

"I don't judge your targets, Mr. Danic. I'm just following orders."

"Well, I'm refusing your order. I won't kill Sori Katsu."

271

The car swerved to the side of the road, throwing Antony to the floor. He raised himself and faced Cate again. The window between the driver and the passenger portion of the car opened. Antony pulled his gun in his left hand and his dagger in his right. He pointed the gun at the driver and placed the dagger at Catelyn's throat.

"One more move and I'll slice her throat," he said to the driver. "Do not trigger the silent alarm, either. Give me one reason to suspect you, and I'll drain her blood on the seat." The driver looked at him and then at Catelyn. The driver leaned toward her, and Antony drove the tip of the blade into her white skin. The flesh gave with a slight pop. She gasped but remained perfectly still.

The driver stopped moving. "I'm sorry, Catelyn. I—" he began.

"It's okay. Just do what he says."

"Catelyn, huh?" Antony said.

She turned her head. Blood ran in a rivulet down her chest and seeped into her tank top, where it mixed with the drying, salty sweat from her yoga workout.

"Too much information, Mr. Danic," she whispered.

He smiled at her words. She was wrong—he had worked with too little information for years. He was through taking orders. He turned his head toward the driver. "Go to the industrial area south of town. There are some warehouses on the west side."

The driver looked at Catelyn again, and she nodded slightly. He turned to the front and Antony felt the car begin to move again.

"Don't do anything heroic or stupid. If you try any of your fancy driving tricks, I'll decapitate Miss Hurst," he said to the driver. "Where *do* you get your orders, Cate?"

She closed her eyes and remained silent as the car drove to the other side of town.

"Turn right here," Antony said, "and then take a left." The car turned and he surveyed the area. There was an abandoned warehouse—he had seen it as he was running a few weeks ago. "There. Turn right and stop behind that building." He gestured with the muzzle of the pistol. "Park and turn the car off, then toss the keys on the floor in front of me." The keys landed on the floor. He took a knee and knelt on them. The pain would be temporary. "Now, crawl into this section and sit by Miss Cate."

The driver complied, and Antony resisted the urge to pull the trigger. *It would be a lot easier to kill him and just get it over with,* he thought. Then he realized if he would do that, he should go ahead and kill Sori, too.

"Hey, driver," Antony said, "pull up on that seat belt until it's fully extended."

The man looked at him like he was crazy.

"Do it!" Antony ordered.

The driver pulled on the seat belt until the metal clip dangled on the floor. Antony reached over, still pointing the gun at Cate, and cut the strap.

"Tie her feet together," Antony ordered. "Make it tight."

The driver took her feet and pulled them together, then wrapped the belt around twice and began to tie a knot.

"Pull it tight," Antony said.

The driver did, and Antony saw her flinch. "Now tie her hands behind her back."

"You won't get away with this, Antony," Catelyn said as he tested the bindings.

"I already have. Now cut two more seat belts." After the driver did so, Antony took the belt and said, "Put her in the jump seat and fasten the seat belt."

The driver did as he was told, yet he handled her with care. Whether he did it out of duty or concern, the effect was the same.

"Now follow me. Bring the straps," Antony said, pocketing the keys and opening the door. He looked around before stepping out, then gestured with the pistol.

The driver followed him out of the car, his face a mask of frustration. All of a sudden, he lunged toward Antony, who fired the pistol low. The driver cried out and fell against the car, his leg bleeding.

"Antony, no!" Catelyn said from inside of the car.

"Did you think I was kidding?" He pulled the wounded man to the trunk. "Open it."

The driver leaned against the car and took the keys from Antony. He noticed that the man's hands shook, probably from the pain from the leg wound. *No self-control at all,* Antony thought. "Sit." He holstered his pistol and took the strap in his hands. "Hold out your hands."

Antony took the strap, wound it around the man's wrists three times, and tied it, then pulled on the knot as tight as he could. He took his fist and slammed the driver in the gut. The man grunted and slid into the trunk, his feet in the air. Antony took the second strap and tied his feet together, then rolled him to the side. He was about to shut the trunk when he saw a black laptop bag. He grabbed it and slammed the trunk lid shut.

He got back in the car and opened the case. *Jackpot!*

"That's my private property," Catelyn said angrily.

"I know. I'm helping you use it," Antony said as the computer booted. The screen remained black. He looked at her, and she sneered. He scooted toward her and grabbed her fingers. "Which one, Cate?"

"I'm not giving you that information, Mr. Danic." She spat in his direction.

"Fine." He grabbed the index finger on her right hand.

"It won't work. If you try it and it doesn't work, then it will shut down and won't reboot for fifteen minutes."

"I'm a very patient man, Cate. I'll just keep trying every finger until I get it right. And meanwhile, your driver will bleed to death from his leg wound."

"You're inhuman, Antony, a cold-blooded killer." She jerked her hands out of his grasp.

"I know, and yet, what are you? You're the one who tells me to kill. Which is worse?" He grabbed her right index finger again.

"That isn't the correct one," she hissed.

"You're lying. You're right-handed, and the pad is on the right side of the computer." She squirmed out of his grip. Growing tired of her games, he grabbed her hands, took one of her fingers on her left hand, and pulled the finger at an odd angle until he heard the bone snap and her cry of pain.

"I hate you," she said as tears streamed down her face.

He leaned the computer up and slid her right finger over the sensory pad. The screen turned blue.

"I don't care, Cate," he said. "Now tell me the password, or I'll break all your fingers."

"You won't get away with this."

"I don't care what you think." He pulled on another finger.

"D-A-M-A-S-H-I-I underscore M-E-I. It's Japanese. "

"Too much information, Miss Hurst," he said and started to access the computer. He pulled out his mini-computer from GA Tech and typed, "If I hook you up to this laptop, can you access the files without harming yourself or being detected?"

"Yes," Mat replied.

Antony pulled out the cable and linked the computers together. The screens flashed and Antony watched with interest. He heard the driver yelling and kicking at the inside of the trunk.

'If you don't shut up, I'll shoot your other leg and then your foul mouth!" he yelled and the noise stopped. The screen returned to his screensaver and the mini-computer beeped.

"I'm finished. Disconnect me," Mat said.

Antony pulled the cord out of the port and shut Cate's laptop, then placed it back in the bag. He reached toward her, but she hissed and moved away from him. He unbuckled her seat belt and grabbed her by her waist. She struggled as his arms wrapped around her.

"Keep it up and I'll shoot you in the leg like I did him." He opened the door a second time. He opened the trunk and laid her next to her driver. The relief in the man's eyes was obvious. She stared at him, her eyes wet and red.

Antony felt a pang of regret. *If they do die, at least it will be together.* He unholstered his pistol and whacked the driver on the head. The man fell limp.

"Have a nice life, Catelyn Hurst," Antony said before he shut the trunk. He locked the doors and took off running. When he reached the river, he threw the keys in. He ran from the industrial area north to his home.

"Gage, I need you," he said into his other phone. "Things just went south. Elite and I'll be on the train north toward Sydney ASAP."

"I'm on my way. Mat will triangulate your position with your phone. Get rid of your Corporate phone and earpiece," Gage said.

Antony pulled his earpiece out of his pocket, dropped it, and stepped on it. It crunched with a satisfactory sound. He threw his phone onto the pavement and stomped on it. Just ahead of him, a heavy street sweeper was making its way down the road. The phone shattered beneath the big wheels and then was sucked up in the giant vacuum. Antony grinned. Leaving this job brought him even more relief than he'd imagined it would.

He used his personal phone to dial the matching phone in Elite's suitcase. It rang until it went to voice messaging. He flew up the stairs to the train, swiped his card, and got on the north train just before the door shut. It was afternoon and the train was deserted—in a few hours it would be packed. His phone rang.

"Yes?" he said.

"Hurst Enterprises is funded in part by a larger corporation named The Trade," Mat said. "They are linked to various criminal activities, including drug trafficking and money laundering. Hurst Enterprises seems clean, but the monies they have received in the past are filthy."

"Thank you," Antony said. "Anything else?"

"I believe The Trade is somehow associated with the drugs on that Trans-World Flight. But I don't have definite proof. On a good note, the limo isn't listed as missing yet. I'll stay in touch."

"Thank you, Mat." He stood as the train entered the station next to his building. The doors opened and he bolted down the stairs, around the corner, and through the doors of the apartment building, then up the stairs, not waiting for the lift.

37

"Elite!" he yelled as he burst through the door. "We need to go now!"

The dishes in her hands fell to the ground as she turned. He slammed the door shut.

"Antony. What?"

"Go now—grab your bag."

"What happened?" she asked.

He looked her over. She wore capris, a T-shirt, and sandals. The sandals would have to go. "I refused a hit."

"Refused? Why? You've got a lifetime contract."

"I know. I just couldn't do it."

"Who?" she asked as he pulled the two bags out of the closet. She reached in and placed another small bag on top of her suitcase.

"What's in there?" he asked.

"Sunday clothes. Who?"

"Go change your shoes to more sturdy ones. I don't know if we'll need to walk. And grab a sweater, too."

"Antony, you're changing the subject. Who did they want you to kill?" she asked as she walked down the hall.

"The High Elder," he said as he looked at the bags by the door.

She stopped and stared at him for a moment. "The High Elder? Why would they want to kill him? He's inn—"

"Innocent—I know. Just like Kyo, El." Antony rummaged through his pockets and pulled out his phone from Gage, and the paper with the address for the yoga studio. Elite had paused in the hallway, her expression somewhere between worried and terrified. "Go change your shoes," Antony said. "The train to Sydney leaves in less than fifteen minutes."

She turned and walked into their bedroom. He unlocked his office, holstered his personal pistol, and loaded his smaller pack with .357 ammo, leaving the Corporate-issued rifle and pistol in the corporation lock boxes. They were bugged just like his phone and earpiece. He took the GA Tech laptop and put it in the soft case, and then into his pack, checking the side pocket. The chip and laser instrument were still there. *The risk is worth it now.* He shut the safe and put the corkboard flush against the wall.

He locked the door and walked down the hall. When he entered the living room, he paused. Elite stood there, her face pale and her eyes wide. The man from Huahine was next to her, his arm around her neck, a pistol pointed at her head. Antony had his pistol aimed at the man's face before he could think.

"Don't move," the man said in a gravelly voice. He was the same man who'd followed Antony into Reverend Miller's church.

"Catelyn," Antony muttered under his breath. She must have gotten out of the limousine already.

"Your handler? No, this concerns people much bigger than your little Miss Catelyn."

"Let me guess—you have another message from Corporate," Antony said.

"You totally botched the hit in London."

"No one told me that he was traveling with his family. I was told to take him out and given the specs on the car—what else was I supposed to think?" Antony looked at Elite and tried to mask his fear. She didn't need to know how terrified he was. Tears edged her eyes.

"Corporate thinks you're getting lazy, that you're not dedicated to your job anymore."

"It was a mistake. It could have happened to anyone."

"But not you, Mr. Danic. They expect perfection and are not getting it. I was sent to motivate you."

Elite jumped as the man pulled the trigger.

Antony pulled his own trigger numerous times. One bullet ripped through the man's jaw and another hit his shoulder. He didn't see where the others entered. Elite fell to the floor as the man crumpled next to her.

Antony dropped to his knees. "Elite!" He crawled to her and pulled her into his lap. Her head was bleeding profusely, her shoulder growing red. She flinched. "Elite!" He placed one hand on her belly, and she opened her eyes.

"Antony, we never decided on a name for the baby." Her hands trembled, and her chest shook with every breath. He brushed her hair from her face.

"No, we didn't. What name do you like best?" He closed his eyes for a moment. Tears broke free and slid down his face. If she was asking about the baby's name, did she know she was dying? He knew the wound was too severe for her to survive. She had maybe a few moments before she was gone. The thought tore a hole in his chest—it felt as if the man had shot him, too.

"I like Lucius," she said. "It means pillar of light." It was her current favorite from the long list they had debated lately.

"It's perfect. I love it," he said, then kissed her.

Her body shuddered and she looked at him. "I love you, Antony," she gasped. Then she fell still. He pulled her to his chest as a sob escaped his throat. She was gone from him forever.

"I love you, Elite," he whispered.

He became aware of raspy breathing behind him. He laid Elite gently on the floor and knelt by the man, his gun pointed at his head. Antony looked at him and smiled. "I'd finish you now, except I think I'd like to see you suffer a little."

"Just the messenger," he choked out.

Antony looked at him. *If only it had been me instead,* he thought, *and she could make it to Gage's and live in Sydney safe from harm, our son would keep her company and take care of her in her old age just like Gage and his mother. Maybe she'd even marry again, someone who could be bound to her. Someone who made her completely happy.*

If I was dead . . . He shrugged off his pack and pulled out the chip Gage had made for Elite and the control module. He took the chip and placed it in the wound at the back of the shooter's head. After pressing the ON button, he selected "Antony Danic" on the screen and pushed ENTER. He watched in fascination as the man morphed and changed, taking on his face, hair, and skin color. The clothes were okay—Antony would wear something like this. He searched the man's pockets and pulled out his wallet, then replaced the guy's ID with his own. He looked at the man, who was beginning to struggle to breathe.

"Goodbye, Antony," Antony said. He stood and slung his pack over his shoulder.

Wait! Think about how Viper would see the scene, he thought. His pants were saturated with Elite's blood—his shoes, too. He needed to change. He stepped to the edge of the widening circle of blood and slipped off his shoes. He grabbed a garbage bag from the kitchen, then picked up his shoes and placed them in it. He rushed into the bedroom, pulled his clothes off, stuffed them in the bag, and tied it shut. He jumped in the shower—there was too much blood to just wipe himself off. When he finished, he pulled on pants and a shirt. He grabbed another pack and added some clothes and a few survival items. It would be a decoy. *Two bodies, two packs . . . the Danics never made it out of the apartment.* He turned to leave and stepped around the dead man.

"Goodbye, my love," Antony said, dropping the decoy pack by Elite's suitcase. He knelt and removed her phone, most of the money, and the credit card. He stopped when he touched a folded piece of paper. He pulled it out.

Her list. He pocketed it, then slung his new pack on his back over his everyday pack and headed for the door. He heard a crunch as he stepped on something. A piece of a plate lay on the floor. The plates Elite had been carrying when he first opened the door were shattered all over the floor. He didn't remember setting the master lock. He replayed the last fifteen minutes in his head.

His wife and his child were dead, the baby too young to survive outside the womb. Antony's life and dreams had shattered like the dishes on the floor. Not for the first time, he wished it was him lying dead next to her. Their misery would end together.

He reached for the door and looked back for a moment. Elite's body was white now, and the blood had stopped seeping. He looked at the body that resembled him and froze— he couldn't leave the chip behind. He wouldn't let someone get hold of that technology. Not only would it reveal Mat's research, but Antony would lose his advantage.

He squatted just outside the circle of blood by the man and closed his eyes as he dug in the wound at the back of his head. He found it after a few seconds. He dropped the chip back in its bag and washed his hand in the sink. So they would know he wasn't dead—big deal. He could hide. He'd make himself invisible; he was good at that. He waited for the body to morph back, but not even a hair changed color. The body still looked like Antony.

Antony, go! Someone's coming! He heard Elite's voice as clear as day in his head. Whether it was his imagination or not, he wasn't going to stay around long enough to find out.

Not the lift—use the stairway. Go out the back exit and take the train to Sydney. It was her voice. He knew it like he knew the beat of his own heart.

"Elite?" he croaked as he ran for the stairs.

38

Antony placed the bag containing his bloody clothes and shoes in the large furnace in the basement of his apartment building. The evidence would soon burn into ash that would be indistinguishable from dust. As the bag started to disintegrate, he pulled the appearance module out, selected one of the looks, and started the program. His skin tingled almost like an itch as he morphed into a man with darker skin, a heavier face, lighter hair, and brown eyes.

He'd have to have the tattoo removed, but that was a small matter in the whole scheme of things. He still wondered when he had received it—that memory lapse really bothered him. At least it was just ink on skin, not some sort of homing beacon like he had suspected at one time.

He slammed the door shut and ran up the stairs to the lobby. Using the back exit like he often did, he stepped out into the daylight. He heard sirens as he hurried away from the building and bounded up the stairs to the gates of the train station. He ran his access card across the scanner and pushed through the turnstile, then rushed past the first train to one heading north, toward Sydney. It was crowded—people were just starting to come back from lunch. He walked through the car and entered the next one before he found a seat in the back. Sitting on the edge of his seat, too tired to remove his pack, he rested his elbows on his knees and looked at the floor.

As the adrenaline ebbed away with every beat of his heart, intense pain replaced the numbness of the last hour. He shook his head, remembering it was just this morning when he'd met Catelyn at the yoga studio. It seemed as if days had passed since then. Memories of the day's events bombarded him as he sat, from the snap of Catelyn's finger to Elite's gasping breath and wide eyes as the bullet tore through her head. He heard himself yelling "No!" as she fell, and saw himself pulling the trigger until the man fell to the floor next to her.

Elite was gone and he would never see her again—never touch her skin, hear her laugh, or lay his hand on her belly. He squeezed his eyes shut against more memories and clenched his fists as a slow, steady anger built in his chest.

"Elite," he groaned between clenched teeth, holding his head in his hands.

As the train approached the northern edge of Canberra, the crowds had thinned considerably. Just a scattering of people were left in the car.

"You're now entering Wollongong," the automated voice said. The train stopped at the station, and two police officers stepped on. One tapped a guy near the front of the car and said something. The guy pulled out his ID and handed it to him. The cop looked at it and handed it back. Antony stood and moved toward the door. He wasn't in the mood to face anyone right now—it was probably for something completely unrelated anyway.

He stepped off the train and walked to the restrooms, hands in his pockets, eyes straight ahead. After a moment, he opened the door and walked from the train station into the city.

I should find a hotel and get some sleep. He laughed at his gut reaction. After today, he didn't know if he would ever sleep again.

He looked up in time to brush shoulders with a policeman. "Sorry," he said and kept walking. Ahead of him, another policeman stood at the corner, his thumbs hooked in his belt loops. Antony turned down a side street and resurfaced on a main road, only to see two more cops, leaning against their patrol shuttle.

Antony was beyond nervous. What if someone had found the bodies already? What if the appearance chip's influence had worn off? What if Catelyn had reported him hours ago? What would happen to Elite's body? Antony's will stated that Gage had possession, but if there was an investigation, Gage might not be able to get her body. What if she was never laid to rest? What if her body, and their son's, were put in an unmarked grave, or worse yet, not buried at all?

Antony turned down a side street and stopped, his lungs burning. He tried to suck in a deep breath before a panic attack hit. "Get a grip," he growled at himself.

Ahead of him was a fuel station. Once again, he wished he and Elite had a car. *The police would have stopped you a long time ago,* he told himself, *if they knew the make and model registered to the dead man lying on your living room floor.* Antony walked toward the station. Perhaps he could call a cab and take it to Gage's house in Sydney.

Just then, a young man pulled up on a nice-looking motorcycle and filled the tank. After snapping the lid closed, the biker turned and headed for the store. Antony watched as he walked past the food section, probably heading for the restroom. The bike was a thing of beauty, if you could call black leather and enamel paint contrasted with bright chrome beautiful. Antony could take the bike and be long gone. He only hesitated a moment at the thought that what he was planning on doing was stealing. With the crushing pain in his chest, he didn't care anymore. He jumped on the bike, turned the key, and took off down the road that headed east into the outskirts. In less than a minute, he was out of town. He turned onto a lesser-used road, pulled down on the throttle, and sped into the surrounding forest as the sun began to descend in the sky. He could hide in the outdoors—he had lived in it for weeks at a time in the military. He could survive until Gage came to get him, or refuel and make it to Sydney himself.

"Tag—you're it!" Elite said. She touched him and dashed away into the deserted park.

Antony frowned and shook his head as if he could shake the memories away. The bike wobbled and he righted himself before he tipped it over. He stared ahead at the scenery as the minutes passed.

"I couldn't find any shoes I liked," she said. He saw bright pink toenails peeking out from under the billowy white dress. His hand rested on a few of the dozens of buttons that ran down the back of her dress. He kissed her shoulder and she sighed.

"Stop it!" he screamed. The speedometer bounced off the right side of the arc of numbers. "Just stop it!" The memory burst like a bubble. The little-used road turned into a lined highway, and in the bike's headlight, the sign read, "Nyngan 20 K."

Antony could see the little outback town as the bike sputtered and lost power. He looked at the gauges and saw that the petrol dial sat on empty. Using the momentum of his bat-out-of-Hades ride, he coasted another few miles before the bike came to a silent stop. He jumped off, letting the bike fall to the side. He kicked it and heard the metallic scratch as it slid on the blacktop a few inches. He kicked it again and again, the pain in his foot and the damage he was causing to the bike feeling satisfactory to him in the moment. When his foot hurt too much to abuse the bike anymore, he turned and walked along the road toward the glowing town in the distance.

On the outskirts of town sat the local bar, lit like a carnival. Noise, and the smell of food, emanated from the open door. It was exactly the kind of place Antony wanted to be, invisible in the middle of everyone. No one would notice a lone man sitting at the bar. He could get some food and rest before working on the next leg of his plan. He would have plenty of time to think about how to get to Gage's home in Sydney. When closing time came around, he would find another form of transportation and head east again. Maybe he'd even buy some gas for the bike and ride it north and then east into Sydney, away from Canberra and anything associated with it.

He stepped into the dark, smoky room and made his way to the bar.

"What's yer poison, mate? First drink is on the house," said the older man behind the bar. Some of his teeth were missing, and it had obviously been several days since he'd bathed.

"Do you serve food?" Antony asked.

"Sure, we have the daily special." The man pointed to a sign taped to the mirror. "You want one?"

Antony nodded.

"No drink?"

"Vodka straight."

When the drink was ready, Antony took it and sat near the end of the bar in the back of the room so he could see the door. Soon, wrinkled tan hands set a plate with food and another tumbler of vodka in front of him, and he accepted it as the empty glass disappeared.

"Do you think they would mind if I added cayenne to this dish? It looks so boring," he heard Elite ask him at a chef's school in Paris. The head chef turned red when he tasted her dinner, but Antony liked it better than the others.

He pushed the half-eaten plate of food away. He pulled a few bills out of his pack and laid them on the bar as the bartender took the plate and brought another tumbler. Antony drained it and the next one, finding the more he drank, the less he could feel his heart.

Another glass appeared and Antony waved the man away, his head spinning and his stomach rebelling.

He held her hand at the ultrasound. She looked into his eyes as he squeezed her hand. They were having a boy. No words needed to be exchanged—the love in her eyes made him melt.

He slammed his hand on the bar top and pushed himself away with a scratching of the wood stool on the tile floor. "Stop it!" he said. "Just leave me alone!" He hit his head with his fists.

"The fund-raiser is Friday. I was hoping you'd be here this year. Some people think my husband is imaginary."

"Leave me alone, please!" He squeezed his eyes shut.

"Hey, mate, you all right?" Somebody touched his arm.

Bang! Elite gasped as the bullet ripped through her head.

"Don't touch me!" Antony said, throwing off the man's hand.

"Sir, we're going to have to ask you to leave." Another man cupped his elbow, and he twisted out of the man's hold and faced him. Antony grabbed the gun in his waistband and cocked it, then held it to the man's forehead. The bar went silent—only the scratch of country music could be heard from the jukebox.

"I said don't touch me," he growled.

"I'm not looking for trouble, mate. Just put the gun down and we'll talk."

Antony shook his head. "No!" He pushed the barrel of the weapon into the skin at the man's temple. Another man approached from the side—Antony saw the flash of movement to his right. "Stay out of this," he said.

"Listen to him. Just let him go and we'll pretend it never happened. We'll call a cab for you, and you can just go home."

An image of Elite on the floor, bled white, flashed through his head.

"Why can't you just leave me alone?" Antony said.

He opened his eyes and his breath caught—the man from Huahine stared back at him. His finger pulled at the trigger and he met the resistance of the safety mechanism. His finger froze, the trigger still unpulled.

"You're a murderer." Elite's voice echoed in his head.

"No!" he said and shook his head. "No, I'm not. Please, you need to believe me. I promise, El. Never again."

The image faded and the man who tried to escort him out of the bar appeared again. Antony closed his eyes and pressed the gun harder into the other man's head.

Someone knocked Antony's hand to the side as someone else grabbed him and pulled him back. A policeman dove toward the hostage as the gun fired and the mirror behind the bar shattered. Antony reached out and hit the face in front of him as someone wrestled the gun from his hand. He gasped as he received a hit to the gut. He grappled and threw his fist at anything in his reach until something hard hit him on the side of the head and things went black.

39

Antony stood next to a wooden desk. He blinked as the retinal burn flashed behind his eyelids. He felt the ink on his fingers like dirt. The world teetered and he stepped to the side to stay upright, the handcuffs and shackles rattling in the silence of the tiny rural police station. An officer looked up from his computer and stood.

"Can I put him back in a cell now?" he asked.

Another officer looked up—he held an ice bag on his face. "Sure. Put him in number 1."

Antony looked at the two little cells and smirked. They had numbers for them when there were only two? His body ached and his head hurt and spun. His stomach violently protested the amount of liquor he'd consumed last night. Light slowly seeped through the windows to the left of him—it was probably close to dawn. They must have left him to sleep after he passed out last night. He'd awakened this morning on the floor of the holding tank, his shoulders and hips aching.

The officer led him into the cell next to the desk, and Antony sat on the bed. The officer pulled out a ring of keys and unlocked the handcuffs, then the shackles. Antony rubbed at his wrists as the door slammed shut.

"Don't I get a phone call?" Antony asked.

The officer laughed.

"When the local attorney arrives, he will help you arrange for bail," said the older officer with the ice bag.

"Bail? You arrested me?"

"You pulled an unregistered gun on someone and fired it," the young man said. "Yeah, we arrested you."

"You resisted arrest, too," the older cop added. "You were like a mad man—like you were seeing things that weren't there. Care to elaborate?"

Antony shut his mouth and looked at the floor. He couldn't explain last night, and no one would believe his story when Antony lay dead in his apartment. He had lied through the recent interrogation, stating the name and address on the fake ID, hoping Mat had a past for him to match the fingerprints.

The older officer opened Antony's smaller pack and pulled out his GA laptop. How he wished Mat was aware of what was happening. He was thankful that at the last minute, he'd thrown the bag with the bloody chip in the furnace with the clothes. The officer pulled out the suturer and dropped it next to the green computer, then removed the first-aid kit, the energy bars, and packets of water.

How did I get here? Antony asked himself. *What happened?* He traced his fuzzy thoughts backwards. *His bike ride into the desert, the train to Sydney, running from his apartment, Elite's body on the rug. The man with the gun—the man from Huahine.*

The officer opened Antony's larger pack and pulled out two sets of folded clothes. *Putting his laptop in his bag and changing his clothes.* Another pair of shoes. *Bursting through the door, telling Elite they needed to go, that she needed to change her shoes.*

The officer pulled out a larger first-aid kit. *Running from the warehouse and the limo with Catelyn and her driver in the trunk.* A bag with food and water. *Breaking Catelyn's finger, jumping in the limo.* From the bottom of the pack, the cop pulled out a black object wrapped with filmy plastic. *Standing in front of the yoga studio.* A heavy black book fell from what turned out to be Antony's suit—the one Elite kept cleaning in hopes he would go to church with her. *Opening the manila envelope.* Scriptures like the ones Kyo Yuji threw at him in the upstairs room. Brand new, though, the pages unmarked and stiff, unlike Elite's well-used ones. *"Sori Katsu, Natani," the paper read.*

That had been the turning point of this horrible day—the call to kill a High Elder. *If I hadn't gone to the yoga studio, if I hadn't refused the call, if I hadn't let stupid things get to me, if it hadn't been for Sori Katsu . . .*

Elite would still be alive.

The door opened and the bell hanging from a metal bar rang as the door hit it.

"Can I help you?" the older officer asked as he laid the suit on top of the pile of things from Antony's pack.

"I'm here to bail out my employee," said the voice with the unmistakable Aussie accent.

Antony looked from the scriptures to Gage's face and ran a hand through his hair.

"We haven't even called the local representation yet. How'd—"

"When my friend here goes out to get a drink and doesn't return to the motel room, I usually suspect he has gotten a little drunk and thrown in the can," Gage answered.

"He's not going anywhere. He pulled an unregistered weapon on a guy."

"It's registered. I've got the papers here—you can check it." Gage handed the officer the papers. "And I'll have your badges for refusal to release a federal agent." He pulled out his wallet from his pocket and flashed an official-looking ID card.

"Agent?" the younger officer said. "He doesn't have any ID on him that said—"

"Would you carry ID if you were on assignment?" Gage asked.

Antony shook his head.

The older officer paled and grabbed at his keys. "Don't just stand there! Get him out! Get the release papers!" he barked as he opened the door to the cell.

The other officer reached for the papers and placed them on the desk, setting a pen next to them. Antony stepped out of the cell and braced himself against the desk, then signed an unreadable scrawl on the line indicated. The older officer placed Antony's belongings back in the bags in a haphazard manner and could barely zip the larger one shut. Antony took the bags and shouldered them.

"The pistol, please," Gage said.

"Oh!" The younger officer opened the safe in the wall, stripped the evidence tag off the weapon, and handed it to Antony.

He took it and nodded, turning to the door.

"Thank you, boys, and have a nice day." Gage said and shut the door, making the bell ring.

"That was great," Gage said a few minutes later. "They fell for it hook, line, and sinker."

Antony stared silently out the front window of the rental shuttle. Hearing Gage's voice made the pain in his chest more real. Perhaps there was a reason he was headed west, away from Sydney.

"Look, I'm sorry about Elite. I can't tell you—"

"Then don't, Gage. Don't tell me that you know how much it hurts, or how I'll begin to feel better. Nothing you or anyone says right now will change things. Just please—don't say it."

In his peripheral vision, Antony saw Gage nod and shut his mouth.

After the town was far behind them, Antony turned to his best friend. "The body still looked like me? Did you see it yourself?"

"No one but Mat could tell the difference between you and that guy. She says the DNA message must have stayed in the body because it died before you pulled the chip out. By the way, where is the chip?"

"Incinerated."

"I've filed a petition as executor of the will for possession of the bodies," Gage said. "They are tied up in red tape for now, but I plan on getting them and dealing with them as the will specifies. Is that what you want?"

Antony said nothing, just stared straight ahead.

"I guess your silence means you don't care what I do. Okay then, I've left the company as it was and your credit card draws directly from your profits." Gage continued to drive.

Antony reached over and clasped Gage's shoulder. "Did you fly your plane here?"

"Of course I did."

"Good. Let's take a flight to Natani," Antony said.

"Natani? Why?"

"Nothing to worry about. I just need to go there."

"Antony, I—"

"Drive me to the local airport then. I'll find a pilot who will take me, no questions asked."

"Fine," Gage growled. "I'll fly you."

40

Antony stepped from the plane onto the graveled road. The air was warm, and the tall grass on the side of the road swayed in the ocean breeze. He cinched down the straps of his pack and stepped away from the road in the direction of the village he had seen from the air. He had used the pilots' lounge in Broken Hill to shower and change clothes while Gage took a nap on the orange vinyl couch. Antony had spent a lot of time in silent contemplation these last few hours, eating the food Gage ordered for him but saying almost nothing.

"Antony, wait!" He heard Gage clamber down the stairs. "Don't do this."

Antony looked straight ahead. He'd paid Gage for the flight—more than needed, actually. A myriad of birds chirped in the trees, and the plants gave off a pungent, green smell.

"Think it over, mate," Gage said. Antony could hear his friend's footsteps behind him. "Antony! Killing him isn't going to bring her back."

Antony stopped and turned, his eyebrow raised. "What makes you think I'm going to kill him?" He adjusted his pack. "Go home, Gage. Send me a message when they release her body." He turned and walked into the trees.

The foliage grew thick where the meadow ended, and it seemed he had stepped into a different world. It reminded him of the pictures he and Elite had seen of the Amazon jungle. After that, a trip through the Amazon had made its way onto her list. Memories of her weren't any easier to deal with now that he was sober, but he felt less violent. Sleep evaded him, and he hoped that one day, the movie that ran in his head of the last ten years would run out of scenes to remind him of what he lost, and stop altogether.

"If you trample the greens, the taro won't grow," a voice said as Antony entered a clearing. He stopped and looked down at neat rows butted up against the green of jungle. The old man squatted, a tool in his hand as he dug at the plants. "That row there needs weeding." He gestured with the miniature shovel.

"How do you know what is plant and what is weed?" Antony asked.

"Real plants grow slow and steady, storing energy to feed the food. Weeds grow as if they had no care in the world." The man pulled up a yellow-green plant and threw it to the side. "Welcome to Natani, Antony."

How does he know who I am? Antony wondered. He hadn't changed his appearance from when he was arrested. Sori Katsu had the knack of making him question things.

"I'm not Antony anymore. He died with Elite." He laid his pack on the ground and squatted, like Katsu.

"I'm sorry to hear that. Mrs. Danic was a woman with a good heart. So, if you're not Antony, what should I call you?"

"I . . . I don't know. I haven't thought about it." Antony pulled at a tall weed. It resisted his efforts, and he had to yank on it to get it out. "Look, I didn't come here to fulfill some dream of yours. You're not looking at a future High Elder. I came here to ask you some questions." He grabbed another weed.

"I see. Well then, ask away. We have plenty of rows to occupy our time." Katsu moved to the next one.

Antony looked—there was row upon row of taro. "Does your God punish you for bad decisions?"

"Well, we're skipping the pleasantries and going for the heavy hitters." Katsu chuckled. "I'd say no, he doesn't punish those who don't know better. He allows you to suffer the aftereffects of those bad decisions, yes. Those God punishes are those who know truth and disregard it."

"Define knowing truth," Antony said.

"Are you asking about your case?" Katsu rocked back on his heels.

"I keep thinking that I'm being punished for years of atheism, that Elite's death is God's way of forcing me to acknowledge his presence."

"Are you acknowledging God's presence?"

"I don't know. Elite believed we exist as something after we die. And after I told her goodbye, just before I left her body there at our apartment, I heard her voice. She told me to leave, that someone was coming." Antony paused, reliving the moment in his head. "I know it was her. And I didn't just hear her voice—I felt her there with me, warning me, guiding me."

"We exist in spirit form after our body dies," Katsu said, "so I'm not surprised Elite was still there, helping the man she loved. Her death was a direct circumstance of your chosen occupation, but it was not God's punishment." The old man adjusted his hat to shade his face. "It all comes down to agency. God allows us to choose right or wrong, and when we choose wrong, sometimes innocent people are hurt."

Katsu dug at a weed and pulled it out, then went on, "I believe that although the circumstances are tragic, you would not be here today, asking these questions, if things didn't happen the way they did. While God didn't plan her death, he knew that in the aftermath, you would begin to ponder and ask questions."

"I don't understand. According to your scriptures, taking a life is a sin. How can you say I'm not being punished?"

"Have you killed anyone since reading that passage?"

"I didn't read it, but I know what your Ten Commandments say."

"You were an atheist. One cannot be held accountable for what they do not know. To do that is to deny you agency."

"Why is choice so important?" Antony asked. He moved on to another row. It felt good to remove the sun-blocking weeds, letting the plants have sunlight.

"Because if God forced you to obey his rules, you wouldn't learn anything on your own, and you wouldn't grow because of it."

"So you believe God gives you the rules and expects you to learn and grow of your own accord?"

"Doesn't that make more sense than forcing you to obey? God respects our intelligence. He knows we have in us the potential to make the right decisions. So he gives us scripture outlining the rules he wants us to follow, and provides us with people to explain the rules and guide us out of chaos into organization."

"Like you."

"Yes, like me, but I'm not particularly special," Katsu said.

Antony raised his eyebrow.

"God knew I'd listen when he called. That's all."

Antony fell silent, things Elite had told him for years echoing in his head. What she said resonated in him, words and ideas burning in his chest like they did when he went to church, but this time it wasn't uncomfortable. "How do you know?" he said quietly.

Katsu stood, made his way over the rows of taro, and stopped by Antony. He squatted again, reached out a hand, and touched Antony's sternum just below his collarbones. "You feel it here," Katsu said.

The burning increased, bringing tears to Antony's eyes. Katsu stood and offered a strong hand to pull him from the ground.

"But I'm a sinner. I'm a murderer—a monster," Antony said as they walked toward the village. "How can someone like you forgive me for what I have done?"

"It's up to God to forgive you, not me." Katsu walked at Antony's side, carrying a wooden hoe. "A penitent heart and the sincere desire to be forgiven is what's required of us at the beginning. I believe God will tell you his intentions for you eventually. When he does, I'll be here to help you understand and fulfill his desires."

"I wasn't planning on staying here. I've got things to do."

"Things like what? Seeking revenge?"

"No, I'll not shed blood again. I promised myself— promised Elite. That part of my life is over." Antony thought of her list and the things remaining on it.

He closed his eyes. The memories were threatening to take over again. He tried to think of anything except his wife and baby. A memory flashed through his mind—he was standing on the sidewalk, his body covered in sweat, the paper with Sori's name on it in his hand.

Antony took a deep breath. "Your life is in danger. I was asked to kill you, like I killed—" He stopped. Killing Kyo Yuji had been one of the darkest things he had ever done. He'd almost lost Elite over that hit.

"Killed Kyo? I know," Katsu said. "I think both he and I knew he wasn't meant to live for long. My life is always in danger. It's part of the calling."

Antony walked beside him for a while. He could see the trail disappear into the jungle ahead of them.

"Who ordered Kyo's assassination?" Katsu asked.

Antony flinched. He had never been asked such a question, but he knew he at least owed Katsu that much information. "My former corporation, Hurst Enterprises. I don't know why—I was never given a reason."

"Hmm. Hurst Enterprises—never heard of them. I'll have to ask my friends if they have. Either way, what's done is done and there's no going back."

"I'm sorry. He was innocent, and I didn't care." Antony shoved his hands deeper into his pockets.

"Again, you didn't know. Your life before now was one of logic, science, and facts. Now you can learn to use your heart and faith to guide you instead."

Antony thought about Elite's voice telling him to go. Was that what Katsu meant?

"Can I bury her here?" he asked after they walked in silence for a time.

"I think Elite would like that."

41

The sound of a jet engine overhead woke Antony from a deep sleep. Gage was here. Antony grabbed his blanket and began to throw it off when he remembered Katsu's request—"Don't leave your room in the morning without thinking of at least one thing you're thankful for."

Antony slid out of bed, knelt at his bedside, and closed his eyes. "Today I'm grateful Elite and Lucius will have a place for their bodies to rest peacefully," he said.

He opened his eyes and looked at his hands, which were shades darker than they used to be. Katsu and he had agreed that while he lived here, for his safety, he should continue to look like someone else. A quick addition of a compression module on his vocal chords from Mat before they left Australia had changed his voice, too. Antony Danic was truly dead, and he didn't know how he felt about it.

Students were rising and dressing for breakfast. This morning Antony would go straight to the training area without breakfast. Katsu had taught him about fasting and asked him to try it from dinner last night until the feast after the funeral. Antony obliged, ready to try anything once. They had talked for long hours over the last few weeks, sometimes late into the night. Even if some things were hard to believe, Antony was beginning to understand. Every night, he lay in his bed, staring at the stars out his window and asking Elite to give him some answer, to tell him the choice he had made was the right one. She never answered him directly, but at times when he was silent, alone, and contemplative, he felt she approved of what he was doing.

He had promised Katsu he would stay until her body was laid in the ground, and that day was today. Antony looked at the room he lived in. Was he doing any good? Where was his future? Certainly, he was not meant to be a High Elder like Katsu.

Antony's work clothes, dirty from hours spent irrigating last night, hung over his chair to dry. His workout clothes hung in the small closet. The teachers asked him to train with them, to teach them things he knew. So far, he enjoyed it.

He pulled the plastic off his suit and laid it on his bed, the white shirt so stark in contrast to the black jacket and tie. *I'm finally wearing the suit you bought me, El,* he thought as he pulled on the shirt.

Once he was dressed, he opened the door and stepped out onto the green grass of the village. The teachers were practicing in the courtyard, and students filed out of the dorms into the pavilion to get plates of sticky rice, fruit, and fish. A priest and priestess dressed in red robes walked down the gravel path to the temple, where the red-lacquered spire stood sentinel over the village.

Antony felt an immense sense of peace. A feeling of belonging settled in his gut and he smiled.

Katsu met him halfway across the grass. "Son, I thought you'd like to come with me for a moment."

Antony followed him into the church building behind the pavilion, to a small room where two black caskets lay on tables.

"Your friend told me to inform you that the man's body was cremated, and the second casket is empty."

Antony nodded. He didn't want that murderer's body anywhere near Elite's.

"I'll leave you alone for a while." Katsu said, then stepped out of the room.

Antony stood at the open casket and looked in. Technology and an expert mortician had made it possible for him to touch her one last time. Her hair was expertly styled, and the color was a soft auburn—she would have liked it. She wore a light blue, short-sleeved dress that draped over her belly. Her left hand with her wedding ring lay over her right, placed at the top of her rounding belly. The ring was crooked, and he straightened it.

"Elite, it's me. I . . . I know I don't look the same, or sound the same, but for security reasons, I've got to be someone else. I wish you were here. You could help me choose another name and a way to look. I'm really bad at things like that." He laid his hand on top of hers.

"I miss you so much. I wake at night, expecting to feel you next to me, and you're not there. The bed is so cold and lonely." He paused as his hands swept over her belly. "I'm sorry. I know you probably hate me. I promised nothing would happen to you, and I let you down. I'm sorry, El. I didn't know. I'd have killed him the instant I saw him, but I was stupid. I didn't . . ." Antony laid his head on her belly, his tears wetting the fabric of her dress.

"Please forgive me for not protecting you. Forgive me for being who I was. It wasn't fair for me to be such a vile creature when you were so loving and kind. You were everything human that I wasn't. I was a monster and you loved me anyway. And for that, I thank you.

"When I told you that you were my salvation, I meant it. I have a new life here. I'm learning to use my skills in a good way, and I'm teaching and learning all sorts of things. Katsu is making sure I'm working every day toward being forgiven for my past sins. I have to admit, sometimes I feel as if it's pointless and that I'll always be a monster. Then there are times when I feel a degree of hope. I hope you're happy with the road I'm taking—it seemed the only logical one. Oh, El, I miss you so much."

Antony fell silent. He lay there until Katsu came with a few men and took the closed coffin out of the room. Then Katsu silently returned. The men stood behind him, their heads bowed.

"It's time," Katsu said.

Antony looked at her one more time. "I know." He touched her belly. "Goodbye, Son." He kissed his wife's cold lips. "Goodbye, Elite. I love you."

He stood, reached for the lid of the coffin, and shut it. He stopped for a moment and pressed his hands on the smooth black surface, then turned and left the room.

I am dead.

42

Antony stood among the students and teachers at the graveside, Gage at the head next to Katsu. A breeze brushed past them as the day grew warmer. The smell of freshly turned earth permeated everything.

"Mr. Antony Danic and Mrs. Elite Danic had big hearts," Katsu began. "He was a devoted husband, and Elite was a major contributor to this school. It's only fitting that she, her husband, and unborn child are laid to rest here. This is not where her charity ended—she managed an orphanage in Australia that included a women's shelter and respite care facility for children removed from their homes. However, the orphanage was her favorite work.

"She and her loving husband and unborn son were cut down in senseless violence. With her passing, a light in the heavens has truly gone out. God is keenly aware of all of us. Not one sparrow falls to the ground without His notice. Antony, Elite, and Lucius Danic, we bid you an earthly farewell and look forward to seeing you again when our own souls reach heaven. Amen."

Katsu pulled the fabric covering off the headstone. The names of the deceased were carved in English and Kanji. Several guests each took a handful of dirt and dropped it on the caskets, and a few of the women dropped flowers. Antony moved forward and stood next to Gage for a long moment. With his head shaved and brown eyes, Antony was unrecognizable. He had turned his voice modulator off, so he hesitated about making contact, unsure whom or what to trust anymore.

"Thanks for coming, and for bringing her," he said quietly, staring straight ahead. "Mat tells me you had some trouble with the police after you dropped me off."

"Ant—" Gage started to say.

"Shh. Please don't expose me." He had changed his appearance again since Gage dropped him off, finding something he was comfortable with for the long term.

"Um, yeah, I had a little trouble. They thought I had motive to kill Antony, since we were partners in a million-dollar business."

"Sorry. How did everything go?"

"Fine. I listed the apartment and sold the furniture and donated the money to the orphanage. I donated Elite's clothes to the women's shelter. I boxed up and kept their personal effects and Antony's clothes. They are in my basement."

"How's the business?" Antony asked.

"Good. I left everything as it was structured—you know, sixty-forty. Left the credit card account open, just in case."

"But he's dead," Antony said as he walked toward the dorms, away from the crowd.

Gage followed. "Yeah, I know, but it didn't feel right."

"I don't need anything here, really," he said when they were far enough away.

"Here? You're staying here? I've got plenty of room in my home in Sydney. Or you could live in my vacation home in Perth."

"I know, but I belong here—for a while. I'm learning things I need to know. I'm welcome here."

"You're welcome in Australia, too."

"I know, Gage, but I can't go back there right now. It's still too raw, too new."

"I understand. I wasn't able to go back to Auckland for years."

"I'm glad you understand. I want to live here for a while, where she is. Spend time with her, with my son. You can come and visit sometimes, and we'll always be connected by computer and by blood."

"You mean that stupid blood-sharing thing we did as teens?" Gage laughed.

Antony smiled. "Yes, that's exactly what I mean. But it wasn't the blood sharing that meant something—it was our intent, the desire to have a brother. That is what really matters."

"Yeah, I guess."

"You guess?" Antony paused as he looked back at the gravesite, then turned to his best friend.

"What?" Gage removed his suit coat.

A line of sweat trickled down Antony's back. "Did Mat send anything with you, for me?"

"Yeah, but I don't understand why." Gage handed him a thick manila envelope.

"I need a new name, identification, and life."

"Why? Antony is dead. Your blood, DNA, iris, and prints aren't on file with any country. Why, when you're the perfect invisible man, do you want an identity?"

"I want some permanence. My identity would only be known to you, Mat, and the people here at the center." He looked at the crowd gathering in the pavilion. The women of the village had laid out a feast, and four men in red robes shoveled dirt into the grave.

"Seems petty, to ruin it for some peace of mind," Gage said.

Antony shook his head. "Something bad is happening at Hurst Enterprises, especially their connection to this 'Trade' entity. Antony was once a part of that. He made some bad, even horrible decisions. Now I" —he held up the envelope— "will do everything in my power to correct that."

ABOUT THE AUTHOR

C. Michelle Jefferies practically grew up in a library, and she spent her early years reading books with her mother. When Michelle was ten, she realized she wanted to write stories instead of just reading them. In high school, she met another writer, who inspired her to write a full-length book instead of just short stories. Michelle finished that 189-page handwritten novel the summer of her junior year.

After graduating from high school, she married her best friend and started a family. She put her writing on the back burner during those early years to raise their seven children and to volunteer as a lactation counselor in the community. When her children were old enough for her to spend a few hours on the computer without them burning the house down, Michelle returned to writing, and she hasn't stopped since. She can often be found writing or editing with a child in her arms or under her feet. With a passion for secret agents and all things Asian, she writes futuristic thrillers and urban fantasies about bad boys turned good. She also enjoys beating herself up in karate class as she works toward her black belt in tang soo do.

The Summer
We Crossed Europe
in the Rain

Also by Kazuo Ishiguro

KAZUO ISHIGURO

The Summer
We Crossed Europe
in the Rain

Lyrics for Stacey Kent

ILLUSTRATED BY
BIANCA BAGNARELLI

Alfred A. Knopf
New York
2024

THIS IS A BORZOI BOOK
PUBLISHED BY ALFRED A. KNOPF

Copyright © 2024 by Kazuo Ishiguro
Illustrations copyright © 2024 by Bianca Bagnarelli

www.aaknopf.com

Knopf, Borzoi Books, and the colophon are registered trademarks
of Penguin Random House LLC.

Library of Congress Control Number: 2023946402
ISBN: 978-0-593-80251-9 (hardcover)
ISBN: 978-0-593-80252-6 (eBook)

Jacket illustrations by Bianca Bagnarelli
Jacket design by Faber

Manufactured in the United States of America
First United States Edition

Contents

Introduction

I've built a reputation over the years as a writer of stories, but I started out writing songs.

This earlier career of mine began in earnest at the age of fifteen, when I wrote a Leonard Cohen-style song called 'Shingles' (the sort encountered beside the sea, not the painful skin affliction) and performed it to bemused schoolfriends gathered that evening for a domestic table tennis tournament. After that I became unstoppable, and by the time I began work on my first novel, *A Pale View of Hills*, in my mid-twenties, I'd written well over a hundred songs.

The songs were mostly ghastly. But I look back now on this songwriting era of my life as an apprenticeship for the career I came to have. I see today a clear line leading from the songs of my adolescence, through the handful of short stories I wrote at the University of East Anglia the year I turned twenty-five, all the way to my latest novel. It was as a songwriter that I passed through the typical phases authors often negotiate early in their careers; in song, not prose, that I journeyed through my introspective, autobiographical period, then into my 'experimental' purple-prose one. (Delirious stream-of-consciousness lines yelled over thrashing jazz chords.) Eventually, I settled into a more pared-down style. Fewer and simpler chords. Understated, almost mundane lyrics, with emotions placed *between* the lines, only occasionally pushing to the surface. That was my arrival point as a songwriter, and I took these same priorities into my early fiction. It's more or less where I am today, over forty years later.

I was fortunate to receive a first-rate education at my state grammar school. But I didn't grow up steeped in literature in the way I found many of my fellow writers had done when I first emerged on the British book scene of the 1980s. Even by the time I published my third book, *The Remains of the Day*, aged thirty-four, vast hunks of the accepted literary canon of the day were still unfamiliar to me. On the other hand, I'd soaked up by then a huge amount of cinema from different countries and periods (but that's another story), and committed to memory the words and music to around two hundred songs. I loved the way I could utterly lose myself inside a song; the way a song would not so much tell me a story as plunge me right into the midst of one, as a participant groping to find my bearings. Bob Dylan, Leonard Cohen, Joni Mitchell; Irish and Scottish songs like 'Wild Mountain Thyme', 'The Lowlands of Holland', 'Mountains o' Mourne', 'Donal Og'; Robert Johnson's 'From Four Until Late', 'Love in Vain', 'Come On in My Kitchen'; Jimmy Webb's 'By the Time I Get to Phoenix', 'Wichita Lineman'; about a dozen sublime Antonio Carlos Jobim songs; Hank Williams's 'Cold Cold Heart', 'I'm So Lonesome I Could Cry'; Jimmie Rodgers's 'Miss the Mississippi and You'; Gordon Lightfoot's 'Early Morning

Rain'; Kris Kristofferson's 'Sunday Mornin' Comin' Down', 'Me and Bobbie McGee'; Hoagy Carmichael, Rodgers and Hart, Gershwin, Harold Arlen, Cole Porter; 'Cry Me a River', 'Nobody Knows You When You're Down and Out', 'Moon River', 'My Funny Valentine', 'In the Wee Small Hours of the Morning'. On and on and on.

If you're reading this and you're someone starting out as a novelist, please understand I'm not necessarily recommending you take a crash course in the history of the popular song. And certainly not at the expense of the great works of literature. I'm just describing to you what happened to me and the path down which I chanced to come.

In any case, here's a question I've often asked myself: did those endless hours spent bent over a guitar bestow any unique benefits on my later novel-writing life? And if so, what were they?

I feel the answer to the first part is 'yes' and, after reflection, I think I can identify several things gained. Not 'advantages' necessarily, more stylistic preferences I can recognise as deriving from a sustained exposure to songs and songwriting at a formative stage. For example, the fondness for a certain kind of first-person voice. Or the tendency towards narrative vacuums and gaps; an oblique approach to the releasing of information; and that placing of emotion 'between the lines' I touched on before. I don't have space here to go into them all, but I do want to focus for a moment on one particular influence of songs that's increasingly preoccupied me as time has gone on.

I've noticed a lot of discussion, in writers' groups and manuals, around the writerly techniques needed to grab a reader's attention, then to hold it – sometimes relentlessly, sometimes subtly – through to the denouement. Likewise around pacing, the use of mystery and suspense, ways to map compellingly a character's psyche. All good and proper, and I have nothing against any of this. But it surprises me how little gets said concerning what for me is a fundamental question about a story's impact on a reader: how do you create a story that lingers in the mind for days, months, even years after a book is finished?

This may be a matter of taste. A story that lingers long in the mind may not be *better* than one that doesn't. But because of my background in song, the longevity of a story's impact has always been of paramount importance to me. When I struggle to put a novel together, I'm often struggling to figure out not so much how to grip the reader (though that too), but how to say what I wish to say in a way that might *haunt* people for a long, long time.

It's probably already clear how this near-obsession comes from songwriting. A song lasts only a few minutes. Its impact can't afford to reside just in what happens during the moment of direct contact. A song lives or dies by its ability to infiltrate the listener's emotions and memory, and, like a parasite, take up long-term residence, ready to come to the fore in moments of joy, grief, exhilaration, heartbreak, whatever. No one aspires to write a song that

[handwritten note in margin:] wouldn't love to do this with photography

x

catches the attention only while it's being heard, then gets forgotten. That's not how songs work.

Although I've often tried, I've yet to identify the magic ingredients – the elements in a story that will ensure that it lingers and haunts. Conversely, I remain unsure why certain books are so gripping while you're reading them, yet so hard to recall even a day after you've finished. If I could just work this out – if I could bottle the magic ingredients – I'd not only resolve a question that's nagged me for years, I'd have the Giant Key to great writing.

As I say, I'm unable to name the essential elements for you here. But my hunch is that great songs – even halfway decent ones – can provide us with a clue.

I've often wondered, for instance, if there isn't something in the unresolved, incomplete quality of so many well-loved songs that's significant here. In the world of prose fiction, there's a strong impulse to achieve completeness; to tie every knot, answer every question, to leave no loose ends hanging. By contrast, in the world of songs, there's a much lower bar when it comes to literal sense-making. The tiny number of words available, the internal logic of the melody, the emotional context imposed by chords and chord sequences mean that the ability of a song to connect has little to do with, say, convincing psychological back stories or even the clear readability of the scenes unfolding before us.

It occurs to me that good songs may haunt the mind not despite their incompleteness, but because of it. The experience of entering a song can be strangely reminiscent of lived experience – filled with bafflement, corners one can't see around, longed-for resolutions that hang out of reach. And yet a good song, like a good story, must at the same time offer at least a small catharsis; a shape to place over scattered incoherence; an emotional vocabulary where one didn't exist before.

I first became an ardent fan of the American jazz singer Stacey Kent when I heard her 1999 album *The Tender Trap*. I proceeded to buy her earlier albums and go to her concerts. And when in 2002 I appeared on BBC Radio 4's *Desert Island Discs*, I chose a Stacey Kent track as one of the eight with which I wished to be marooned on my lonely desert island. At this point I'd met neither her nor her husband, Jim Tomlinson. But following the broadcast, a request came from her record company: would I write the liner notes to her forthcoming album? I accepted immediately and sat down to articulate why Stacey's music had come to mean so much to me. Here's a part of what I wrote back then:

Stacey's singing never lets us forget these songs are about people. Her protagonists come to life so fully in her voice you sometimes have to remind yourself the CD has no visuals. She has, in fact, much in common with today's finest screen actors who, assured of the camera's ability to pick out detail, portray complex shades of personality, motive and feeling through subtle adjustments of face and posture. Like them, Stacey has complete mastery of her tools, but hardly allows us to be aware of them. In song after song, we find a route to the emotional heart of the music without having first to admire her technique . . . She conveys as well as any singer I've heard the sense of a person talking to herself; the faltering hesitancies, the exuberant rushes of inner thought.

I was nervous she'd not like my take on her art, but thankfully she did. At least, she graciously gave me that impression. Not long afterwards, my wife Lorna and I met Stacey and Jim, and we became friends. Even so, I was surprised when they approached me with the idea of my writing lyrics for original material that Stacey could perform.

I found myself in their north London house one afternoon in 2006, sitting at a large table, boardroom style, with Stacey, in wraparound sunglasses, presiding as chair. They explained to me they were about to change record label – to the legendary Blue Note – and wished their first album there to mark a new era for them. (The album, *Breakfast on the Morning Tram*, went on to earn platinum status and a Grammy nomination.) They told me they'd loved covering the Great American Songbook over the years, but were now ambitious to record original songs written expressly for Stacey. Jim had many ideas on the musical side, but neither he nor Stacey felt comfortable about writing lyrics. Dauntingly for me, as we sat around that table they began to recite examples of what they considered to be woeful original lyrics people had sent in to them. I wasn't so sure I could do any better, but my old yearning for songwriting came rushing back and I told them, yes, I'd love to try.

Several interesting issues immediately confronted us. What should a modern-day jazz song look like? To what extent should we attempt to evoke the pre-World War II heyday of the Great American Song, and the musical and lyrical vernacular of that era? (Things being 'swell', barmen addressed as 'buddy'.) And where, geographically, would our songs take place? We came to the view that our kind of jazz song should reflect the world we ourselves lived in. That despite Stacey being American, we'd locate our songs largely in Europe, sometimes even the Far East. That the lyrics should stay away from pastiche and evoke contemporary settings and situations, even if that meant imagery that was incongruous, even surreal, in a jazz-song context (bullet trains, ice hotels, rucksacks, moorland cattle). The songs would, for now, be exclusively love songs. And there was one other instruction I received that day.

Stacey told me that although she'd been an admirer of my novels for many years, she'd noticed they were often 'pretty sad'. This was all very well as far as my novels were concerned. But when I wrote words for her to sing, there was one important remit: however sad, however bleak the song became, *there had to remain an element of hope.* Even if only a tiny sliver – she held up to me a forefinger and thumb to illustrate – because that was what she, as an artist, needed to work with. ⌈She needed that sliver of hope to reach into the hearts of her audience.⌋

I remember thinking that day, 'Okay, this is profound.' It was an insight into not only the art of a sublime singer, but into something even bigger, something about us all.

What follows in this volume are my lyrics to sixteen of the songs Jim Tomlinson and I have created for Stacey since that first discussion. I must say here that I've often felt ambivalent about the practice of publishing on printed pages the lyrics of songs created to be performed. It's rare that a song lyric, isolated from its melody, orchestration and performance, can satisfyingly double as something to be read. And it remains my belief that a song lyric is not, and works quite differently from, a poem. Mindful of this challenge, my editors and I have attempted to create with this book something fresh and unique by persuading the brilliant Italian comics artist Bianca Bagnarelli (with whom I've collaborated before, and of whose work I've become an avid fan) to bring her own vision and dimension to each song.

And it's my wish that after looking through these pages, you'll want to experience, if you've not done so already, the recorded versions of our songs via the QR link provided. The songs' musical side is entirely the work of the magnificently talented Jim Tomlinson – composer, saxophonist, flautist, bandleader, arranger and record producer. Eleven of these songs – the other five are works-in-progress – have appeared on various Stacey Kent albums over the years and have been performed, often many times over, in some of the most vaunted venues around the world, such as the Birdland Jazz Club in New York, Ronnie Scott's in London, La Cigale in Paris and the Blue Note Tokyo.

My hope is that you'll find here a gateway into our special world. Something that will amuse, move – perhaps even haunt.

Kazuo Ishiguro,
21 September 2023

The Summer
We Crossed Europe
in the Rain

I Wish I Could Go Travelling Again

I wish I could go travelling again
It feels like this summer will never end
And I've had such good offers from several of my friends
I wish I could go travelling again

I want to sit in my shades, sipping my latte
Beneath the awning of a famous café
Jet-lagged and with our luggage gone astray
I wish I could go travelling again
I want a waiter to give us a reprimand
In a language neither of us understand
While we argue about the customs of the land
I wish I could go travelling again

I want to sit in traffic anxious about our plane
While your blasé comments drive me half insane
I want to dash for shelter with you through the tropical
    rain
I wish I could go travelling again
I want to be awakened by a faulty fire alarm
In an overpriced hotel devoid of charm
Then fall asleep again back in your arms
I wish I could go travelling again

But how can I ever go travelling again
When I know I'll just keep remembering again
When I know I'll just be gathering again
Reminders to break my heart?

I wish I could go travelling again
It feels like this summer will never end
And I've had such good offers from several of my friends
I wish I could go travelling again

The Changing Lights

Were we leaving Rio
Or were we in New York?
I remember bossa nova in the breeze
We were in the back seat
Of a cab we couldn't afford
You were holding my old rucksack on your knees
You leaned towards your window
To see the traffic up ahead
'These commuters here,' you said
'Could be the walking dead'
And we vowed to guard our dreams
From all the storms that lay ahead
From the winds of fear and age and compromise
And we laughed about the hopelessness
Of so many people's lives
As we slowly moved
Towards the changing lights

It was near Les Invalides
Or perhaps Trafalgar Square
It was late at night, the city was asleep
You were clowning in the back seat
With some friends we'd found somewhere
The kind back then we'd always seemed to meet
There were those in this great world, you said
Just fated to go far
And among the lucky ones were we
Inside that car
And your friends began to sing
'When You Wish Upon a Star'
And you clapped along like you didn't have a care
But once I turned to glance at you
As we drove across that square
And your face looked haunted
In the changing lights

Was it last September?
It was autumn more or less
You were waiting to cross some busy boulevard
Talking on your phone
To your family, I guess
Your briefcase tucked up high beneath your arm

As I approached you turned around
A question in your eye
As though I might ignore you
And just simply walk on by
But we smiled and talked awhile
About each other's lives
And once or twice I caught a wistful note
Then you moved towards the crossing
As the cars slowed to a halt
And we waved and parted
Beneath the changing lights
We waved and parted
Beneath the changing lights

So Romantic

You always had a taste for those movies
Like *Casablanca* and *Song o' My Heart*
Where a complicated world or the call of adventure
Forces true lovers to part
When the hero turns his back so stoically
On all the happiness they might have had
You always considered it so romantic
But I just considered it sad

It was so like you to choose such a moment
The sun setting over the square
A pavement café, the local children at play
The sound of an accordion somewhere
You suddenly said Fate was pulling us apart
Then you shrugged, like there was nothing more to add
I suppose you considered that so romantic
Well, I just considered it sad

Perhaps you're living in America now
Perhaps you're in Timbuktu
A small part of me, even after this time
Has never stopped waiting for you
To live in this state of hoping
When hoping seems so utterly mad
I can't help but consider that so romantic
Though I know I should consider it sad

The Ice Hotel

Let's you and me go away to the Ice Hotel
The Caribbean's all booked out
And that's just as well
Once I'd have been much keener
On Barbados or Antigua
But just now I think the Arctic will suit us well
Let's you and me go away
To the Ice Hotel

They've built it all with ice that's pure and clear
The sofas, the lobby, even the chandelier
A thermostat guarantees
A steady minus five degrees
What other place could serve our needs so well?
Let's you and me go away
To the Ice Hotel

Romantic places
Like Verona or Paris
They'll always lead you astray
You'd have to be a novice
To ever trust Venice
And those dreamy waterways

And what the tropics can do, I know only too well
So let's you and me go away
To the Ice Hotel

Heavy clothing at all times is the expected norm
Even candlelight at dinner is considered too dangerously
    warm
And when the time comes for us to sleep
We'll spread out our reindeer fleece
And curl up together on an ice block carved for two
But then in the morning, provided we've made it
    through . . .

We'll step out together
To watch the sun rise over
That vast expanse of cold
And who knows, if we're lucky
We may find ourselves talking
Of what our futures may hold
This is no whim of the moment, I want you to realise
Let's go away to that palace made of ice

Let's you and me go away to the Ice Hotel
The Bahamas are all booked out
And that's just as well
I don't think we're quite ready
For Hawaii or Tahiti
And when we will be, only time will tell
Let's you and me go away
To the Ice Hotel

Breakfast on the Morning Tram

So here you are in this city
With a shattered heart, it seems
Though when you arrived you thought you'd have
The holiday of your dreams
You'd cry yourself to sleep if you could
But you've been awake all night
Well, here's something you need to do
At the first hint of morning light
Walk right across the deserted city
To the Boulevard Amsterdam
And wait there for what the citizens here
Refer to as the Breakfast Tram

Climb on board
You'll soon manage
To find at the far end
Of the carriage
The most wonderful buffet
There's everything
You'd want to eat
You can take a feast
Back to your seat
Whatever you can fit onto your tray

And the mist on the windows will start to fade
As the sun climbs higher in the sky
And you can sit back with your *café au lait*
While outside the waking city clatters by
So things didn't quite meet expectations
But you're bound to conclude
Upon reflection
There's no reason you should give a damn
Just treat yourself
To a cinnamon pancake
Very soon
You'll forget your heartache
When you have breakfast on the morning tram

It'll be quite quiet
When you first get on
But as that tram keeps
Moving along
It'll fill with people starting on their day
They'll be laughing and joking
As they eat
They'll be passing plates
Along the seats
Your night of heartbreak will soon seem far away
And even though you're a stranger
They'll make you feel right at home
They'll be offering to refill your coffee

They won't have you sitting there alone
They've seen many others
Just like you
And each one of them
Has had it happen too
So just enjoy your scrambled eggs and ham
Treat yourself
To a cinnamon pancake
Very soon
You'll forget your heartache
When you have breakfast on the morning tram

And even though you're a stranger
They'll make you feel right at home
They'll be offering to refill your coffee
They won't have you sitting there alone
Because they've seen many others
Just like you
And each one of them
Has had it happen too
So just enjoy your fresh croissant and jam
And don't neglect
The Belgian waffles
You'll soon forget
All your troubles
When you have breakfast on the morning tram

Craigie Burn

A sunken lane, a muddy track
A grey sky over the moorland
It was much the same when we came this way
Arm in arm last autumn
Those may be the very same cattle
Silhouetted on the horizon
Around that abandoned four-wheel drive
Just where the land stops rising
Well, you see I'm walking here again
Though I said I'd never return
Searching for something I dropped here that day
I walked with you to Craigie Burn
I walked with you to Craigie Burn

So how have I been since that little occasion?
I'm sorry I've been out of touch
I've been working in a developing nation
And though it didn't pay very much
My days were filled with urgent events
I thought I'd found my true calling
Like a bird caught mid-flight by a barb-wire fence
I kept going for a time before falling

But here I'm back on these moors again
Searching through the bracken and the fern
For something precious I dropped here that day
I walked with you to Craigie Burn
I walked with you to Craigie Burn

I suppose you would say it's a hopeless task
And even if I found it again
What would be left of a thing like that
Out here in this wild terrain?
But even though a year has gone by
Since that morning it was lost
It was made of something enduring and strong
To weather the rain and frost
I just wish I was holding it here in my hands
So our happiness could return
And we'll never let it slip the way we did that day
I walked with you to Craigie Burn
I walked with you to Craigie Burn

A sunken lane, a muddy track
A grey sky over the moorland
It was much the same when we came this way
Arm in arm last autumn

The Summer We Crossed Europe in the Rain

You say it's the way these passing years have treated you
That the weight of the dreams you once carried has now
    defeated you
That our candlelit dinners will all just be reheated through
Our quarrels and disappointments just get repeated too

Well, I've packed our bags, I know I should have
    consulted you
But pretending to bargain would have only insulted you
So do just as I say
We'll go away today
The fire still burns whatever you may claim
Let's be young again
If only for the weekend
Let's be fools again
Let's fall in at the deep end
Let's do once more
All those things we did before
The summer we crossed Europe in the rain

Remember that hotel, the crooked balcony door
From where we stood and watched the market in the
   downpour
Sharing warm baguettes
On sunny cathedral steps
Dancing the tango while waiting for our train
Let's be young again
If only for the weekend
Let's be fools again
Let's fall in at the deep end
Let's do once more
All those things we did before
The summer we crossed Europe in the rain

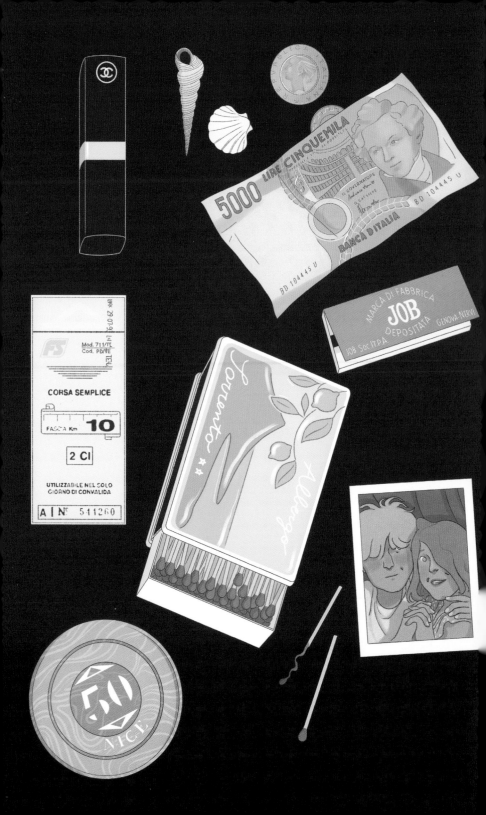

Let's do once more
All those things we did before
The summer we crossed Europe in the rain

Bullet Train

Your head against my shoulder
You've fallen asleep again
Beside me on this dream train
They call the Shinkansen
Tokyo to Nagoya
Nagoya to Berlin
Sometimes I feel I lose track
Of just which hemisphere we're in
And this town outside the window
Looks like the one that we just passed
They call this the bullet train
But it feels like we're not moving
Though I know we must be moving
Yes, I know we must be moving
Know we must be moving, know we must be moving
Pretty fast

That steward with his trolley
Now going down the aisle
He was a schoolfriend from my home town
I was in love with for a while

I thought I heard some talk
He'd settled in New York
Became some kind of Wall Street super-lawyer
So why's he looking so relaxed
Serving beverages and snacks
On this train from Tokyo to Nagoya?
And why's it taking so long
For the night to fall?
They call this the bullet train
But it feels like we're not moving
Tell me, are we really moving?
It feels like we're not moving
Feels like we're not moving, feels like we're not moving
At all

The man there on the platform
In that town we just came through
He looked exactly like a teacher
From way back in senior school
Everybody loved him
A gentle inspiring man
So what's he doing out here
In Nowheresville, Japan?
There's so much empty land
After all that urban sprawl
They call this the bullet train
But it feels like we're not moving

It still feels like we're not moving
Feels like we're not moving
At all

Your head upon my shoulder
You're fast asleep again
Beside me on this dream train
They call the Shinkansen
Tokyo to Nagoya
Nagoya to Berlin
Sometimes I've no idea
Of where I am or where I've been
We're so lucky to have found each other
In this world of steel and glass
They call this the bullet train
But it feels like we're not moving
Though I know we must be moving
I know in truth we're moving
Know in truth we're moving
Way too fast

I'm so glad you're here beside me
On this bullet train
Dreaming on my shoulder
Let me hold you closer
On this bullet train
As the night grows colder
We're headed to the future
On this bullet train
But are we growing older
On the bullet train?
On the bullet train
On the bullet train

Best Casablanca

It was raining in the cinema, rain sliding down the screen
It was raining in the cinema, rain sliding all down the
    screen
But I didn't mind it, if anything
I thought it added something to the scene

Someone behind me was complaining to the attendant
    with the light
Someone behind me was complaining to the attendant
    with the light
Attendant said, 'We'll fix it soon
But you'll just have to bear with it for tonight'

Someone in my row was saying how it happened just this
    way the week before
Someone in my row was saying how it happened just this
    way the week before
Now he could hardly tell a happy scene
From a sad one any more

The actors looked so bleary, even the big stars failed to
    shine

Actors all looked so bleary, even the big stars failed to shine
Their faces out of focus
Their eyes looked tear-stained just like mine

Attendant said to me, 'Miss, maybe you'd care to change
   your seat?'
Attendant said, 'Excuse me, miss, maybe you'd care to
   change your seat?
There's so much rain streaming down your cheeks
I can see it pooling by your feet'

I said, 'Oh, I don't mind it, these things just happen from
   time to time'
I said, 'Oh, I don't mind it, these things just happen from
   time to time
You have some kind of maintenance problem
And I have a melancholic turn of mind'

Who needs reminding how sweet it all felt at the start?
Who needs reminding how sweet it all felt at the start?
Who wants to see a feel-good movie
When it just keeps pouring in your heart?

It was raining in the cinema, rain sliding down the screen
It was raining in the cinema, rain sliding down the screen
But I didn't mind, it was the best version
Of *Casablanca* I've ever seen

Postcard Lovers

Lately I've become such a postcard lover
Especially of the ones I get from you
And if these days they don't come quite so often
They charm me more than ever when they do
I'll picture you beside a sunny harbour
Waiting for a boat to come to shore
Your finger lingering on a postcard spinner
In the doorway of a tacky tourist store
Or whiling away those warm enchanted evenings
Writing in the corner of some café
Those careless collections of words and feelings
You happened to feel like sending me that day
I save every card
Although it gets hard
To keep order
Among these random souvenirs
It amazes me some
The way we've become
Such postcard lovers
Divided by the oceans and the years

Have you found yourself some wonderful companion
And all the happiness that heaven allows?
Or are you homesick for this grey and drizzly nation
As you walk home amidst the evening crowds?
The postcards I send to you from my own travels
Can hardly match the ones you send to me
But at least I give you news of what I'm doing
And open my heart to you occasionally
Looking back through all these cards you've written
From every far-flung corner beneath the sun
They say so little of the life you're really leading
So little of the person you've become
But they still bear the traces
Of those special places
We once kept for one another
Deep within our hopes and our fears
It amazes me some
The way we've become
Such postcard lovers
Divided by the oceans and the years

Catherine in Indochine

I dreamt that I had lost you and become a movie queen
Searching through the ruins of a movie we'd once seen
Like Catherine in *Indochine*
Like Catherine in *Indochine*

I was lying in a room under spinning ceiling fans
Haunted by the shadows of strange servants' hands
Lost in the darkness of old colonial France
Like Catherine in *Indochine*
Like Catherine in *Indochine*

There were lush plantations, there were shady deals
A rickshaw standing in the rain with broken wheels
Propeller planes waiting in the burning fields
For Catherine in *Indochine*
For Catherine in *Indochine*

Five Césars and an Oscar too
An international cast and crew
I'd let them all go just to get back to you
Like Catherine in *Indochine*
Like Catherine in *Indochine*

Let me wake up by your side and stare into your eyes
Let's flee this port before the war arrives
Let's watch from the deck and see if this town survives
Like Catherine in *Indochine*
Like Catherine in *Indochine*

I dreamt that I had lost you and become a movie queen
Like Catherine in *Indochine*
Like Catherine in *Indochine*

Gabin

Gabin
Hooded eyes
A slow Gitanes
Weary deserter on the run
Gabin
You came up to my room
And we passed the afternoon
Remembering Gabin
Jean Gabin

Gabin
A high window
An empty gun
Comrades all perished one by one
Gabin
You didn't want him to get away
I was so angry with you that day
As we watched Gabin
Jean Gabin

Gabin
Marseilles or was it Milan?
They were showing *The Sicilian Clan*
Or *Voici le temps des assassins*
Gabin
We were quarrelling as the lights came on
But held each other as we walked home
After watching Gabin
Jean Gabin

Gabin
Hooded eyes
A slow Gitanes
Weary deserter on the run
Gabin
You came up to my room
And we passed the afternoon
Remembering Gabin
Jean Gabin

Tango in Macao

You said there'd be shutters
And rusty ceiling fans
And broken-hearted gangsters
With roses in their hands
There would be tango in Macao
That's what you told me
And I believed in you somehow
Believed all your baloney
We've come halfway round the world
I guess I'm stuck with you for now
I'm not saying that you lied
But it was definitely implied
There would be tango
In Macao

I don't know how it happened
You got past my defences
And brought me all this way
On distinctly false pretences
I asked our concierge, he said
There's nothing like that now
And neither has there been since before
The days of Chairman Mao

You'd be a man true to your vow
At least that's what I thought
You said we'd tango in Macao
But we've done nothing of the sort

But we've still an evening left
To salvage this somehow
We have one last chance to find
Some tango in Macao
Perhaps there'll be a club
Down one of these dark alleys
Where they tango really close
Like they do in Buenos Aires
Or down by the harbour
Along the cobblestones
We'd dance by the lamplight
To a wind-up gramophone
Then there'd be tango in Macao
Just the way you told me
Oh yes, we could tango in Macao
All you have to do is hold me

You said there'd be shutters
And rusty ceiling fans
And broken-hearted gangsters
With roses in their hands
There would be tango in Macao
That's what you told me
And I believed in you somehow
Believed all your baloney
We've come halfway round the world
I guess I'm stuck with you for now
I'm not saying that you lied
But it was definitely implied
There would be tango
In Macao

Voyager

Wasn't this a voyage to remember?
Not a moment to regret
Now we can almost see the harbour
But this thing may not be over yet
The sun's still shining on the portholes
The stewards are still balancing their trays
The old professor's still charming the widows
With his jokes and his European ways
And this ship's still filled with card sharks
Gold-diggers by the score
So you'd better keep me close beside you
Till you're safely back on shore

Handsome men in white tuxedos
Exhibiting all their naivety
Should never walk into ship's casinos
Should never lock gazes with a woman like me
It went so against my tested system
So against the roll of my weighted dice
To lose my heart to my intended victim
And to gamble on paradise

But wasn't this a voyage to remember?
Travel in the finest style
So till we reach terra firma
Won't you hold me for another little while?

Millionaires, adventuresses
Black ties, Chanel dresses
Dances that feel like caresses
And this incessant pull of the tide . . .

The sea kept calm, but my heart kept on tossing
Till I let go of my professional pride
Such are the hazards of an Atlantic crossing
When the moon's rising on the starboard side
Some lose their fortune in the Depression
Some lose their fortune in a game
Maintaining a poker expression
As they draw closer and closer to the flame
Oh, but wasn't this a voyage to remember?
I wish we could live it all again
And we could stay here on this deck forever
I wish this voyage would never end

Wasn't this a voyage to remember?
Not a moment to regret
Now we can almost see the harbour
But this thing may not be over yet

Waiter, Oh Waiter

Waiter, oh, waiter
Please come to my rescue
I cannot understand a word that's written on this menu
Not that I'm unaccustomed to this kind of smart cuisine
But what you handed me is in a language I've never seen
And the way my companion here keeps gazing over at me
Makes me feel like I'm drifting further and further out to
    sea
Everything looks so frightening
Everything here looks so nice
Oh, waiter, please waiter
I really need your advice

Waiter, oh, waiter
I feel so embarrassed
If this is really French, it's not the kind they use in Paris
What is this crab and lobster foam, what's in this *cassoulet?*
While my companion's so at home, so terribly au fait
I need some words of wisdom, I need you to take my side
For very soon I know will come the moment to decide
Won't you help me through this menu?
Won't you please just catch my eye?

So, waiter, oh, waiter
Please help me out tonight

Underneath that stiff tuxedo
You must be human too
You'll have had your days of heartbreak
And days when your dreams came true
So, waiter, oh, waiter
Please help me out tonight

Waiter, oh, waiter
Please come to my rescue
Oh, let this be the sort of thing your service can extend to
Not that I'm unaccustomed to this kind of smart cuisine
But this menu is as baffling as anything I've ever seen
And the way he looks across at me with his sardonic gaze
Makes me feel I'm drifting further out into the choppy
    waves
Everything looks so frightening
Everything here looks so nice
Oh, waiter, please, waiter
I really need your advice

Underneath that stiff tuxedo
You must be human too
You'll have had your days of heartbreak
And days when your dreams came true

So, waiter, oh, waiter
Waiter, oh, waiter
Waiter . . . waiter . . .

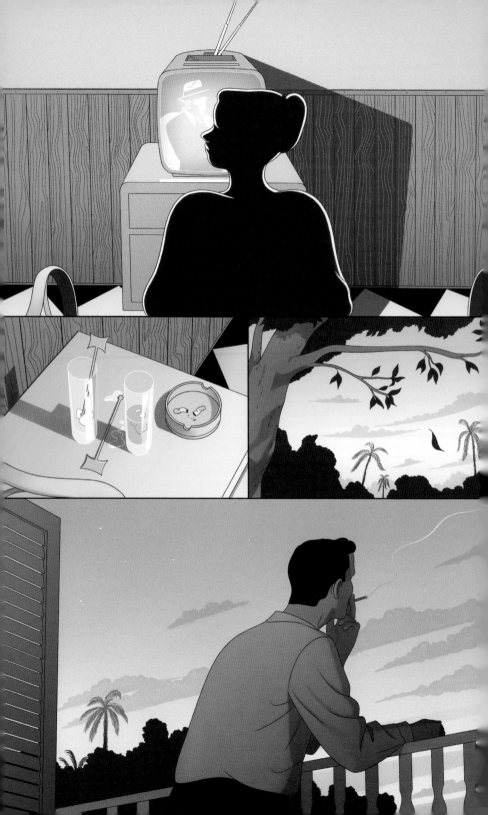

Turning Noir

How long will you stay out on the balcony?
I wish you'd come and sit down here next to me
Then we could watch together this old romantic comedy
I'll fill you in on what you've missed so far
It started out light-hearted and amusing
Though things have now grown darker and confusing
These lovers, are they really on a road of their own choosing?
Do they know what's in the trunk of their own car?
Is there something here I'm just not seeing
Or are things turning noir?

I love to sink into this flickering black and white
These 1940s kisses, the moody neon lights
But why are these limousines waiting in the night?
Who's that raincoated figure beside the bar?
The evening's growing chilly, though the breeze is still
    quite pleasing
But would she keep that silver pistol in her bag for no
    reason?
And you're still on the balcony, leaning out to the horizon
Careful not to lean too far
I wonder, is this just the turning of the season
Or are things turning noir?

Are you searching the sky for a warning?
Or dreamily gazing at a star?
I can only see your back from where I'm sitting
Can you see our days ahead from where you are?
Is this just the way the day turns into evening
Or are things turning noir?

I love to sink into this flickering black and white
These 1940s kisses, these moody neon lights
If only you'd come in now, close the door onto the night
I'll fill you in on the story so far
It's escapist entertainment
So it will all turn out right
Or are things turning noir?

Stacey Kent is an American jazz singer with an international reputation that has seen her perform in over fifty countries. Her collaboration with Kazuo Ishiguro began in 2007 with the platinum-selling, Grammy-nominated, *Breakfast on the Morning Tram*. She was awarded the Chevalier de l'Ordre des Arts et des Lettres in 2009, and is the recipient of many awards including, most recently, the Prix Ella Fitzgerald at the 2023 Montreal Jazz Festival.

Jim Tomlinson is a British tenor saxophonist, clarinetist, flautist, producer, arranger and composer. He studied PPE at Oxford University and music at the Guildhall School of Music. His solo album, *The Lyric*, won the BBC Jazz Awards Album of the Year in 2005. He is married to the singer Stacey Kent.

London, 2007 © Jim Tomlinson

THE SUMMER WE CROSSED
EUROPE IN THE RAIN

THE KAZUO ISHIGURO / JIM TOMLINSON
SONGBOOK

PERFORMED BY STACEY KENT

Scan the QR code to listen
on your preferred streaming platform

Your personal information will be processed in
accordance with our Privacy Policy located here
penguinrandomhouse.com/privacy

HH 29 07 93 L4

Mod. 711/TL
Cod. PD/VE

FS

CORSA SEMPLICE

FASCIA Km **10**

2 Cl

UTILIZZABILE NEL SOLO
GIORNO DI CONVALIDA

A I N° 541260

5000 LIRE CINQU

BD 104445